The BOOK BOYFRIEND

CARINA ROSE

THE BOOK BOYFRIEND
Carina Rose © 2021

No part of this book may be reproduced or transmitted in any form or by any means, including photocopying, recording, or by any information storage and retrieval system, without the written permission of the author, except for the use of brief quotations in a book review.

This book is a work of fiction. Names, characters, places, and incidents are products of the author's imagination or are used fictitiously. The use of artists, song titles, famous people, locations, and products throughout this book is done for storytelling purposes and should in no way be seen as an advertisement. Trademark names are used in an editorial fashion, with no intention of infringement of the respective owner's trademark.

Editor: James Gallagher, Castle Walls Editing
Formatter: Tami Norman, Integrity Formatting
Cover Design: Sommer Stein, Perfect Pear Creative

TABLE OF CONTENTS

Prologue	1
Chapter 1	4
Chapter 2	12
Chapter 3	19
Chapter 4	29
Chapter 5	35
Chapter 6	48
Chapter 7	59
Chapter 8	71
Chapter 9	84
Chapter 10	97
Chapter 11	103
Chapter 12	114
Chapter 13	121
Chapter 14	129
Chapter 15	136
Chapter 16	141
Chapter 17	149
Chapter 18	158
Chapter 19	165
Chapter 20	173
Chapter 21	181

TABLE OF CONTENTS

Chapter 22 190
Chapter 23 197
Chapter 24 206
Chapter 25 213
Chapter 26 220
Chapter 27 228
Chapter 28 236
Chapter 29 243
Chapter 30 253
Chapter 31 261
Chapter 32 268
Chapter 33 279
Chapter 34 287
Epilogue 296
Preview – Once Upon A Kiss 304
Other Books by Carina Rose 313
About the Author 314
Contact Carina Rose 315
A note from me 316
Acknowledgments 317

This book is dedicated to those who took a chance and did it.

PROLOGUE

She did it. Finally. Callie's trembling fingers hovered over the keyboard as she stared at her laptop's screen. Months and months of sleepless nights, some tears, and part of her heart and soul had been poured into her first and, for all she knew, her last romance novel, *Ready to Fall*. Callie took a deep breath and read what she had just typed.

He turned and looked at the sea of guests at the large outdoor wedding before he heard the minister formally declare his brother off the market. In the past, weddings would make Hudson break out into a cold sweat, but today that hadn't been the case. Could it be that he was ready to share his life with someone? To take the chance and fall in love in hopes of not losing it? To give up the life of one-night stands and unemotional sex for a true relationship? And what woman would be ready for a man like him?

Perhaps being the most sought-after bachelor was overrated? A few weeks ago, that thought would have made him laugh out loud. That one woman could win his heart. But today, after witnessing his brother, someone he admired, recite his vows, Hudson Newman decided he wanted that for himself... that it was time for him to open his heart.

He glanced around the marquee tent, and although he had dated more than one guest and a bridesmaid, no one there was the one for him. It wasn't as though he expected to easily find his soul mate, but that wouldn't deter him. Excitement coursed through him as he thought about all the possibilities and the fact that he, too, was ready to fall.

A glorious smile spread across her face as she typed *The End*.

Relief, exhaustion, and a major sense of accomplishment flowed through Callie. Her friend had told her she could do it, but believing it herself had been a completely different reality. It wasn't as though she didn't think she was intelligent enough to pen a story, but to have the courage to share it with the world? Someone might as well have challenged her to bungee jump out of a helicopter. No, even that seemed easier.

Not to mention that *Ready to Fall* wasn't your typical romance, if one at all. It mostly revolved around the hero of the book as he traveled his path to self-discovery—his awakening, so to speak. It actually sounded more like male fiction. *Was that even a thing?* Marketing-wise, Callie wasn't sure. Plus, there were a few bedroom scenes that were a bit risqué but made him all the more swoony.

Granted, Hudson didn't get his happily ever after at the end of the book, but he was happy for now—and on his way to finding true love. Research showed that was good enough for the genre. Plus, she'd already plotted out the second book, which would show Hudson falling in love and possibly getting married. She loved the idea of establishing a character and following their arc.

Being able to breathe life into her characters and live through their eyes had been liberating... fictionally, of course. She never frequented adult clubs, nor did she own any "toys" of the grown-up variety. Callie preferred old-fashioned courtship, and then if she clicked with a man, she'd consider a relationship. Despite her belief that marriage wasn't for everyone, Callie looked forward to giving her character that moment—even if she didn't want that for herself. Which could be the very reason she'd been single for so long.

Shaking her head and getting back to the topic at hand—her manuscript—questions aside, she knew an honest opinion would be needed before hitting "Publish." And there would be only one person for that job: her best friend, Gina. She had been Callie's biggest cheerleader since day one, always telling her to believe in herself and that she could do it. After a few deep breaths, she sent the document in an email and prayed Gina liked it.

Callie closed her laptop, took a sip of her wine, and decided to let the words fall where they may.

CHAPTER 1

Three months later

Callie still couldn't believe she'd done it. She remembered the day she finished *Ready to Fall*. It felt as though it were a lifetime ago rather than a few months. In that time, she'd had her book edited and formatted. The perfect steamy cover had been created, and then she'd read it over and over again and given it to Gina for a final read. Thankfully, Gina loved it. And Callie knew that despite being her best friend and maybe a bit biased, Gina would tell her the truth—even if it hurt.

Gina gave her a warm smile. "Sweetie, don't stress. You've got this. Plus, you have me." Much to Callie's surprise, Gina had told her she belonged to several online book groups and, being her typical self, had integrated herself among bloggers and book influencers. She knew how to market books and understood that side of the business much better than Callie could have ever imagined. Still, that didn't put her at ease.

"Thank you, but I'm just so nervous."

"We're at a spa," Gina said, winking at her nail tech, who most likely thought the pair had had one too many mimosas. The woman ignored her boisterous client and continued tinting Gina's toes. "I understand your anxiety, but trust me, between my connections and ad placements, you're on your way. I'll go as far as to say *cheers* to the next bestselling author."

Callie tentatively clinked her glass against her best friend's and rolled her eyes. "That's a bit much. I'd settle for a few sales."

Gina downed half of her mimosa in one fluid swallow. "Trust me. Pretty soon, Lily May will be a household name."

At this rate, Callie was sure her eyes would stay pointed toward the ceiling. But that was Gina. The believer in manifesting your destiny. *Believe it will happen. Visualize it.* Two lines Gina had said on more than one occasion. Callie, on the other hand, didn't buy into watching the angle of the moon or deciding which spice to burn or whatever her best friend said to do.

The only thing Callie had manifested was thankfulness that she had a day job. "Let's not get ahead of ourselves," she said as the manicurist misted Callie's toes with a quick-drying solution. Deciding to take the day off from her job as the membership coordinator at an elite country club, and head to the spa where she'd be forced to stay away from her computer and the tempting refresh button, had to be Gina's best idea ever.

Callie knew to keep a level head and not to expect too much, regardless of Gina's enthusiasm. Everyone in the one authors' forum that she'd decided to join said the same things—*Gaining readers is a marathon, not a sprint. Do not put too much stock in your debut book. Do not waste money on advertising, but just keep writing.* One went as far as to say, *The market is completely saturated, so don't get your hopes up.* A few comments, including that one, were not very kind-spirited. If it weren't for her constant pom-pom-waving best friend, Callie may have kept her story in her hard drive and not sent it out into the world.

"Have faith, sweetie. PR is my specialty. Plus, along with everything else, I may or may not have contacted my sorority sister at the morning show in DC... and a different contact at the *Chronicle*... and may have sent a hundred or so copies to a few social media influencer friends of mine."

"You did what? And where did you get copies?"

"Please..." She waved her glossy pink-tipped fingers in the air and blew on them for good measure. "Your password wasn't that difficult to figure out. I went in and ordered some advance copies. Plus, the morning show needed a little spicing up. More than one of the hosts, including my sorority sister, Morgan, read and loved it. Who was I to say not to talk about it? Same with the influencers. Look, if you want to be in the game, you need to get in the game. Benchwarmers don't win titles."

"You're unreal."

"Let's see how unreal I am." Before Callie could say the word *no,* Gina pulled out her phone, going against everything they said they wouldn't do for fear of ruining her day. She watched her bestie quietly scroll and tap her screen; meanwhile, the lump that formed in Callie's throat continued to expand.

Callie kept looking at her best friend, hoping to get even the slightest hint as to what was happening with her book. Then, much to her dismay, Gina slowly lowered her phone and let out a breath before turning her head toward Callie.

"What? Is it bad? Do I not have a sale? Are the reviews horrible? Do I even have reviews? Should I have not released today, since it's a Thursday?" Callie dropped her head into her hands before peeking through two of her freshly manicured fingers. "Go ahead, rip off the bandage. I can take it." *Lord knew she had already survived hot wax being used in places where it didn't belong.*

When she saw her bestie's shoulders release any stature they had, she almost told her to keep it to herself. But it was too late. "Look, this is your first book," Gina started off saying in a soft, almost motherly tone. Callie looked up and nodded, doing her best to not look disappointed. "It's such a major accomplishment to even write a book. Not to mention a romance that even had me blushing… and I'm not the *good girl* in our twosome." At that, Callie forced a smile at her friend's claim. She had stepped way out of her comfort zone to write *Ready to Fall,* much like she had in the waxing room. Gina went on, "I'm so proud of you. I absolutely loved your story, and you know that I declared your sexy hero, Hudson Newman, as my own. I mean, how could I not? Who wouldn't want a tall, dark, stunningly handsome, and successful man who is looking for love? I can't wait for book two!"

When Callie had created her book's hero, she'd merely put on paper the type of man she'd want. The sort that had eluded her. She'd kissed a few frogs over the years, and it wasn't as though she were looking for Prince Charming—she just wanted a man who knew her worth and appreciated it. Gina was right. What woman wouldn't want a man like Hudson? He was perfect… and sadly lived only in her imagination.

"Yes, I know. Thank you, and despite him being fictional, he's all yours." Doing her best not to smudge her freshly tinted Tiffany Blue toes, she sat up a bit straighter, ready to slide out of the large leather chair and go home to drown her sorrows in a big vat of hazelnut-flavored chocolate. She was beyond thankful that she'd decided to use a pen name. At least people who knew her wouldn't look

The BOOK BOYFRIEND

at her with sympathetic eyes. Finally upright, she forced a smile. "I appreciate your support and for everything you did."

"Sweetie, I'm not sure how to tell you this, but you better sit your cute butt back down, because once we leave here, you have a lot of work to do."

What could she possibly need to do? Who wanted to do anything after so many hours of work had failed? It only proved why she loved her day job. It was stable and brought in a steady paycheck. The only person she had to rely on to make money was herself, not the spending habits of others. Still, Gina looked so convinced at her statement. "Why?" Callie finally asked.

"Because, my friend… you… are… trending!" Gina's boisterous voice had others in the salon turning their way. Her voice hitting fever pitch, she beamed: "Your book isn't ranked yet, but trust me, when it is, it's going to be fantastic, because your social media is blowing up."

Callie's jaw dropped. "What?" She grabbed Gina's phone and couldn't believe what she saw. Early readers and bloggers were posting and tagging her all over the place.

> *Lily May's debut book is fire!*
>
> *Oh, Hudson… I'm ready to catch you.*
>
> *I'm calling it… Hudson Newman is the hottest book boyfriend of the year… no, the CENTURY!*
>
> *Where can I find my own Hudson? *fans self**

"Oh my gosh!" Callie finally said, handing Gina her phone.

"You're so lucky I'm not the type to say, 'I told you so.' You know what, forget it. Who am I kidding? I'm exactly that type. I told you so. All you needed to do was burn that negative energy and manifest the positive."

Callie's blonde hair bounced as she bobbed her head, still in shock. "And have the best bestie ever."

"Well, yes, that goes without saying. Get ready, Cal, because you, my friend, are on your way to becoming a bestselling author, and everyone is going to want a piece of you."

A sudden bout of panic tickled each one of Callie's nerves. It wasn't just a saying that a person could feel the blood draining from their face, because if she had to guess, Callie looked more like Casper than her usually rosy self. Her head spun and suddenly Gina's silhouette had doubled… no, tripled.

"Cal, honey, are you okay? Here, drink this." After a quick nod, Callie closed her eyes, took a few deep breaths, and accepted the bottle of water from Gina, who added: "We've got this."

"We? Will you help me?"

"Consider me your personal PR person. Heck, I'll go as far as being your agent. Granted, I'm a novice to the book world, but I'll figure it out. Clearly I did something right with your ads and early copies." She stood and helped Callie out of the leather recliner. "Let's get out of here and strategize. We have work to do. We need to strike while the iron's hot."

Again, all Callie could do was blink. The only plausible explanation was that she must have been dreaming. After practically floating out of the salon, they hopped in Gina's car and were in Callie's apartment in record time. Gina plopped down on the sofa. "Okay, I think having a publisher would be beneficial."

Callie snort-laughed, knowing how hard they were to come by. Gina didn't know that she had queried the book's synopsis to a few, only to be rejected. "You make it sound so easy."

"Numbers talk. And from the looks of this, you're going to have the numbers."

Once again, and still shocked, she couldn't disagree. "I'm no longer sure I want a publisher. Everything is happening so fast. Let's put a hold on the publisher search. What else?"

They spent the rest of the day adding to Callie's to-do list, and by the time Gina left, Callie didn't bother checking on her book's ranking. Instead, she climbed into bed and prayed that when she woke up in the morning, today wouldn't be a dream.

CHAPTER 2

On a normal day, Callie didn't need to force herself to focus, but ever since she'd released her book two weeks and three days ago, everything had seemed to tilt on its axis. Where she used to receive few emails unrelated to a subscribed list, she now received more than one hundred... per day. She had been getting requests for everything from the links to her character Hudson's social media pages—something she thought to be a bit extreme—to readers asking for more.

Gina, who sat next to her, sifted through a different email account, clicking and typing away.

"What are you doing?"

"Creating your reader group and posting the link to your newsletter."

"A what? In where?"

"Group." Her flat reply had Callie furrowing her brows. "Seriously, Cal, how do you not know this stuff? Authors create online groups so their readers can stay up to date and also chat about your books. Don't worry, I made myself the admin."

Callie exhaled and then counted to five. It wasn't as though she were annoyed with Gina. She wasn't annoyed at all, just confused. "I feel like I'm a fish out of water here, G. I woke up one day and decided to finally put my thoughts down in somewhat of an organized fashion. Then released it a couple of weeks ago. I never expected anything like this would happen. It was just a story that I thought of. We all know…" She raised her hands and made air quotes. "*That* guy."

"The hot guy?" Gina asked, with a tilt to her smirk.

"No, the guy who doesn't want a relationship. The player. The BMOC, the one that turns every girl's head but refuses to turn his. And… ," she continued, with a palm facing Gina. "I'm not saying that guy is a jerk. He's someone who knows what he wants and what he doesn't. It's just in *Ready to Fall* he takes a look at it and figures it out, you know what I mean?"

She nodded. "Yes, and hold that thought, because whatever you're going to say to me, we need to write it down for our publisher pitch."

"I'm sorry, the what? I thought we put a pin in that."

"Yes, we did, but being prepared is key. Did you not appoint me your agent?"

Callie nodded and then laughed. "Yes, over a few mimosas. Like I said before, I'm not sure I want a publisher, Gina. Maybe in the future we can revisit it. Do you know how many people say this is a fluke? And need I remind you that you, my friend, have a full-time job, as do I."

Gina placed the laptop she'd been working on aside and stood. "Callie Richardson, I'm going to give this to you straight." Callie cocked a brow at her best friend's sudden motherly tone. "You let me worry about the naysayers. You do you. People can be mean when they feel threatened. Yes, you're the newbie, but that doesn't automatically make you a one-hit wonder. Nothing in life is guaranteed. I'll say it again: you just do you and let me handle the rest. Got it? Plus, you wrote one of the sexiest book boyfriends ever. That has been a constant in reviews. I've read them all. Okay?"

Callie nodded.

The pair sat in Callie's living room, going over the first newsletter, which included a "thank you to readers" letter and a few teasers. Gina wanted to make sure the momentum continued, which Callie could understand. Again… axis tilting. They ordered takeout, and before they knew it, the sun had been replaced by the moon.

Gina went back to her apartment, and Callie decided to call it a night. She tossed her glasses on the side table, locked up, and dragged her butt into the bathroom. When she stared into the mirror, she sighed. Her usually shiny blonde hair seemed

The BOOK BOYFRIEND

lackluster, most likely from her constantly running her hand through it, turning it into a frizz-fest, and her eyes bordered on gray rather than their usual green hue. In short, she was exhausted. Forgoing her nightly skin-care ritual, she brushed her teeth and crawled into bed, not believing the weekend was already over.

Callie got in her car and headed to Birchwood Assisted Living Center, where her grandmother now lived. Ever since she'd written *Ready to Fall,* she had wanted to tell her nana all about it. After all, if it wasn't for her always encouraging Callie, who knows if she ever would have written the book.

Visiting her grandmother lately had become more and more concerning. Yes, Alzheimer's was a tricky and cruel disease. The first time she didn't recognize Callie had scared the living daylights out of her. Her grandmother had taken care of her, and she was the one constant in her life, so to have her not know her own granddaughter's name took the word *sad* to a completely different level.

Priscilla Livingston was the epitome of grace and class. She always did for others, despite losing her husband at a young age and having a daughter who, after leaving her with her two children, went off to who knows where doing who knows what. Yet her grandmother stayed strong through it all.

Callie pulled up to the large white apartment-like development, parked her car, and got out. She had hoped to get Nana flowers but didn't want to miss her appointment time. The staff did their best to keep their residents on a schedule so they wouldn't get confused—which she appreciated.

When she strode through the double doors, the familiar scent of cleaning products wafted around her as she made her way to the check-in desk.

"Hi, Callie."

"Hi, Monica. How's she doing today?"

The sweet nurse gave Callie a reassuring smile. "Today is a good day. Priscilla just got her hair done and is due to go for a walk. She's in the community room. You're more than welcome to take her."

"That would be wonderful. Thank you." She signed in, clipped a visitor's badge to her purse, and headed down the hall. Sounds of chatter filled the large room. A couple of residents were playing checkers, some playing cards. Others were sitting in chairs, looking out the window, enjoying the sunny summer day.

When she spotted her grandmother sitting in her wheelchair, a large smile spread across her face. Callie waved to a few familiar faces and then prayed her nana would recognize her.

"Hi, Nana."

"Callie." She stretched out her aged hand.

Tears welled in Callie's eyes as she stared at her favorite person. Callie took her hand. "It's so good to see you. Your hair looks beautiful."

"I just had it done."

"Miss Priscilla, it's time to go for a walk. Would you like Callie to take you?"

"Oh yes, that would be wonderful."

Callie gripped the handles of the wheelchair and guided them out of the facility and into the immaculately groomed courtyard. They ended up at the fountain in the middle of the perfectly landscaped area, surrounded by benches.

Callie wanted to tell her about the book, and she was about to when her grandmother said, "I can't be out here too long because Alan will be looking for me soon. He just went to get some apples for me to make pie. That man loves my apple pie. Did you remember to take the turkey out of the oven?"

Callie's heart dropped. Alan was her grandfather, who'd passed away before she was born. And just like that, her grandmother was gone. Each time was getting quicker and quicker. Callie almost wished she could move in with her so she'd be around for the better times.

Per usual, Callie played along. "Yes, Nana. I did."

"That's my sweet girl. Now let's go. We don't want to miss the parade."

With a lump in her throat, Callie wheeled her grandmother back inside to a nurse stationed in the community room.

Most likely noticing Callie's despondent expression, the sweet woman asked, "Time for a rest?"

"Yes, I think she's had enough for today."

Callie squatted next to the chair. Her grandmother's eyes seemed to focus on the door leading out into the hallway. "I'm going to go now, Nana. I'll see you soon, okay?" When she didn't respond, Callie stood and kissed her grandmother on the cheek, thankful that she had gotten to spend a little bit of time with her.

CHAPTER 3

Hudson Newman had a daily routine: wake up, work out, shower, coffee, office… in that order. Ever since he was young, he'd stuck to schedules. In his opinion, order surpassed chaos and boosted productivity any day of the week—and sometimes on weekends. It was something his father, an ex-marine, had drilled into his head as a child, and it stuck.

Monday-morning traffic greeted him as he pulled onto the highway to head toward work. Despite there being a coffee shop not far from the gym, and even having a pot in his office's break room, Hudson preferred the brew at the smaller, independently owned café next to the building where he worked.

It was a perfect summer day: clear skies, warm

air, and low humidity — a rarity in Virginia. Not that Hudson spent much of his time out of the office. Still, he could appreciate it. As a military brat, he had been all over the world. He'd had his share of brutally cold winters and rainy springs. When he and his family had settled in Virginia, he'd welcomed the seasons. What he wasn't fond of was the traffic. If he didn't like to be in control of his destiny, he would take the Metro to the office.

Twenty minutes later, he pulled into his assigned spot and headed toward the small café. The familiar smell of arabica beans and freshly baked pastries greeted him as soon as he walked in and stood in the short line. It didn't matter how many people were in front of him. Annie, his usual barista, looked up as though she sensed his presence. Hudson smiled, and her face flushed pink. *Interesting.* She whispered something to her coworker, Jen, and he swore she batted her eyes. Hudson pivoted, thinking someone was behind him, but there wasn't.

He'd been going to that café since it opened. Never had she batted anything at him, let alone blush. Maybe she'd had too much caffeine that morning or possibly needed more.

Finally his turn, he stepped up to the counter.

"Hi, Mr. Newman." She had worked the counter for the past two years and usually had his large black dark roast coffee ready for him. But today she placed a small espresso in front of him, along with a white pastry bag.

"Good morning, Annie." A bit confused, he looked at the tiny coffee and bag before bringing his attention back to her. "What's this?"

"Espresso with a twist of lemon and a blueberry scone." Hudson thought the shop might be having a special, but then she added, "Your favorite."

Hudson chuckled. "Annie, have I ever ordered an espresso or a scone?"

She shook her head.

"Right, because I prefer my usual: large dark roast, black… to go. Are you okay?"

"Yes, umm… sorry. I just thought, well, because of… you know… in the…"

He cocked his head to the side.

"Never mind." She fumbled with the lid on the cup before he took over and secured it himself. "It's on the house."

Still a bit confused, but running out of time, he handed her a five-dollar bill, thanked her, and walked out. His phone dinged, signaling that he had a meeting in twenty minutes. He hustled around the corner and into his office building. The vast marble lobby echoed with soft chatter and the hum of the elevator taking employees to their designated floor.

After saying hello to the security guard, he noticed a few women staring at him. It wasn't an uncommon occurrence, but their sniggering had been. He smiled, and he swore that one of them, much like Annie, had blushed. He'd seen them before but didn't know them. Still, that reaction had never been one he'd received from either woman.

Hudson pressed the "Up" button, and once the brass door closed, he hit the number twelve. As the illuminated numbers climbed, he sipped his coffee, savoring the full-bodied nutty flavor.

The car arrived on his floor, thankfully without any stops along the way. On a high-pitched ding, the doors slid open, dropping him off steps away from the receptionist's desk.

"Good morning, Caleb."

"Mr. Newman, sir, good morning."

Hudson turned and headed toward his office, passing cubicles on the way. Being one of the executives at Logan Enterprises, he prided himself on knowing everyone in the company's name. Despite being only thirty-one, he'd climbed the ranks quickly, but that didn't make him better than anyone. Hudson also knew that taking an interest in a colleague, regardless of the level of seniority, made a difference in how work got accomplished.

The familiar tapping of a keyboard alerted him that his assistant, Keira, was busy at work.

"Good morning," Hudson said. "Welcome back. I hope you had a nice vacation. For the record, you're not allowed to take a week off again." He laughed, but she clumsily stood, sending her chair into the back wall and almost knocking her large tumbler of coffee onto the floor. Hudson darted forward, but Keira righted it before it soiled the gray-patterned carpeting.

"Everything okay, Keira? I was only kidding."

"So sorry, Mr. Newman." Keira replaced the cup

back onto the desk and straightened her spine. She started rattling off his schedule, which he already had memorized. Except at the end of it all Keira said, "I put your mail… and packages on the table in your office. The mail room put them in my cubicle, not knowing I was away."

Hudson's brow furrowed. "Packages?"

Keira's face flamed red. "Yes… er… you have quite a few. I opened them, but…"

He watched his assistant twist her fingers together.

"I wasn't sure what to do with all of it. I'm sorry, sir. I can—"

Hudson put his hand up. "I got it. Why don't you take a break."

Not arguing that she had just started her day, she nodded and darted around the corner into the break room, where he heard a few giggles. Ignoring whatever alternate universe he'd arrived at this morning, he made his way to his office, and when he walked in, Hudson couldn't help but notice the abundance of small opened boxes piled up on his table. *What in the world?*

He picked up a box and pulled out a red lacy thong and a small card containing a picture of the tall blonde modeling the gift she'd sent. A bit stunned, he flipped the picture over to find her name and number along with *#ReadyToFall*. Confused, he moved on to the next box. In that one was another red lacy pair of women's underwear, with no picture but a name, number, and, again, that same hashtag. Moving on, thong, thong, thong, matching bra — *That was different* — and then he came upon a heavier box. Hudson flipped open the flaps to find a bottle of cologne — not his brand, but still expensive. And once again, a note with her name and personal information. Why would anyone, in this case Katie, send it to him?

Hudson sifted through more boxes, some including candy, and then he pulled out another pair of panties at the exact moment his colleague and best friend, Jack, walked in. "Not sure red is really your color. You seem more of a sunshine yellow to me."

Hudson dropped the underwear. "What is all of this?" Jack asked, picking up one of the pictures. "Who's Mandi?"

"No clue."

Taking a quick inventory, he had a few dozen panties — all red lace — cologne, and bags of sour candy in the shape of moons, which he'd never liked, even as a kid. And each note looked the same, with the same hashtag. Between Annie, the women in the lobby, Keira, and now the bizarre gifts, if Jack hadn't been enjoying this so much, Hudson would have asked him to punch him to make sure he was indeed awake.

Ignoring the table, Hudson moved behind the desk, sat in his chair, and fired up his laptop.

Jack sat opposite him. "I came in here to discuss the Abbott acquisition. Should I come back?"

Hudson shook his head. The Abbott deal would bring a substantial amount into the business he'd worked so hard to first acquire and then help succeed with Jack by his side.

"No, it's fine. Let me just grab the contract. It should be sitting in my inbox." When he clicked the little white envelope icon, he thought his email information must have been sold or he had been hacked, because it sounded as though someone had run a mallet up and down a marimba.

"What's going on?"

Hudson shook his head. "No idea."

Needing to get back to business, he finally found the contract buried beneath a slew of emails from random women. He had to be getting pranked. If Jack didn't look as stunned as Hudson felt, he would think his buddy had something to do with the anarchy that had started off his day.

Ignoring it and moving on, the pair went over the financials, tweaking a bit here and there until they were satisfied and two hours had passed. Hudson's chair creaked with the force of his body disentangling back muscles that had been in a knot since he'd sat down.

At least he and Jack had made progress and, in their opinion, penned an even better contract. When signed by Abbott's CEO, the company was slated to make seven figures, pushing the chaos of the morning to the back of his mind.

That was, until Jack looked at an incoming message on his phone.

"I don't know how to tell you this, but you're trending," Jack said.

"I'm what?"

"Trending."

"You mean the company? Is it that article again?"

Last month, his picture had been attached to an article that featured a report he'd published. It had gotten quite a few hits, but nothing that would warrant it trending. *Had it gotten republished?*

Jack shook his head and chuckled. "Nope. My sister Natalie just texted me. *You* are a hashtag." He handed Hudson his phone.

Blinking, Hudson saw his name on the right side of the screen, along with the same *ReadyToFall* hashtag written on the majority of the cards and emails. He tapped one of the posts and almost dropped the device onto his desk.

> *I'm ready to catch you. #HudsonNewman #ReadyToFall*

Then clicked the next one.

> *Hottest book boyfriend on the planet. #HudsonNewman #ReadyToFall #mybookboyfriend*

And the next one.

> *Fanning myself. #ReadyToFall #hudsonnewmanhasbeenclaimed #fallforme #HNisMine*

"What's a book boyfriend?" The question had meant to be said to himself, but Jack shrugged. Hudson continued to scroll, reading similar posts, including his name and the same three words, *ready to fall,* preceded by, of course, a hashtag.

The BOOK BOYFRIEND

A faint knock on his door almost made him jump. Keira walked in with a vase full of colorful wildflowers. "Excuse me, sir, but these were just delivered." The strong floral scent quickly permeated the space. Jack earned a glare from Hudson when he let out a loud chuckle.

"Who sent them?"

"Hillary."

Not knowing anyone by that name, he exhaled. "You can keep them, Keira."

"Oh, are you sure? Would you like the card?" When he narrowed his eyes, she added, "Thank you. I'll be at my desk."

Normally, other than the weather or idle chitchat, Hudson wouldn't ask Keira anything personal, but he needed answers. "Keira, just a minute. Do you know what a book boyfriend is?" When she turned, her face flamed red, and she nodded. Still clueless, he prodded, "Do you know why my name would be associated with that term?" Again, she bobbed her head forward. "Care to tell me?"

His usually collected assistant nibbled the side of her lip, averting her eyes from him.

"What's going on, Keira?"

"Um…" She shifted the vase in her hands. "Your name has been used in a book. And an image of you from the article in last month's report has been linked to that character. It's also been posted on social media… with all of his preferences. I'll show you."

She walked out of the office, and when she came back, rather than the flowers in her hand, she had a book. When she flipped it around, he couldn't believe what he was seeing. It wasn't the barechested, headless man on the cover holding a pair of... you guessed it... red lace panties. But it was the title that shocked him—*Ready to Fall* by Lily May.

Keira handed it to him. "Ali, in the mail room, read it and gave it to me to borrow. I just finished it over the weekend. It's a bestseller. I wasn't sure how to tell you." She worked down a swallow. "The hero's name is... well... it's... err..." Both men stared at her. Finally, she completed her thought: "Hudson Newman." She forced a smile, and Jack exploded with laughter.

"Well, on that note," Jack said, slapping his hands on his knees before standing, "I'll be in my office. Have fun with that."

When he stepped out, Hudson looked at Keira. "Thank you. I didn't mean to make you feel uncomfortable."

"You didn't. Is there anything I can get you?"

"Yes, a copy of that book... and Lily May's contact info."

CHAPTER 4

*H*udson spent his weekend reading *Ready to Fall* for the second time. The first had been as though he were in a fog. The words seemed to bleed into one another. Most likely due to the ire that simmered in his veins with each sentence that his eyes scanned. A bit calmer, yet still annoyed, he read the ending: the part, he was convinced, that had sent his life into a spiral of courtship.

He turned and looked at the sea of guests at the large outdoor wedding before he heard the minister formally declare his brother off the market. In the past, weddings would make Hudson break out into a cold sweat, but today that hadn't been the case. Could it be that he was ready to share his life with someone? To take the chance and fall in love in hopes of not losing it? To give up the life of one-night stands and unemotional sex for a true relationship? And what woman would be ready for a man like him? Perhaps being the most sought-after bachelor was overrated? A few weeks ago, that thought would have made him laugh out loud. That one woman could win his heart. But today, after witnessing his brother, someone he admired, recite his vows, Hudson Newman decided he wanted that for himself... that it was time for him to open his heart.

He glanced around the marquee tent, and although he had dated more than one guest and a bridesmaid, no one there was the one for him. It wasn't as though he expected to easily find his soul mate, but that wouldn't deter him. Excitement coursed through him as he thought about all the possibilities and the fact that he, too, was ready to fall.

Hudson shook his head. *The author clearly doesn't know me,* he thought. Hudson had a sister, not a brother, and wanting a relationship had been the furthest thing from his mind. Lily May wrote that *her* Hudson was ready to fall in love. Hence his current plight. The uncanny part that stuck in his throat had been her description of him, which had been spot-on: six-foot-two height, light scruff, brown hair, deep-blue eyes, and a fit physique.

Now Hudson sat at his desk sifting through business emails that Keira had forwarded to him. The woman deserved a raise for taking on the task of filtering through proposals of a personal nature. Yes, a few women had proposed marriage. A couple even went as far as sending rings, which Keira promptly sent back. She also had the horrible task of fielding dozens of phone calls that had nothing to do with business. Of course, she'd never complain about it. From what he could tell, she felt sorry for him.

After scrubbing his face with his hands, Hudson sipped bitter coffee that he'd poured for himself from the carafe in the break room rather than enjoy the smooth blend he'd been used to from the café. Sadly, he hadn't frequented the establishment in the past ten days. He rolled his chair away from his desk and got up to stare out his window. The cloudy day outside mirrored his disposition. His life had been in constant disarray for almost three weeks, which felt more like a year. How could one book spark such a frenzy? Granted, if he were the romance-book-type reader, he may have a different opinion. It had been well written, and if he were being honest, Hudson was put in a good light, and maybe he would have thought differently if the character wasn't using his physical characteristics and his name… and if his ordinary life hadn't blown up.

At first he thought maybe it had been an ex of his that had taken on the pen name and made him the hero of their book. Then Jack reminded him that if his exes thought he was a hero, they'd still be together.

Jack sat in Hudson's office, babbling on about his weekend. It all sounded like white noise until he hit him with, "You do understand you're a chick magnet now, right? The woman I was with Saturday night had a copy of *Ready to Fall* on her coffee table. When I asked her about it, her face turned bright pink."

Hudson glared at his so-called best friend and business associate.

"Yes, that was my reaction as well. Then she started reading it to me. I've been in the locker room with you, and let's just say that Lily May has exaggerated a bit."

Hudson lifted his hand and extended his middle finger. Jack laughed; then a knock on the door halted their conversation. Keira stood in the doorway, holding yet another box. His office had continued receiving gifts, making it look as though a bachelorette party had thrown up in it. Panties, bras, books on the best Kama Sutra positions, sweets that were the character's favorites, massage oils… and a few *toys* to spice up the bedroom. On top of that, there were pictures attached with some of the gifts.

"Excuse me," Keira said, taking a step in. "This just came for you. Also, I finally tracked down Lily May. I had to use one of your contacts to find her."

He didn't care if she used every name in his electronic phone book. The only thing that mattered was he finally could confront the person who had turned his life on its head. He just hoped she lived in the US. Although, at this point, he'd travel to Timbuktu if he had to. Then Keira handed him the slip of paper, and he studied the name on it: Callie Richardson. Nope. Didn't ring a bell.

"Are you sure this is her?"

"Yes. I found her agent, Gina Greco, on social media. She works for a public relations and marketing firm. It's the same firm that handled Genevieve Markus's hat business."

Hudson's brows furrowed.

"You remember Genevieve? She is Lincoln Jenson's sister. He works for the investment company that handled the Garrett deal."

Hudson rolled his hand, doing his best to spur her on without being rude.

"Right, anyway, Gina Greco, who is also Lily May's agent, works for that company. When I went on Gina's page, I looked at her followers and found a picture of her at lunch drinking champagne with a woman. The book, *Ready to Fall,* was sitting on the table. She tagged the author, but when I did a reverse image search, it brought me to Callie Richardson's social media page."

"So what you're saying is Lily May is really Callie Richardson?"

A beaming smile spread across his assistant's face as though she had just found the Holy Grail. *Then again, maybe she had.* "Correct. And according to what her page said, she works at Shadow Oaks Country Club."

Hudson could have been knocked over with a light breeze. *She's local?* He'd been to that country club on more than one occasion. It hadn't been difficult, since it was in the same town as his office. *Had Callie Richardson seen him? Did she actually know who he was?* Keira continued, "When I looked up the club's directory, I confirmed that she works in the membership department."

"Remind me to never get on your bad side. Dang, you could be a private investigator," Jack said with wide eyes. Hudson couldn't agree more with his best friend.

Keira smiled before she added, "There's also a start-up petition that people are signing to have the book adapted into a movie. That's sort of exciting."

He thought it was anything but exciting. "Thank you, Keira. You'll be getting a bonus in your next paycheck. Also, please keep all of this to yourself. Oh, and please clear my schedule."

"Yes, sir, and thank you."

Keira floated out of his office, and Jack leaned back in his chair. "What are you going to do now?"

"Go have a little chat with an author."

CHAPTER 5

From her office, she heard her boss chatting with two of the club's board members. Per usual, they were discussing the scores they'd posted over the weekend and the upcoming tournament. Their dedication to the sport was unrelenting. Callie didn't mind playing golf if she had to, but she much preferred tennis. Although, she'd been so busy, she didn't get much time to do either.

Callie had a few appointments scheduled for potential members. She'd surpassed her quarterly goal, and the quarter wasn't over for another two months. Maybe when Gina had talked to the stars, she'd manifested success in this area of Callie's world too. Whatever the reason, she couldn't have been happier… nor could her bank account.

She had always prided herself on working hard.

That was how she was raised and hadn't faltered. *Life is what you make of it and what you put into it,* her nana used to say. Callie loved her more than anything and took her words to heart.

A knock on her door pulled her out of her thoughts. When it opened, her assistant, Gwen, popped her head in. "Cal, there's a Mr. Newman here to see you." Callie's brows furrowed. "He said you would know who he was."

The snort-laugh that flew out caught her off guard, and now Gwen's brows were the ones drawn together. "Is it Gina?" Callie asked, rolling her eyes. "I swear she kills me."

Her chuckle died when Gwen tilted her head. "No, I haven't seen Miss Greco today. And unless she morphed into a six-foot-something male model that has turned the head of every female and some men that he's walked by, I can assure you it's not her. I asked Mr. Newman what it was regarding, but he said you would know. I thought maybe you scheduled something… personal."

Still confused, Callie assumed this was one of Gina's antics. Knowing her, she'd hired a Rock Hudson look-alike to come to the office. Callie hoped he didn't burst into song or something worse. The last thing she needed was for someone at the club to find out she was a romance author. Shadow Oaks Country Club was one of the most exclusive clubs in Virginia.

Faking realization, she feigned recollection and snapped her fingers. "Right, right, Mr. Newman. Feel free to send him in."

The BOOK BOYFRIEND

Her assistant nodded and walked out, probably thinking Callie was a few golf balls shy of a dozen. She picked up her phone, ready to send a text to her best friend as to what she was up to, when the most gorgeous man stepped into her office.

All she could do was blink. And stare. And blink a few more times. Her mind wandered to the hero in her book, and then went down the line as she studied the man in front of her. Tall… check. Soft brown, sexily styled hair… check. Deep-blue eyes that didn't need the sun to sparkle… check. Looked like a dream in a tailored suit… check. Model-worthy smile… nope. This man wore a scowl. And why was he carrying a box?

"Hi, may I help you?"

"Lily May?"

Callie's heart leaped to her tonsils. She scurried around him and shut the door before heading back to her desk. The fear of someone hearing him pierced her heart, sending her pulse to ricochet through her veins. "No, you're mistaken. I'm Callie Richardson."

"Right." His towering frame should have intimidated her, but instead she felt her heart racing—and not from fear. A ghost of a beard shadowed his jawline, which currently ticced on the right side. Before she could stop him, he opened the box, dumped the contents on her desk, and let the box fall to the floor. Piles of red lace, sour candy that she'd written about in her book, pictures of scantily clad women… She narrowed her eyes, not believing what she was seeing. Then something purple rolled off her desk and landed on her floor with a thud. *Is that a —* Callie gasped and rushed to pick up the box.

"What are you doing?" she gritted out. As quickly as she could, she put everything back into the container and covered it, as though the panties and the rest of the items had sharp teeth, ready to strike. She set it on her desk. "Who are you?"

The stunning stranger with the familiar name crossed his arms, accentuating his broad chest. "Hudson Newman. The man you wrote about. The man whose life you've turned upside down thanks to your silly book."

Callie's eyes narrowed. *Silly?*

"How dare you use my name? My likeness." He flicked his attention to the box before shifting his eyes back to her. "That box is one of more than a dozen. I could stock a women's lingerie store… among other things."

Callie propped her fisted hands onto her hips. "I have no idea what that has to do with me."

"Do you or don't you use the pen name Lily May?"

Callie could feel the earth shift beneath her feet. How could this man possibly know her alias?

There was nothing more she disliked than lying, and she was also horrible at it. Each time she told one, her left eye would twitch. It was why she'd never gotten away with anything as a teenager.

"What would make you think so?"

She had been so careful to cover her tracks… or so she thought.

"Are you saying you aren't her?"

His deep voice left a heavy weight in the air. Despite the pounding in her rib cage, and knowing once she admitted it, everything could blow up… and not in a good way, what else could she do? Callie knew she had one choice. Come clean and then beg for his silence.

"Yes. I wrote it. But Mr. Newman, my book is fictional, as are my characters, and I prefer no one know I'm the author." All she could picture were parents pulling their kids out of her class at the dance school.

"Well, my name isn't fictional. My life was nice and quiet, just how I liked it. I'm a man who appreciates order, and your book disrupted all of that. Do you know I've received marriage proposals? I have women sending pictures to my office email dressed in all sorts of ways… and I haven't had a decent cup of coffee in three weeks."

"Things could be worse than women throwing themselves at you. Plus, I'm sure it's not the first time." He cocked a brow and an oddly sexy smirk appeared. Callie wanted to smack her forehead or him. Yes, him… definitely, him. Ignoring her slip-up, she gave him her own grin. "Most men would be here with flowers to thank me. Also, I have no idea what your lack of knowing how to make coffee has to do with me."

"You think I should thank you? With flowers? Are you kidding? You used my name… not a common one, I might add. Your hero looks like me.

Dresses like me. Is a businessman like me. Except guess what?"

Callie was afraid to ask, so she remained silent.

"I'm not looking for love or am"—he lifted his fingers to make air quotes—"ready to fall. What I am ready for is getting my life back. I can't go into my favorite café without everyone acting like they've witnessed some sort of second coming."

Ignoring all else, she blinked a few times, not completely understanding. "You read my book?" Callie could feel her cheeks redden, and she felt a surge of pride. Like a fool, Callie added, "Thank you. I'm a bit surprised. And like I said, I used a fictional name." A sweet memory sprang to mind. "My grandmother and I would watch Rock Hudson and Paul Newman movies. They were her favorite actors. Hence, Hudson Newman. So I'm sorry if you're inconvenienced, but I promise it's just a coincidence. It actually says that in the front of my book." Callie almost recited the copyright disclaimer about all names and places being fictional. Instead, she sat down, rolled her shoulders back, and looked at the gorgeous man, who, if she had a muse for her book's hero, would look like the man in front of her, but that was beside the point. "Now, if you don't mind, I have work to do."

She watched as he lowered his arms and gripped the edge of her desk. The end of his charcoal-gray tie brushed the papers she had been working on.

"I, too, have work to do, and I can't do it. Thanks to you and your fans."

His deep, gravelly voice would have turned her on if he hadn't sounded like a school principal ready to send her to detention. "I'm sorry, but what do you expect me to do about it?"

"I'll tell you what you're going to do about it. You're going to delist the book. I happen to know someone who could help with that."

Callie huffed, then defiantly shook her head. First, Gina would kill her. Second, her sales were still climbing. Third, she was proud of what she'd done. Regaining her backbone, she crossed her arms in front of her chest. "I'm not doing that. Figure out something else."

His intimidating glare wasn't going to make her budge. How dare he walk in and be so demanding. She thought that if they were in a different scenario, like one in her book, his alpha male personality would be a major turn-on. Except, they weren't in a book they were in her office which made everything ten times worse. All she needed was for someone to walk in. Then, throwing her completely off guard, he looked her square in the eyes. "Are you single?"

"What? Why? I'm not sure what my relationship status has to do with anything."

Hudson didn't flinch a millimeter. Instead, his eyes bore into hers, goading her to answer. An aviary of tiny winged creatures decided to use her spine as a xylophone. Doing her best to squash the goose bumps ready to sprout, she answered blankly: "Not that it is any of your business, but yes, I'm single."

"Not anymore, you're not."

A full-blown guffaw died on her lips when the intensity in his gaze doubled.

"What are you talking about?"

"You're now my girlfriend."

The man standing before her may have been the most gorgeous man she'd ever seen. And he must emit some magic pheromones, because her body had never reacted to anyone as it did to him. Too bad he was delusional.

"I beg your pardon?"

"You heard me."

"What makes you think I'd agree to that?"

"Here are your choices: delist the book or date me."

No way had she heard him correctly. Short of sticking her finger into her ear and wiggling it around, she simply shook her head. This man was clearly used to getting what he wanted. Bummer for him that the last thing Callie wanted was a boyfriend. Except there was a shift in him. His tense, penetrating, sky-blue eyes softened. He let out a breath, never breaking their ocular connection. Callie began to feel a bit responsible for the dark circles beneath his eyes. Something she thought had to do with the coffee comment, but date him?

"I'm sorry. I really am. However, I'm not delisting the book. And I'm not dating you. Plus, how will us being together solve your problem?"

"If I'm off the market, your fans will leave me alone."

The man was stunning. Women had to be tripping over themselves to get his attention. "I'm sure you can find another willing participant. It's not like you're hard on the eyes."

Hudson cocked a brow.

"Generally speaking, of course."

He nodded. "Of course." Hudson took a step toward her. "Yes, you're right. I could find someone to date, but this arrangement will be just that. An arrangement. No expectations. No feelings. No disappointment."

She really couldn't argue that point. "For how long?"

"For as long as it takes."

This time her sarcastic laugh didn't die on her lips; instead it rang loudly in her office. "That is the most ridiculous thing I've ever heard. I hate to break it to you, but determined women aren't dissuaded by another woman hanging on the arm of the man they want. If anything, it will spur them on."

Callie knew this to be true. The last man she dated had been gorgeous. Not as beautiful as the one standing in her office, but it never mattered if she were holding his hand or if his arm were slung around her shoulders. Women who set their eyes on him didn't stop because of it. She never understood why, because if Callie saw a man was taken, she would not even consider making a move. When she glanced up at Hudson, there was no doubt that women would continue to pursue him. Nor did he shift his stance.

Would she want to go through that again? The simple and definitive answer was no.

"It won't work," she stated emphatically.

"It will. If you don't agree, I'll be forced to—"

Her hand flew up into the air. "Fine, I'll date you." The thought of taking her book off the market felt more terrifying than accepting the alternative.

Hudson nodded, his lips twitching almost into a grin. What in the world had she just agreed to? Granted, the man was easier on the eyes than her favorite ice-cream sundae, but date him? He could be a sociopath.

"Wait. First, how do I know you're not a sociopath? Let me see some ID."

Great, Callie, like a driver's license will have his mental stability stamped on it. Name: Hudson Newman.... not a sociopath.

Without hesitation, he reached into his inside suit jacket pocket and pulled out his wallet. Why that move was sexy she had no idea. He plucked out his identification and handed it to her. She glanced at it but only had the time to see his name was, in fact, Hudson Newman—and that he was an organ donor—before she handed it back to him. At least he was generous.

"Satisfied?"

"I suppose. Look, for the time being, no one can know I'm the author. I prefer to keep that part of my life separate. It could disrupt everything." Technically, if all went well, she could quit her job, but again the phrase *one-hit wonder* bounced around in her head.

"Yes, I know how annoying disruption can be."

Callie couldn't help but frown. "I said I was sorry."

Hudson raked his hand through his chestnut hair, which looked naturally highlighted, giving it a messy yet still-styled look. *How did men do that?* "I'll keep your identity a secret. Tell your agent or whoever to spin a story. Maybe we found each other because of this book. I don't care what explanation you or she uses, just please do it. Unless you'd rather I date her instead."

For whatever reason, picturing Hudson with Gina created a pang of jealousy that slammed into her chest. "No. I'm sure she'll come up with something."

"Great. I'll pick you up after work. We'll go to dinner at Prism, get our story straight, and make sure people see us. How does seven work for you?"

"It doesn't. Look, Mr. Newman—"

"Hudson."

"Hudson," she corrected before continuing, "I'll agree to this plan of yours, but don't start bossing me around. I'll meet you at the restaurant." Callie grabbed a piece of paper and scribbled down her number. "Here."

She handed it to him, stood, and walked to her door, praying he'd follow. When she placed her hand on the knob and pulled it open, he walked up behind her. His manly cologne intruded on her senses, his breath warmed the back of her neck, and the sensations almost made her teeter into the hallway. Taking a chance, she glanced up at him. He'd been so close that if she were taller, her lips rather than the top of her head would have brushed against his chin.

Hudson leaned down and cupped her cheek with his large, warm palm. Callie's nerves sparked to life. She'd never felt such a connection before. Of course, she'd written about it. Maybe she was dreaming. That had to be it. Then he bent down and kissed her temple. She couldn't understand why he did that, or why she didn't mind that he had.

"Until tonight." He shot her a *make you weak in the knees* wink and walked away.

Yeah... she definitely hadn't been dreaming.

Coming out of her stupor, she knew there was one person who could help her... Gina. She'd know what to do. Callie closed her door, grabbed her phone, and called her best friend.

"Hey, girlfriend. If you're calling about the ad samples I sent you, trust me, abs sell—"

"No, G. It's not abs—I mean ads. It's Hudson Newman." She heard a sigh over the phone. "He was just here. In my office."

"*Who* was there?"

She knew she sounded ridiculous. Callie may as well have said that Santa Claus had walked in with the Tooth Fairy trailing behind him riding on Aladdin's carpet. "Hud-son New-man," she said, annunciating each syllable. "I thought it was a joke, or you set something up when Gwen announced him, but then he stepped through the door and, quite frankly, straight off the pages of my book. Except my guy wasn't as grumpy."

"You lost me."

Callie went on to explain everything that happened. From Hudson getting gifts from Callie's overzealous readers, gifts that still happened to be in her office, to his ultimatum to her now having a fake boyfriend, to the fact that they were going out to dinner.

"First, he can't make you delist the book."

"G, you don't understand how upset he was. He said he knew someone. Hudson suggested having you spin a story about us that looked plausible. You need to come with me tonight. We're going to Prism. You've always wanted to go there."

"First, I'm proud of you for not agreeing to delist the book. And if he's as hot as your guy, then kudos to you! And second, as much as I would love to join you tonight, I have a date with Jordan from accounting."

"You don't even like Jordan from accounting."

"That's not true. I like *parts* of him."

Despite Gina's not being able to see her, Callie's nose crinkled. "You're ridiculous."

"Look, you've got this. I'll call you tomorrow, and you can tell me all about it."

Callie said goodbye and ended the call. She had a feeling it was going to be a long night.

CHAPTER 6

*G*orgeous. Why hadn't he asked Keira to give him a link to her picture before he burst into her office? Callie Richardson was beyond beautiful. Blonde hair, pale-green eyes that darkened to a deep emerald when she became annoyed, and legs that seemed to go on forever even though she was easily seven inches shorter than he was. Her navy dress accentuated every curve—making his heart race. And her glasses made her look like every man's sexy-librarian dream.

Despite her elegant appearance, asking her to be his girlfriend shocked him. He had every intention of forcing her hand to delist the book. Why, then, did he hope that she'd agree to go in that direction instead? He saw the worry lines form and could feel her stress regarding her pseudonym. All Hudson wanted to do was reach forward and run his thumb across her skin to smooth the indentations.

He couldn't remember the last time a woman had that effect on him. If he had to guess, it would be never. Naturally he has had girlfriends, but none who made his heart race like Callie had. Maybe it was annoyance. It didn't matter. Right now their arrangement was a means to an end.

As far as her identity, he had no interest in outing her. And from what he could surmise from the bit of research he'd done after leaving her office, her PR pal should be able to spin the story without compromising her position.

Thinking back, Hudson thought he'd noticed a bit of jealousy in the romance author when he'd mentioned dating her agent rather than her. For someone so adamant about not being his girlfriend, it appeared she sure hadn't wanted him to be with another woman. *Curious,* he thought.

One thing he knew, her skin had felt soft beneath his lips. Aside from the fake-relationship proposal, the last thing he thought he'd do was kiss her. When he noticed her assistant looking at him, and two men chatting at the end of the hallway, Hudson figured there was no time like the present to start their charade. The quicker people saw them in public, the better. But even so, she'd been at work, hence the peck to her temple.

It wasn't lost on him that the foreign feelings that instantly hit him square in the chest were everything he had told her he didn't want. Callie's attitude toward him hadn't been one that he'd been used to either. Everything about her was different from all other women he'd known. And for whatever reason, that intrigued him.

Hudson took a sip of his bitter coffee and brought his focus back to work. Five minutes later, Jack walked in and sat down across from his desk.

"How was the meeting with the author?"

"Please, make yourself comfortable."

Jack laughed but didn't move. Hudson didn't blame him. If the tables had been reversed, he would have acted the same way. At times, it was difficult to take the "frat" out of the boys.

"What happened? Did you tell her about all the gifts you've been getting? Speaking of, I just saw a pair of fuzzy handcuffs on Keira's desk. Unless our dress code has changed, I'm assuming they're for you. Of course, if you don't want them, I'd be happy to take them off your hands—no pun intended."

"You're ridiculous. My meeting with Callie didn't go as expected. I thought I'd tell her to just delist the book and the problem would be solved."

"Good idea. Wait… you *thought* you'd tell her? She's not taking the book down?"

"No. In hindsight it wouldn't have worked anyway. The damage has been done."

"Okay, so what's plan B?"

"I asked her to be my girlfriend."

He stuck his index finger into his ear and shook it. "I'm sorry. I must be hearing things. Did you say 'girlfriend'?"

The BOOK BOYFRIEND

"If I'm off the market, this will all stop."

Jack moved his leg to rest his ankle on his opposite knee and plucked something off his pants. "You clearly don't know women."

Hudson thought back to Callie saying that some women wouldn't be deterred by the announcement, but he would make sure they would be. "It will work—it has to. We're meeting for dinner tonight to discuss logistics."

"Is she pretty?"

No, Hudson thought, *she's gorgeous.* "Very, but that's not the point." Jack's chuckle caused an immediate glare from Hudson. "What? Go ahead and say what you're thinking."

"I'm not thinking anything."

Sure he isn't.

"I wish you good luck."

"Thanks, can we get back to work now? We have the Lansdowne merger meeting in a few hours. Let's start there."

For the rest of the afternoon, Hudson did what he could to keep his mind off Callie. Except it wasn't that easy. He needed to play his cards right because he had a feeling both she and Jack were correct. Maybe other women wouldn't be turned off by a man having a girlfriend. All he knew was he needed to make sure that they were.

Hudson lifted his highball glass and sipped his bourbon just as a blonde caught his attention. He stood and watched Callie approach him. She was dressed a bit more casually in a pale-pink top and white pants, her hair pulled back in a ponytail that swished as she walked.

"Hi, Callie," he said, pulling out a chair for her.

"Hi, and thank you."

They both sat down and stared at one another.

"Couldn't you have picked a more secluded table? We may as well be sitting under a spotlight."

Hudson glanced around and shrugged. "That can be arranged. I know the chef, and I'm sure that Josh would accommodate us."

"Of course you do." Callie unfolded the linen napkin and laid it on her lap. "I still can't believe this is happening."

Hudson could feel her tension roll off her in waves. Lifting his hand, he signaled for the waiter, who took Callie's drink order. "Which part? The part where you wrote a book that everyone's talking about? The part where you used my name as one of your characters, turning my life upside down? Or the part where we're now dating?"

"I didn't use *your* name per se, nor did I intend to flip your life on its head. But the rest of it. Yes. Not to mention the part that you found me. That's terrifying."

Hudson arched his brows.

"You're not terrifying. Well, you were a little scary in my office, but the fact that it was so easy for you to do. I never asked: How did you know I was Lily May?"

"I didn't at first. My assistant, Keira, can take all the credit for that. She followed a trail left behind on social media and then did a reverse image search or something. Sad to tell you that it didn't take her long. I suggest you tell your friend not to post pictures of you. What are you going to do if you have to make a public appearance?"

Callie let out a long breath and frowned. "I don't know. Not do one?"

Her small voice had him wanting to pull her into his arms.

"Like I said, I never in a billion years thought this could happen. Let alone have my little book explode. I meant no harm, you know."

"Have you been writing for a long time?"

She shrugged. "I guess. Hasn't everyone in one way or another? We all have thoughts, and whether we write them in a notebook and shove them in a drawer, in a letter, or just in our minds, we all have a story to tell. That's why there are so many authors. But to answer your question, have I dreamed of being a writer my entire life? No. I had an idea, and rather than keep it in my nightstand, and with Gina's encouragement, I went through the self-publishing process. Everything that came afterward could never have been predicted. I will say, it is eerie looking at you, though."

"How do you mean?" Hudson knew exactly what she meant. As he read the book, it was as though he almost believed the character had been physically based on him.

"Aside from your clear hatred of romance, it's as though you stepped right out of my book. When you walked into my office, I thought for sure Gina had sent you as a joke or something."

He remembered Keira mentioning Gina as the name of her agent and friend. "No joke."

"Clearly." The waiter came back with Callie's white wine and rattled off the specials, to which he ordered the steak and Callie the chicken. She thanked the waiter, who took a moment or two too long to appreciate Hudson's date.

"That'll be all, thank you."

Callie shook her head. "You're so gruff."

"Believe it or not, I'm usually not. And I don't mean to be. Nor do I hate romance. What I dislike is disruption." Hudson took a cleansing breath. He could tell by the remorse etched on her face that Callie hadn't meant any harm, but that didn't negate the fact that his life had been turned on its head. "We need to get to know each other."

A woman hastily weaving her way through the restaurant caught his attention. Her determined strides made him realize the brunette was heading straight for their table. His hackles rose. Pushing his chest out, he prepared himself to ward off whatever the woman had to say. *Another reader?* Maybe it was a good thing. That way Callie could see what he'd been going through. However, aside from Annie's odd behavior, this would be the first woman to actually do anything in person.

Callie must have noticed the eager female, but

rather than an adverse reaction, like Hudson, she popped out of her chair and greeted her with a hug.

After their bonding moment, the woman brought her attention to Hudson, who arched a brow. She stepped around Callie and extended her hand. "Wow, no wonder you're getting gifts. I'm Gina Greco, Callie's best friend and agent."

Hudson stood and took Gina's hand, giving it a small shake. "Nice to meet you. My apologies. I was unaware you'd be joining us." He raised a finger, signaling the waiter to come to the table. "Can we please get another chair and place setting? It looks as though we'll be three for dinner, and please bring a bottle of the chardonnay my lovely companion is drinking and another glass." He looked at Gina. "If that's okay with you, of course."

She nodded.

"Fantastic. She'll also need a menu."

"Oh, I'll just have whatever she's having."

"Very well." The waiter nodded and walked away.

In a matter of seconds, their twosome had grown by one. "So what brings you here tonight, Gina? I may call you Gina, right?"

"Of course… Hudson." She smiled, and Hudson tipped his glass to her before taking a sip. "My best friend, having been given an ultimatum, brings me here tonight."

"I thought you had a date?" Callie asked, seeming a bit put off by Gina's surprise arrival.

"He got stuck at work. So what did I miss?"

Callie brought her up to speed, including how

Keira had found her. Gina apologized profusely and immediately made their picture private on her social media accounts. The server returned with their wine, and Gina took a sip, set her glass down, and rolled her shoulders back. "I'd like to make sure I understand everything, Hudson. You'd like to make it known that you're off the market, correct?"

"Yes, that's right."

"Fine. That means you'll need a media splash. Callie, you, of course, don't want to be linked to Lily."

"Right," they both said simultaneously.

"Hudson, how do you feel about morning shows?"

Hudson and Callie both stared at Gina as though she had two — no, three — heads. He needed more of an explanation.

"That's quite a broad question. Care to elaborate?" Hudson glanced at Callie, who shrugged.

Gina rolled her eyes as though he bored her. Not a typical reaction, but he'd take that over the alternative, which he'd been the target of lately.

"I'm going to call my friend Morgan," said Gina. "We went to college together. She loved the book, is one of Lily's biggest fans, and follows all of Hudson's social media pages. She talked about the book on her show the day it was released. Morgan is local, but the national network picked it up. I'll see to it that it happens again."

Callie finally spoke up. "I can't go on that show,

G." Her voice wavered, and Hudson had to stop himself from placing his hand on hers. *What was that about?*

"Sweetie, you won't need to." She pointed her red-tipped finger at Hudson. "You, on the other hand, are a different story."

Hudson had a feeling that would be the case. Her phone dinged, and when Gina looked at it, she smiled before tapping out a reply and tucking it back into her purse. "Well, I need to go."

Callie's eyes sprang wide open. "Wait, what about dinner?"

"I'll be fine. You kids have fun. Get your stories straight. Keep it simple so you don't mess it up. Hudson… I'll send you the preapproved questions that Morgan will be allowed to ask you. You do your part and play the dutiful boyfriend or *your* idea won't work. Cal, don't worry. Trust me."

Gina kissed Callie on the head and then looked at Hudson. "You really are very much like the fictional character… in the looks department. I hope you're as good a guy. My girl deserves the best… real or not."

Hudson wanted to say that none of it was his fault, but with the way Callie seemed so taken aback with everything, he stayed silent. Instead, he stood and extended his hand to Gina. "Pleasure meeting you. I'll look forward to your call."

"Very nice. I'll get your number from Cal. Bye." She wiggled her fingers, and just as quick as she came, she left.

"Nice girl," Hudson said, bemused. The server

came to their table, balancing a tray with their dinners. When he went to set Gina's down, Hudson asked him to box it up instead.

"Gina is the best. She'll figure all of this out. Then we can go back to our normal lives."

Hudson nodded. Despite a thousand questions rattling around in his head, they sat in companionable silence and enjoyed their dinners. Every so often, Callie would lift her pretty green eyes to meet his. If he were actually in the market for a girlfriend, she did check all his boxes. Beauty aside, she was confident and sharp—and other than not wanting her alias outed, she seemed fearless.

On that note, he lifted his glass and glanced at hers, signaling for her to do the same. When she did, Hudson voiced his thoughts: "Congratulations on your bestseller. It takes a lot of guts to do what you did. I realize I've been so wrapped up in my own issues that I neglected to acknowledge your success. I'm not a mean guy, Callie, but—"

"You need order."

"Yes."

Callie nodded. "Well, as your temporary girlfriend, I hope to restore that for you."

Girlfriend. That word usually made him want to run for the hills. Except when she said it, rather than bolt, he gently tapped his glass against hers. "Let's just hope that Gina's plan works."

"To Gina's plan."

They both took a sip, and Hudson prayed it didn't all backfire.

CHAPTER 7

What in the world was I thinking?

Callie paced her living room, wondering how everything had gone with Gina and Hudson. Her thoughts raced all day, and she could barely concentrate at work. She hoped a sunrise yoga class would clear her head—except that hadn't been the case. Instead, her mind kept rounding the proverbial track back to her friend and fake boyfriend.

Every few seconds, she'd glance at her phone gripped tightly in her hand, hoping a text would come in. She almost felt sorry for Hudson, because Gina had the tenacity of a shark. It wasn't very often her bestie didn't get what she wanted. When they were at dinner, Callie had been shocked when Hudson had agreed to Gina's plan. Then again, she hadn't given him much choice. The man wanted his single status abolished, and what better way than broadcasting it on television.

Gina also didn't let Callie forget that *Ready to Fall* would be front and center. Despite the rave reviews and eye-popping sales numbers, Callie still feared the possibility that her book would get decimated by review trolls. Some of the meanest people hid behind their keyboards, ready to tear someone apart. At times, she wondered if they'd been bullied in school, which made her sad. Still, it didn't give them the right to be so mean because they had the platform to do so.

When her phone finally dinged, Callie almost dropped it.

> *Hey. We're all set.*
>
> *How was your meeting?*
>
> *Fine. I will say, the man is stubborn.*
>
> *Tell me about it.*
>
> *Interview is all scheduled for Friday. I'll be working on your ads. Like I've said, we need to strike while the iron's hot. Oh, I do need you to sign some paperbacks. I promised them to Morgan.*
>
> *OK. I'll do it tonight.*
>
> *Also, they asked for a picture of the happy couple.*

Callie's heart paused before it kick-started against her ribs. Of course they'd want to see his girlfriend. Anyone could challenge him and say that it was fabricated. A half laugh flew out of her,

The BOOK BOYFRIEND

since their relationship had indeed been fabricated. Just as she was going to text and ask what the plan was, Gina sent another message.

> *I've scheduled a photo shoot for tomorrow evening. We'll do it at Hudson's home.*
>
> *What?!!*
>
> *Don't worry, it will be fine. Just a casual night at your boyfriend's house.*

Callie sighed and begrudgingly typed back, *Fine.*

Rather than worry about the new man in her life, she needed to worry about the one who started it all… the fictional Hudson Newman. She needed to start on the sequel.

Callie sat down at her small desk, staring at her laptop. The open page should have a few hundred words on it. Instead, it felt as though the glaring white screen mocked her. When she first thought about a sequel, she couldn't stop the ideas from flowing. It hadn't mattered if she were in the shower, in her car, or in line at the market; the images kept playing out like a movie.

In one scenario, Hudson would meet a smart businesswoman who challenged him rather than fall at his feet. In another, they would take romantic trips, watch movies, and enjoy quiet nights together. And at the end, he'd sweep her off her feet with the most romantic proposal, and they'd live happily ever after.

Callie smiled, remembering how easily it had all seemed to come to her when she'd written *Ready to Fall*. No outside influences or preconceived story lines, just honest words on paper. Now, after meeting Hudson and agreeing to his request, or really, his ultimatum, her ideas died a quick death.

She let out a long, lingering breath, closed her eyes, and pictured him. Despite the reason for his visit, she couldn't deny how sexy he looked in a suit. And that kiss to her temple still played over and over again in her head. His height even sent shivers up and down her spine. That was what she needed to channel, and that was exactly what she did.

Three chapters and almost ten thousand words later, Callie removed her glasses and tossed them on her desk. Her tired eyes watered, her fingers ached, and when she reached her hands toward the ceiling in a much-needed stretch, she swore she heard a few vertebrae shifting. Proud of what she'd written, she was heading into her bathroom to take a shower when her phone dinged. Thinking it was Gina, she almost ignored it, not wanting to hear about photo shoots or anything book related for a few minutes. Except when she glanced at the screen, she sighed.… Hudson, or as she listed him in her contacts, *Book Boyfriend*.

> *Hi. Have you spoken with Gina?*
> *Yes.*
> *Everything OK?*
> *Yes, fine.*
> *Is that "fine" girl talk for the opposite?*

Callie couldn't help but laugh. She pecked away.

> *I'm good, thank you. I just finished writing. I'm tired, hungry, but before anything else I'm in need of a shower.*

*Ahh... so my girlfriend gets hangry?
#thingsIshouldknow*

Callie's empty belly toppled over a few times before coming to a rest. Her thumbs hovered over her phone as she decided what to type back. Then she smiled and tapped out:

*A boyfriend would be a bit more sensitive and empathetic.
#thingsyoushouldknow*

You're correct, my apologies. I'll let you get on with your night.

She set her phone down on the charger, stripped out of her clothes, and hopped into the shower, ignoring her growling stomach.

"Just a minute!" Callie yelled from her bathroom. Her quick shower had morphed into a soothing lavender-infused bubble bath and finished with a quick pedicure refresh. Her gray sweats were cuffed up to her calves, one of her pink camisole's straps kept sliding down her left shoulder, and she did her best to walk on her heels so as not to smudge her pink toenails.

The ding sounded again. Who in the world had been ringing her bell? When she yanked open her door, Callie cursed herself for not looking out the peephole. If she had, she would have pretended she wasn't home. Amusement danced in Hudson's eyes when his gaze roamed up and down her body.

"Green looks good on you. Brings out your eyes."

Green? Callie raised her hand to her face, and the tackiness beneath her fingers reminded her she must have looked like an alien. She'd forgotten about her facial mask, which had five minutes left to work its magic. *Oh my God!* He lifted a white paper shopping bag and said, "I brought dinner."

As though he had been there a million times rather than this being the first one, he walked past her and straight toward her kitchen, setting the bag on the table. "Nice place."

Her one-bedroom apartment wasn't big by any means, but it was perfect for her. When she'd first moved in, the walls were a dull white, which she changed to a creamy gray. She placed area rugs in her living room and dining area, and a runner in the hallway to warm up the light faux-wood flooring. The pictures that hung on her walls were mostly from her grandmother's house. They held many good memories for her.

"Wait, what are you doing here? Did I give you my address?" Callie waddle-hopped toward him, trying to remove the tissue snaked between her toes.

"Gina gave it to me."

Note to self: kill Gina.

Without invitation, Hudson began taking containers out of the bag. The smell of tomatoes and garlic filled the air, making her stomach speak up and fill the quiet space. "I hope you like it. From the sounds of hunger coming from you, I'd say I was in the nick of time."

She crossed her arms and noticed his eyes landing right on her braless chest. On a huff and without saying a word, Callie scurried out of there, headed to the bathroom, and tossed her wadded-up tissues away. "What in the world was he thinking?" she whispered to her Martian-like reflection before scrubbing it away. She hustled into her bedroom, tossed on a hoodie, and closed the door behind her as she went to rejoin her surprise dinner guest.

When she spotted the meal laid out and no Hudson, her heart slowed. Had he left? Why did that notion deflate her? She hadn't really wanted him there, nor had she thanked him. Deep laughter came from her back deck. Taking a few steps closer to the screened-in window, she leaned against her counter and eavesdropped.

"Hi, sweetheart. I know, I miss you too."

Sweetheart? Miss you? Callie felt her brows frowning.

"I'll see you this weekend, I promise." His laughter sounded sweet and somehow full of adoration. "Love you more. Good night."

He turned and their eyes locked. She hadn't noticed his appearance before, but now it was unavoidable. Dark jeans that made his legs look longer than they were, a light-blue T-shirt accentuating the curve of his upper arms, and his masculine silver watch that, for whatever reason, made him even more attractive. Then there was his sexily styled hair and constant five-o'clock shadow that had her wishing she were on the other end of that conversation.

"Sorry about that," he said, sliding his phone into his pocket. "My sister called."

His sister? "Everything okay?"

"Yes, thank you. My niece wanted to talk to her favorite uncle."

Callie had used the word *swoon* in her book. Although she never truly knew the meaning of it until that very moment.

"Does she have more than one? I thought it was just you and your sister?"

"Funny."

She laughed, enjoying their banter. "How old is she?"

"Five going on fifteen. And she does have another uncle on her father's side, but no matter what he says, I'm still her favorite." He winked, and her insides melted like the cheese on the lasagna sitting on her table. Hudson must have noticed where her attention went, because he walked over to her table and pulled out a chair. "Come on, it's getting cold. Where are your dishes?"

"I'll get them." Callie walked into the kitchen, opened her cabinet, and pulled out two plates, then two of everything she needed until she had a place setting for both of them. She set the table. Callie wasn't exactly sure how much he'd brought or if he planned on joining her, but she wanted him to. "This looks wonderful." Then Callie found herself asking, "Would you like to join me?"

"Sure."

"Wine?"

"Yes, thank you."

Once they sat and filled their plates with saucy goodness, they dug in. "Thank you for bringing dinner."

"You're welcome," Hudson said, taking a bite of bread. "I wasn't sure if you liked Italian."

"Not to worry, I love eating everything. Plus, I was starving or, as you put it, hangry. You know, I'm not sure if a boyfriend would say that to his girlfriend."

His chuckle brought a wide smile to her face. "He would if he were honest."

"I suppose. Although maybe a bit more tactfully."

"Noted."

They ate in silence until Callie couldn't help but ask, "What are you going to do if your sister asks about us?"

Hudson wiped his mouth and leaned back in his chair. "Sadly, I need to lie to her and tell her we're a couple. If I don't, she'll need to keep up the pretense. I wouldn't want to put her in that predicament. Dwight would knock me out if I did that to his wife."

"Are you two close?"

"Yes, very. She's older by almost three years."

Callie realized that she didn't know how old he was. Now knowing the distance between him and his sister, she felt weird asking. Instead, she continued to listen.

"Because our dad was in the military, we moved around a lot. Izzy—that's my sister—and I relied on one another. Since our family wasn't always in the same place for too long, it had been difficult to make friends and keep them. Once my father decided to take a job near Quantico, my sister and I landed here. She's married to her college boyfriend, Dwight, and they have Hailey."

"Have they been married long?"

"Yes, ten years. They got married shortly out of college, when Izzy was twenty-four."

That would make him thirty-one. Only two years older than her.

"Ugh."

His groan was in complete contradiction to how he spoke of them.

"What's wrong?"

"It's their anniversary next weekend. My sappy brother-in-law is throwing a party. You're going to need to come with me."

"No way." Callie couldn't imagine meeting his family already. She'd dated a guy for almost a year and met only his second cousin twice removed. Never parents or siblings. "I can't. Make something up. I'm a horrible liar."

Heat flourished beneath her hooded sweatshirt. If she knew her boobs wouldn't come flying out of her tank top, she would have ripped the fleece off. Meeting his family? She could already feel her eye twitching.

Hudson nodded. "Fine, I'll tell them you're giving yourself a facial."

"Good, thank you."

"No problem. What about your family?"

"Well, they won't see the interview. My brother really isn't the morning-show type, nor is he local. My parents aren't in the picture. My mom had me and my brother when she was very young. She wasn't ready to be a parent, and my dad didn't stick around either. They were never married. He lives in California. Sends the obligatory cards when he remembers, but that's really about it. My grandmother raised us."

"You're a twin?"

She shook her head. "No, although some call us Irish twins. He's eleven months older. Tommy lives in Dallas with his wife, Gretchen. They got married late last year. Sadly, we don't see each other too much."

"Tell me about your grandmother."

Callie let out a sweet, yet sad, sigh. "My nana is the best. She's one of those women who knew what to say and when to say it. Everyone loves her. Nana was a schoolteacher, which gave her all the patience in the world. Raising two kids when you should have been gearing up for retirement couldn't have been easy. Tommy was always playing baseball. He was an amazing pitcher. Could have gone pro if he hadn't torn his rotator cuff."

"What did you like to do? Did you play sports too?"

"Me? No, I read books and danced. I wanted to be on Broadway or travel, but I stopped when Nana got sick with Alzheimer's. She took care of us, and Tommy had already moved. He offered to come back, but I convinced him not to. There was no reason why we both needed to be here. Anyway, with everything going on, I lost my edge. So, instead, I took her lead and decided to teach."

"You teach dance?"

"Yes, but not as often as I'd like to."

"I'm very sorry about your grandmother. That has to be rough."

"Thank you. We're very close. When Tommy had away games, we'd sit in her living room watching movies. She loved the classics. Like I mentioned before, Rock Hudson and Paul Newman were two of her favorite actors, hence the name of my character." Callie thought back to how she would talk about the two men as though she knew them. "As far as my pen name, Nana's first name is Priscilla, or as close friends call her, Lily. It's also her favorite flower, and her birthday is in May. And that's how the two names came to be. I hadn't intended on writing a book; it just sort of happened. I went to visit her, and the day started off good, but then it changed, so I never told her about it."

Hudson nodded. "I'm sure she'll be proud."

Callie fought back tears through a smile. "I like to think so. I also think she'll like you. Nana used to be a spitfire and still can be on her good days."

"Much like her granddaughter."

"Well, Mr. Newman, that's the nicest thing you've said to me."

CHAPTER 8

The next day, Hudson stood in his living room, watching Gina and her photographer set up silver and black lighting umbrellas for the photo shoot. Off to the side, Callie sat at his dining table with her back facing him, getting her makeup done. One thing he liked about Callie was that she wasn't all smoke and mirrors. She was naturally pretty, so he had no idea what the fuss was all about.

He cracked a grin when he thought back to the other night at her apartment, when she'd answered the door with green goop on her face. Never in his adult life had a woman he'd known let him see her in such a way. Her shamrock-color greeting was startling, to say the least, and the way she balanced on her heels, forcing her to use her chest as a ballast, would be something he wouldn't forget.

Then how she discussed her grandmother with such endearment. If anything, Callie was the most down-to-earth person he'd ever met. No pretenses, no phoniness, just her. There had been no doubt in his head that everything had been a coincidence. That she hadn't set out to purposely use his name. Still, that didn't negate the fact that his life was a bit topsy-turvy. She reminded him of the way Izzy spoke of family. In fact, he could see the two of them being friends, another reason why she shouldn't go to the party.

"Okay, how are we doing?" Gina asked, walking up to him. Her eyes narrowed. "Did you have your makeup done?"

"You're kidding, right?"

She burst out laughing. "Yes, geez, lighten up." Hudson brought his focus back to Callie, who stood and turned to face them. Stunning. That was the only word that came to his mind. Thankfully, the makeup artist hadn't made her look like an Andy Warhol painting. Instead, muted colors merely accentuated her features.

"You're beautiful," he said without thinking.

Callie tipped her head to the side before her pearly whites appeared between soft, pink lips. "Thank you."

"Sweetie," Gina said, lifting Callie's hands to the side. "You look gorgeous. I'm so happy you decided on those white jeans; seriously, your butt looks amazing."

"It's the heels," Callie said, looking down at her feet. "Are you sure this navy top looks okay? Maybe I should put on the black one."

The Book Boyfriend

"No, it goes with Hudson's gray sport coat." Gina gave him a once-over. "You wear jeans well too."

"Gina, we're ready," the photographer said.

"Okay, lovebirds, it's time."

Hudson and Callie looked at one another. "This should be fun."

Callie just laughed. "You'll get used to her. And let me remind you that being a couple was your idea."

"No reminding needed."

Gina stood next to the photographer barking out directions. First she wanted Callie and Hudson in his kitchen. In one shot, he poured her a glass of wine; in the next they were raising their glasses for a toast, then, of course, taking a sip while staring lovingly into each other's eyes. That last shot took longer than it should have, since Callie couldn't stop snickering.

The camera's shutter mimicked a machine gun, capturing each blink frame by frame as the photographer moved around them.

"Okay, set your wine down on the counter." They followed Gina's instructions. "You two need to kiss."

Callie's eyes widened before sending laser beams of misfortune in Gina's direction. Granted, he had been taken a bit aback by her request, but it made sense if the pair were a couple. They needed to sell this, and Hudson needed her readers to stop sending him things. He admired their dedication, and if it hadn't been so inconvenient for him, he'd think it was cool that Callie's readers loved her words so much.

Without touching, they angled their bodies toward one another. Callie puckered her lips as though she were in a lipstick commercial.

"Sweetie, this isn't spin the bottle in the second grade," Gina said.

Hudson and Callie both snapped their heads toward her.

"Who plays spin the bottle in the second grade?" Callie asked.

Gina waved her hand back and forth. "Whatever. You two need to buck up and sell this."

Callie grimaced. "Geez, you make it sound so tawdry."

Hudson brought his attention back to Callie. "Can we just do this please?"

"Yes, Mr. Impatient."

Taking a breath, her pale-green eyes searched his when she looked at him. He couldn't tell if it was excitement, fear, or a combination of both. Doing his best to ignore the onslaught of shutter clicks, he cupped her cheeks and leaned down. Just as he was about to make contact, Callie burst into a fit of laughter.

Dropping his hands, he took a step back and shook his head. "Really?" During his adult life, and his teen one, for that matter, a woman laughing when he was about to kiss her had never been the reaction. Once again, Callie Richardson surprised him.

She dabbed the skin beneath her eyes to collect a bit of moisture that had escaped. He had a feeling that if she ruined her makeup, Gina wouldn't be pleased. Then, like a prizefighter, Callie rolled her head from side to side as though she needed to crack her neck and bounced on the balls of her feet. He half expected a bell to go off. She shook out her hands at her sides. "Okay, sorry, I'm just nervous."

"Fine," he grumbled. "You good now?"

Callie nodded, giving him the green light. Once again, he cupped her cheeks and leaned in. When he saw her lips turn up at the corners, and her nose crinkle, he should have stopped. Instead, he licked his lips and went in for the kill… so to speak. Despite it not being overly sensual, it didn't prevent his body from coming to life. Suddenly, he became hyperaware of his surroundings, yet he didn't care. Callie must have felt it, too, because her hands wrapped around his wrists, pushing the band of his watch into his left one, and tightening her grip with each second that passed.

Their lips began to move in sync, and he'd bet money that the photographer would assume they've been together for a long time rather than for a short-term fake relationship.

When they broke apart, Hudson and Callie locked eyes. No snickering. No banter. Not anything. Everything just stilled.

Gina cleared her throat, breaking through the silence. "Okay, well, wow." The pair took a step back. "Why don't you two take a break. I think we're all set."

Hudson glanced over to find the photographer closing one of his silver umbrellas and packing a few lenses away in a padded case. Thank God it was over. He steered Callie toward the back door, opened it to the sounds of birds and a few other creatures that replaced the clicking of the camera shutter he'd been listening to.

He stood on his stone patio and took a breath. Callie's perfume mingled with the flowers arranged in the corner pots.

"Your home is beautiful. I figured you'd live closer to the city."

"No, I like it out here. Horse farms and green space. It's only thirty minutes from the office." He paused, thinking about the dream house he would one day design and build. The one he currently lived in was a temporary place to hang his hat. "Depending on traffic, of course."

Callie leaned up against the railing. "So you weren't in the area when you brought me dinner."

"Well, I was on my way home from work, so technically, after a few turns and a couple of miles, I was."

She nodded with a smile. "Any more gifts today?"

"I don't know. The mail room is instructed to send them back. If they don't have a return address, they get donated to a women's shelter."

"You donated lacy thongs to a women's shelter?"

"Don't forget bras. They probably think I have a fetish."

The BOOK BOYFRIEND

Her lips quirked up at the corners. Hudson shook his head. "Go ahead, get it out. I can tell you're ready to explode."

Callie covered her mouth for a minute before lifting her hand toward him. "I'm so… sorry… I know… it's not funny."

Hudson waited for her to get it all out of her system. After a few small hiccups, she straightened herself and let out a whoosh of air.

"Are you done?" he asked.

Callie nodded. "Yes." She cleared her throat. "It just struck me funny."

"Trust me, it isn't funny."

She shrugged. "Right. Well, I'm going to go and get my things. Hopefully Gina's photographer captured enough to make us look believable."

His mind wandered to the kiss and how her reaction appeared to be genuine. A notion he had to get right out of his head. Callie skirted by, leaving a trail of sweet perfume that reminded him of lavender.

"The photographer just left. Thank you for letting us use your home," Gina said, joining him outside. "You and Callie look to be getting along rather well."

"Yes."

"I know you guys weren't involved in a meet-cute and that it's fake, but regardless of the circumstances, a word of warning?"

Hudson nodded.

"Callie is one of the sweetest people I know and

one of the toughest. She'd kick my butt into next week if she knew I was saying any of this, but I'm going to anyway. Don't hurt her. She's doing this as a favor to *you*." He opened his mouth, but Gina lifted her hand to halt him. "You and I both know you wouldn't have a leg to stand on to force her to delist the book. She could have very easily called your bluff, but she didn't. Callie may say I'm way off base, but that's how I see it. So, again, don't do anything that will make me come back here and smack your handsome mug. Got it?"

Hudson thought about what Gina had said. He wasn't sure if she was right or not. Nor when he went to meet Callie did he go in with the ultimatum in mind. It had just fallen into place.

"First of all, I have no idea what a meet-cute is. Second, my intention isn't to hurt anyone. Third, I appreciate the warning. Now, are we done here?"

Gina nodded. "Good luck tomorrow. Morgan has a way of getting people to talk."

"Noted. I'm ready."

Callie stepped out onto the patio. "Everything okay out here?"

"Yes, everything is fine. Just wanted to wrap a few things up," Gina said before stepping inside the house.

When Callie looked at him, he smiled. "Like Gina said, everything is fine. Drive safely, and I'll talk to you tomorrow."

"Okay, good luck," Callie said with a quick wave.

He watched the ladies leave before grabbing a beer and plopping himself onto the couch. Needing a bit of normalcy, he clicked the television on to the baseball game. *Tomorrow,* he thought. After the interview everything would start to get back to the way it should be. At least, he hoped it would.

Hudson arrived at his office earlier than usual. He had told Keira he wasn't to be disturbed because he was being interviewed. There were only a few people in his circle who knew the story: his assistant, who had the loyalty of a Labrador retriever, and Jack, whom he trusted with his life.

Gifts, photos, and invitations to various events still arrived at his office or in his email. It would be comical, flattering even, if it hadn't been so intrusive.

His phone dinged, alerting him he had five minutes before Morgan would be calling him via video chat. He fired up his laptop, opened the webinar-style app, put his earbuds in, and waited. A man wearing a headset popped up in the center of the screen.

"Good morning, Mr. Newman. I'm JJ, one of the associate producers. Before we go live, I'd like to test the microphone and camera. Can you see and hear me?"

"Hello, JJ. Yes, I hear and see you."

He felt his Adam's apple bob and his nerves kick

up. Why this needed to be a live segment baffled him. Hudson had participated in his share of interviews and meetings, and he had been on television once for a charity event, but this was different. This was about him and his relationship, something, if real, he'd never discuss in such a forum.

"Fantastic." JJ put the small mic to his mouth. "All set on three." He looked at Hudson. "Just relax, everything will be fine."

Hudson nodded, and JJ's face was replaced with the show's logo. "Ten seconds," echoed in his ears, right before he heard, "and three, two, one…"

The morning show was set with a small navy couch, a side table, and a flatscreen television next to Morgan. If it weren't for the DC skyline providing a backdrop, it would look like an ordinary living room. Morgan sat on the right side of the sofa, and when she made eye contact with the camera, her red-tinted lips spread into a wide smile.

"When this story came across my desk, I couldn't wait to talk to our next guest. A few weeks ago, romance author Lily May released her debut novel, *Ready to Fall*. A friend of mine who happens to be Lily's agent sent me a copy. Well, let me tell you…" She stopped to lift the book from the table in front of her, then proceeded to fan her face with her free hand. "I couldn't stop reading." She set the book back down. "And as wonderful as the story is, that isn't what this segment is about. Well, not really. What it is about is the hero in the book, or to be more specific, the hero's name, Hudson Newman."

She pivoted on the sofa and angled herself to a different camera. "It seems that although the name is fictitious, it also happens to be the name of a prominent businessman in our community. Who, I'm happy to say, is joining us."

Just then, Hudson saw his face on the screen next to Morgan's. He prayed his heartbeat wouldn't be picked up by the mic on his headphones. "Good morning, Mr. Newman. Thank you for joining me."

"It's my pleasure. Thank you for having me, and please call me Hudson."

"Hudson," she said with a slight lilt in her voice. "So, I'm going to get right down to it. I understand you've been receiving gifts and even a few marriage proposals."

"That's right. Apparently having the same name as a book hero will do that." He nervously chuckled. "But I can assure you, Lily May's character was not based on me. The only common denominator is our name, which is coincidental."

"Have you read *Ready to Fall?*"

"Yes," he laughed. "I have. Lily May sure knows how to write a love story." As annoying as everything had been, he knew that Callie had worked hard on the novel. Throwing her under the bus suddenly didn't feel right. Then he added, "My girlfriend is familiar with it as well."

Morgan brought her hand to her chest, almost thumping the small mic clipped to the collar of her dress. "Yes, that's right, ladies. *This* Hudson Newman has already fallen."

A picture popped up of him and Callie on his back patio. They were both laughing. After all their posed shots, the one Gina decided to send to the news station had been candid, and one he hadn't even known about. He was sure Callie didn't know about it either. Then it flipped to an image of their staged kiss.

When he realized he was blankly staring, he smiled.

"She's a very lucky lady. What does she think of all the attention you've received?"

"Thank you, Morgan. Callie was a bit surprised by all of it but found it to be very sweet. She is a very kind person, and I wouldn't want anything negative to be directed toward her. I'm not implying that would happen—after all, these are fans of romance. Also, I'd like to suggest something, if I may."

"Of course, go ahead."

"Rather than spend the money and send gifts to me, I'd encourage everyone to send the gifts to people who need them." He paused, thinking about the gifts that would be appropriate only for brothels and amended his statement. "I'm not encouraging them to send just lingerie to women's shelters or charities, but rather purchase something they can use or donate the money. I'm quite certain they can use it more than I could." Hudson winked.

"That's a wonderful idea. We will post a list of women's shelters on our website." Morgan once again pivoted toward the other camera. "Thank you for taking the time out of your day, Hudson. Although I'm sure you've broken a few hearts this morning, I wish you and Callie all the best."

"Thank you, Morgan. I appreciate that."

"And now, let's see what's happening on the roads. Ted, how's it looking this morning?"

The screen flashed and JJ appeared. "Thank you, Mr. Newman."

"My pleasure." He pulled his earbuds out of his ears and tossed them onto his desk. His phone dinged with an incoming message from Gina.

> *Great job.*
>
> *Thank you. Nice pictures.*
>
> *I thought so. I'll send them to you.*
> *Gotta run. Have a good day and thanks again.*

Another message came through with the two images he saw just a few moments ago. He studied them, and even he was fooled by how much they looked like a couple. Now all he hoped for was that everyone else would buy it as well so his life would regain some resemblance of how it was before Hudson Newman became a hashtag.

CHAPTER 9

Callie sat in her office, going over new membership applications and numbers, but she couldn't focus. Her mind continued to wander to Hudson's interview. She had no idea he'd speak so highly of her book. Granted, he wasn't as awful as she thought after he had barged into her office that first day, but what she saw today shocked her.

Gina had told Callie that she'd sent pictures to Morgan, but it never occurred to her to ask Gina which ones she was sending. In her mind, she figured it would be of them enjoying wine or staring lovingly at one another. Not the kiss or the candid one she didn't even know about. Oddly, that one had even her thinking they were a real couple.

Since she'd released *Ready to Fall,* Callie had done her best not to look at her numbers. Except this morning, she decided to before Hudson's interview. Her sales had been steady. When she refreshed her screen, they made a big jump. "No way," she said aloud to herself. Moving on, she decided to search her book's title on social media.

> *Wow, I've seen sexy and then there was that interview this morning. Callie is one lucky lady. #CongratsHudson*
>
> *Congratulations! Bummer that you're taken. Hit me up if you guys break up! #stillsexy*
>
> *I guess you can forget my marriage proposal. LOL #offthemarket*

Callie blinked a few times before closing her laptop, and she didn't bother to read the rest of the several dozen comments. She grabbed her purse and headed out to see a man about an interview. Her assistant, Gwen, smiled when she saw her.

"Heading out for lunch?"

"Yes, I should be back in about an hour or so."

"Going to see your gorgeous boyfriend?"

Callie held her breath.

"I know we're at work, but I can't believe you acted as though you didn't know him. You're so sneaky."

The day Hudson came to her office, they hadn't been dating. Once again, she found herself lying. If she were religious, she'd go to confession.

"Guilty." She needed to leave before Gwen started asking more questions that deserved real answers. "Well, I should get going."

"Have fun. You should invite him for a round of golf. Maybe he'll become a member."

Yeah, that's not going to happen.
"We'll see. Bye."

She hustled outside, and once in her car, Callie punched in the address of Hudson's office. Thankful that it wasn't too far, she began driving in his direction. How dumb she'd been to not factor in her coworkers finding out about her relationship. She'd been so consumed with worrying about Lily May's identity and her book that she'd forgotten about her real life. Callie needed to figure it out. Knowing Hudson, he had an exit plan already in place.

Shoving her anxious thoughts away, she rolled down her window and enjoyed the warm breeze until the robotic voice interrupted a song on her radio, telling her she had reached her destination.

She pulled into the parking lot and turned into a visitor's spot. When she looked up, she saw a coffee shop. *That must be where he used to get his coffee.* Deciding to help him and the situation out a bit more, and to thank him for pimping her book on live television, she walked into the café.

Tables were buzzing with customers. Some had laptops open and headphones in; others seemed to be on a break, chatting away or just enjoying their favorite drink.

A young girl looked up at her and did a double take. "Um… hi. What can I get you?"

Callie looked at her name tag and wondered if she knew Hudson. Taking a chance and realizing she didn't know his favorite blend, she said, "Hi,

Annie. I'm here to get Mr. Newman's favorite. Do you know him?"

She nodded. "Yes, I haven't seen him in a while. Well, until this morning on television. You're his… um—"

"Girlfriend. I'm Callie. I thought I'd pop in and surprise him. You know how he loves his coffee." Callie prayed the barista did, because she had no idea what Hudson's favorite blend was or if he took cream, sugar, or some flavored syrup.

"Of course. It's nice to meet you. I'll get it right now. Can I get you something?"

Callie almost let out a sigh of relief, but instead she thanked Annie and decided to get herself a nonfat vanilla latte. Another barista whispered something as Annie prepared Hudson's favorite drink. She wondered what that was about but could only imagine it had to do with her handsome boyfriend. If she were a young woman and a gorgeous man like Hudson came in every morning, she'd miss seeing him too. Had to be one of the highlights, if not *the* highlight of their day.

"Here you go; it's on the house. Please tell Mr. Newman we miss seeing him. And that we're sorry. We hope we didn't make him uncomfortable. It's just the book…"

Callie felt like preening, knowing those girls had read her novel. "It's okay. I'm sure you'll see him soon. Take care, girls." She left a ten-dollar bill in the tip jar and walked out.

The heat from the cups in her hands made her

thankful his office wasn't far away from the café. She walked through the double doors and was greeted by a man wearing a brown uniform, sitting behind a large wooden desk. "Good afternoon, Callie."

Confused, she racked her brain, wondering how he knew her. When she came up blank, she apologized. "I'm so sorry, do we know each other?"

His chuckle eased her nerves a bit. "No, ma'am. I'm Michael. I happened to see Mr. Newman's interview. I must say, the man has wonderful taste."

She felt heat rush to her cheeks. "Thank you, Michael. It's a pleasure to meet you. Is he in? He isn't expecting me." Callie lifted the hot beverage. "Just thought I'd surprise him."

"I believe so. His assistant just left for lunch. Here's a pass. Go ahead on up. Floor twelve."

Callie set one coffee on his desk and clipped the laminated badge with a blue *V* to the bottom of her blouse. "Thank you very much." She picked up the cardboard-wrapped paper cup, and with a straight back and wobbly knees, Callie headed toward the elevator, pressed the call button, and waited for the doors to slide open. Thankfully, when they did, the few people who got off didn't look her way. After what Michael had said, she wondered how many other people had seen the interview. And if that was the case, what type of day was Hudson having? Maybe Gina's idea would backfire and he'd get a different sort of attention.

The Book Boyfriend

Once inside, it took only a few seconds to reach Hudson's office floor. She stepped out, and thanks to the empty reception area, Callie realized she had no idea which direction to go. Then she heard a man chuckle, and then another one. Callie couldn't prevent the smile that grew across her face as she recognized the second one as Hudson's.

Following the voices, she turned to the left and walked past several cubicles. A few employees glanced up over their burlap-paneled walls, but no one said anything. Keeping a strong stride, she made her way closer to his office, stopping just shy of the cracked-open door when she heard a man's voice that wasn't Hudson's.

"You even had me convinced," she heard him say before he added, "And she's gorgeous."

"Yes, very." Hudson's agreement had Callie smiling from ear to ear.

"Well, you're a lucky man."

The aroma coming from the coffees reminded her that she hadn't moved in a few long seconds. Taking a deep breath, she stood in the open doorway. "Knock, knock." Both men's heads snapped in her direction. "Hi, honey. Sorry to just drop in."

Hudson's lips quirked up. He smoothed his tie down, pushed his chair away from his large wood desk, and walked toward her. She held out a coffee. "For me?" Taking the cup from her, he leaned down and kissed her cheek. "Thank you."

The other man also rose to his feet and extended his hand. He was just about the same height as

Hudson, with the same broad shoulders, but he seemed more relaxed… something not that difficult to accomplish around Hudson. "Hi, I'm Jack."

"Hi, Jack. It's nice to meet you." Callie shifted the coffee from her right into her left, and she briefly shook his hand.

Hudson clapped him on the back, and as Jack walked out the door, he said, "I'll see you later."

"It was a pleasure meeting you, Callie. Good luck with this one. He tends to be a little high-strung." Jack glanced at Hudson before letting his chuckle trail behind him.

"I hope that's the right one." She regarded the paper cup in Hudson's hand.

When he looked at the navy logo on the cup, his face lit up. He popped the lid, took a big whiff, and sipped it. A sweet sigh followed his swallow. For a moment, Callie wondered what it would be like to be the cause of that reaction. Not knowing where that thought came from, she blinked a few times and brought her attention to the man in front of her.

"Wow, how did you know?"

"I didn't until I pulled up to your building. Then I saw the café. Annie was all too happy to make your favorite. I think you're missed in there."

"Believe me, I'm the one who misses this." He took another taste. "It's like coming home to an old friend."

She couldn't help but laugh. "Well, now that you're off the market, you should be able to go there without any bizarre happenings. As your girlfriend, I wanted to make sure you could get a good start to your day. I figured if they saw me in the flesh, we could both move on from this and move on with our lives. Plus, they do make a mean vanilla latte."

Despite her nerves at what he was going to say on live television, she also knew this was the beginning of their end. The sooner he stopped receiving unwanted presents, the sooner they could split up. She'd be lying to herself if she didn't admit that she'd miss his witty banter. Not to mention the man was a skilled kisser. Whoever he did end up with would be a lucky woman.

Hudson set his cup down. "I appreciate the coffee, but was that the only reason for your visit?"

Callie shook her head. "No, I also wanted to let you know how appreciative I was for the interview you gave this morning. My sales hit my release-week numbers in just a few hours. I hadn't expected you to boast about my book."

"Yes, well, I didn't feel it right to toss your business under the bus. Like you said, everything was coincidental. Your hero's name came from two actors, while mine came from my mother's maiden name mixed, of course, with my father's."

"I did a bit of research after our encounter, and there are several people, men and women, with your name. I honestly had no idea. But yours came up first in my search."

"Because of a business article I was featured in last year. Our company's marketing team did a great job getting it out there to bring in more clients."

"Didn't hurt that your handsome face was the first thing to pop up."

"Hmm, you think I'm handsome?"

Callie's face flushed, but before she could answer, the sound of tiny feet running in the hallway had them both looking at the door. "Stop running, Hailey," a woman whisper-shouted in an authoritative voice.

A familiar five-year-old bounded into the office. Her ponytail, tied with a red ribbon, swung side to side before she stopped dead in her tracks after spotting Callie.

"Miss Callie! You're here!" She ran up and hugged Callie's legs. When Callie glanced up at Hudson, his eyebrows pulled together. No doubt wondering why his visitor was hugging his fake girlfriend.

"Hailey Margaret. What did I tell you about running in Uncle Hudson's office."

Callie glanced at the woman she knew as Mrs. Webster, and then to Hudson, before looking down at the adorable dark-haired girl. All the pieces started coming together.

As if knowing exactly what to do, Hailey released Callie and jumped into her uncle's arms, then kissed his cheek. He dipped her and peppered her face with kisses, causing a squeal to erupt before righting her in his arms. If Callie hadn't thought he was already the sexiest man she'd ever met, that maneuver just amped it up a million notches.

"Hey, squirt, why aren't you in school?"

She looked at her mom, who answered, "It's teacher workshop day."

He gently tugged her ponytail. "Well, lucky me. So many visitors today. How do you know Miss Callie?"

"She's my dance teacher."

Hudson's gaze flashed up to Callie, who bashfully shrugged before nodding.

"Watch…" Hailey squirmed out of his hold, lifted her arms in fifth position above her head before squatting into a plié. Her little sandals didn't help her when she started to fall forward. Hudson reached out to stop her from hitting the floor.

"How about you show Uncle Hudson the next time he comes over and you're wearing your ballet shoes," her mother said, beaming at her daughter.

"Okay. I know! I'm having a recital. You can come with Miss Callie now that she's your girlfriend. I'm so excited. Does that mean you're going to get married?" The exuberant little girl didn't stop to breathe. Instead, her questions came rapid-fire. "Can I be the flower girl when you do? My friends are going to be so jealous. Can I have a white dress like yours, Miss Callie? Are you coming to Mommy and Daddy's party? Will you dance with Uncle Hudson?"

Everyone stood silent. Hudson ruffled his niece's bangs before crouching down to her level. "Hey, guess what?" She leaned in closer. "Miss Keira has candy on her desk. Why don't you go and get some for yourself?"

She looked at her mother for compliance, and when she nodded, Hailey bolted out the door.

"I'm so sorry about that," his sister said before giving her brother a proper hello with a kiss to his cheek. "We were sitting at the breakfast table watching the morning show when you popped onto the screen. I was a bit surprised, since I didn't know you were dating anyone. And I haven't read that book. But now that I know your name happens to be the lead character's, not sure that I will. No offense to the author, since she clearly didn't know."

"Right. Funny, isn't it? And our relationship is new," Hudson stated as a way of explaining. He looked at Callie. "As you can see, this is my sister, Isabelle. But you already know her."

"It's good to see you again. I never put two and two together. However, now that I know you're related, I see the resemblance."

"Hi, well, to say I'm surprised would be an understatement. And that book…" Callie felt dots of sweat spring up on the back of her neck. "How wild, right? I can't believe women sent you gifts. I mean, I can, I suppose, but wow."

"Yes, *wow* would be an appropriate word."

Isabelle rolled her eyes. "I can only imagine how you handled it." She looked at Callie and laughed. "The man needs his order."

"Yes, I know," she replied, smiling affectionately at Hudson.

"Well, you two are adorable, and Hailey couldn't be more thrilled—as you saw. As far as our party, you must come. It'll be so much fun, and although Hailey will only be there for dinner, she'd love to see you there. Oh, and Hudson, you're lucky that our parents left for their Mediterranean cruise or you'd really have a lot of explaining to do. Mom would want all the details. Speaking of, how did you two meet?"

Before Callie could even come up with a lie, he blurted out, "Coffee shop. We're that cliché couple." It suddenly felt as though their little snowball of a lie was rolling into a massive one.

"Mommy, can we go now?" Hailey stood in the doorway with a lollipop in her hand.

"Yes, sweetie." She kissed her brother. "I promised I'd take her to the museum. I'm very happy for you both. Next time"—Isabelle swatted Hudson's shoulder—"I don't want to hear about your love life on the news. Bye, Callie, see you at class."

"Yes, nice seeing you." She lifted her hand and waved at Hudson's niece. "Bye, Hailey."

"Bye, Miss Callie."

When it was just the two of them, Hudson raked his hand through his hair. "I hate lying," he said to Callie, who felt awful for doing it herself. Although she didn't say much on the matter. "I also dislike my niece being involved. She really likes you."

"I adore her," Callie said. "She's so much fun in class. I should have known she was your niece with the way she always takes charge."

Pride flashed in Hudson's eyes. "Looks like you're going to meet the rest of my family at their party."

"Hudson—" When she saw the determined look in his eyes, she forfeited her argument on why she shouldn't and simply said, "Okay."

CHAPTER 10

Of all the dance classes, Hailey had to be in Callie's? The woman taught one day per week, for God's sake. Some would say it was coincidental, others may say it was karma, and the romantics would say it was fate. All words Hudson wouldn't have chosen. He hadn't been exaggerating when he told Callie that Hailey was five going on fifteen. There hadn't been a doubt in his mind that Hailey had them as good as married, even if neither replied to her earlier question.

Hudson scrubbed his jawline, catching Callie staring at him. "I'm sorry. I never put two and two together. I don't call parents by their first names, and there are two Haileys in my class. It's not an uncommon name."

"Because you know all about those." When her

head reared back, he let out a long breath. "Sorry, I'm just stressed. I love that little girl as if she were my own flesh and blood. This just got a bit more complicated."

"I know. We can worry about all of it when the time comes for us to break up."

He wasn't sure what it was, but Callie seemed more on edge than usual. For someone who didn't crave order as much as he did, she sure did need an expiration date for their relationship. Right now, his niece's feelings came first. "Yes, well, we'll need to tread lightly around Hailey."

"I agree. Her last class and recital is in four weeks."

"Then there you have it. A month should do it. By then, hopefully, the gifts will stop."

Callie nodded. "Okay, a month it is. Then we'll break up, citing we're better off as friends."

"Friends, yes."

She adjusted her purse strap on her shoulder. "I should get back to the club. As it is, I've already extended my lunch hour."

"Did you even eat lunch?"

She shook her head. "No, it's fine. I have a protein bar in my desk." Callie stepped toward the door, but before walking out, she turned to face him. "Thank you, Hudson. Really. That interview went above and beyond anything I could have imagined."

"Yes, well, it was as much for me as it was for you."

A sweet smile grew on her face but didn't reach her eyes. "Yes, of course. I'll see you later."

Per usual, after Callie had been in a room, her gentle lavender scent lingered in the air. Being in his office along with his sister and niece hadn't been on his to-do list. Nor was his sister being adamant about Callie attending her anniversary party.

Jack waltzed in as though he had every right to be there and sat down across from Hudson. Just as earlier, he made himself comfortable.

"Our meeting isn't for another hour."

"I know. I'm not here about that. Care to tell me what is really going on between you and the author?"

"You already know that answer."

A smug smirk spread across his face. "Yes, I do. But the question is, do you?"

"Yes. We will stay together until this all dies down, and then call it quits. Then life will get back to normal." Hudson picked up his pen and started marking up the printed proposal in front of him. Hoping his friend and colleague would get the hint.

He didn't.

"Great. You know who will be happy about that?" Jack asked.

Jack's bemused voice pinged Hudson's patience. Without looking up, he merely moaned: "Hmm?"

"Mark Donnely."

Hudson half expected the pencil in his hand to snap. Hudson had known Mark since college. When he was brought in on the logistics team,

Hudson did everything in his power to not cross paths with him unless necessary. Ever since they'd met, Mark had been a thorn in his side. He belonged to the rival frat, strived to be listed higher on the dean's list, and challenged Hudson each chance he got.

Hudson glanced up at Jack. "Yeah, why is that?"

"I saw them talking before I came in here. I'm not sure, but he may have given her his number."

The thin wood flexed in his grip. Hudson set the pencil down and moved the paper to the side. The mere thought of Callie with Mark annoyed him for reasons he wasn't ready to explore. Whatever the bizarre feeling had been, it needed to be tamped down. Of course, Callie would get his attention. She was stunning; even monks wouldn't stand a chance against her.

Except, hearing that Donnely of all people had spoken to her had him seething. The thing was, giving Jack even a tiny hint that he'd been bothered by it would unleash a different type of fury he wasn't expecting—and which at that moment he couldn't wrap his head around.

So, rather than go down that road, he forced a grin. "Why would you think that would bother me?"

He put up his hands. "Hey, my mistake. I just figured since she was yours and all."

"She's not property. If she wants to make new friends, that's fine with me."

A low rumble turned into a full-blown chuckle. Jack knocked once on Hudson's desk before standing. "Okay, you keep telling yourself that. And if I can say one more thing?" Hudson leaned back and rolled his hand, moving Jack along. "Watch your interview back. Because there was nothing fake about the guy who was talking about his girlfriend this morning."

He walked out of the office, and Hudson decided to call it a day. After he gave Keira a few instructions, he asked her to clear his schedule. Something needed to give, because once again, Callie Richardson had turned his day upside down.

Sweat stung Hudson's eyes as he rounded the corner, finishing up his five-mile run. With each pound of the pavement, he wondered why he couldn't get Callie out of his head. If anything, he should still be annoyed with her. Not only had he just lied to his sister, but he'd also gone on live television, crossed his fingers, and said how happy he was in his relationship.

All of that should have been fueling his ire, but instead Hudson's mind kept rounding back to the image of them laughing, of them kissing in his kitchen. Maybe he should be an actor, because he even started believing they were a couple.

Hudson slowed his steps into a jog before coming to a leisurely stroll in front of his home. He lifted the bottom of his shirt and wiped his brow before heading inside his air-conditioned foyer.

Once he closed the door behind him, he started to relax. He snagged an apple out of the bowl on his kitchen island and plopped himself onto his couch.

"Velma, TV on," he said to the AI device sitting on his coffee table. Afternoon television wasn't his thing — he hoped to find a game to watch — but just as he was going to ask Velma to do that for him, an entertainment show popped on. Morgan was on a screen much as he had been when he was on her show. Since tuning in late, he wasn't sure what had already been said. What he did hear was, "Callie is a very lucky woman." The redheaded host nodded. Hudson couldn't help but to relax into his cushion… sweat be damned. He had taken a chunk out of the apple when a picture of him and Callie kissing came onto the screen. His jaw stopped working the tart fruit. His eyes studied the image. His heart beat wildly. And his body reacted as it hadn't in a long time.

"I will say Hudson Newman, the nonfictional version, could very easily be that book boyfriend, but alas, ladies, he's taken."

The two women laughed before the host sent the program to a commercial.

"Velma, turn on baseball."

Thankfully, the screen changed, and although it was a collegiate game, Hudson didn't care. As long as he could clear his mind for a couple of hours and not think about the sexy and gorgeous author who'd decided to take residence there. Except he had a feeling that would be easier said than done.

CHAPTER 11

Callie stood outside the assisted living home, holding a vase full of calla lilies, and said a silent prayer that her grandmother was up to seeing visitors. Taking a deep breath, she pulled open the door and stepped inside. Per usual, the patterned carpet and plush furniture gave the space a homey look rather than a medicinal one.

The desk nurse, Monica, looked up at her with a beaming smile. "Good morning, Callie. Beautiful flowers. Are you here to see Priscilla?"

"Thank you and yes. Do you know how she's doing this morning?"

Relief flowed through Callie when Monica smiled. "Yes, I was just in the dining room. She just finished breakfast and seemed to be in good spirits."

Callie felt her eyes begin to pulse with tears. Alzheimer's was an awful disease. There were times that she didn't know who it was worse for, the patient or their family. The first time her nana hadn't recognized her broke Callie's heart. Over the past couple of years, it had gotten a bit easier, but it still hurt.

"Can I see her?"

"Of course."

After signing in and affixing a visitor's badge to her shirt, she made her way to room 202. Pushing the door open and seeing her grandmother sitting in a chair rather than her bed was another bonus. The morning sun shone brightly through her window.

Her room looked like a regular apartment less a kitchen. She had a small living room, bedroom, and private bathroom. She was so thankful that her grandfather was smart and had left Nana with the means to afford such a wonderful place. Plus, the sale of her home also helped to cover the cost.

"Hi, Nana," Callie said, taking a few steps inside.

When her grandmother's head turned, the familiar smile that Callie had missed appeared. "Callie?"

She nodded. "Yes, it's me. I brought you flowers." Callie walked over and placed the vase on the small table in the corner before giving her grandmother a hug, which she returned in kind.

"They're lovely and my favorite. You know that's how you got your name."

Another memory, good. "Yes, and I love it. How are you?"

"You know, things could be worse. Edgar made scrambled eggs for breakfast. They were a bit dry, but palatable."

Callie laughed at the critique. "That's nice. I'm sorry I haven't been here."

Nana tilted her head. "You were just here, sweetheart. Don't you remember? You didn't like the eggs either."

Callie's heart sank. She never knew what to do in these situations, so she just played along. "Right, silly me."

"Always forgetting things." Nana laughed. "How's your dancing? Did you join a troupe yet? You know, men love dancers. It's the legs. Nothing a man doesn't love more than legs."

"Nana!"

"Well, maybe breasts."

Callie giggled a bit, shocked by her. "Do they? I'll remember that. And, no, I haven't joined a troupe. I teach classes now. I actually have one soon."

"Right, right. I used to be a teacher too… I think."

"Yes, you were. The best teacher." Callie wanted to tell her about her book and about Hudson. She had a feeling she'd get a kick out of it, but she could tell that her mind had started to drift away. "Well, I should get to my class, but I wanted to come and see you. I'll be back soon, okay?"

"Sure, sure. I'll be here."

Callie leaned down and kissed her cheek, committing to memory the way her skin smelled of the lavender soap that she and her grandmother both loved so much. She was happy that the nurses took such wonderful care of her—since she couldn't do it herself. "Bye, Nana. I love you."

"Love you too."

Before she walked out, she looked back at her grandmother, who once again was staring out the window. Feeling a bit better about seeing her and being able to talk to her, regardless of how short a time, Callie left and drove to the studio.

Thankfully, when she arrived fifteen minutes later, she still had an hour before the class started. It was her time to stretch and work on choreography. Of course, the steps she did would be modified for five-year-olds, but for now, she'd let the music dictate the next sixty minutes.

"Canon in D" began to flow through the speakers and through her body. Letting the music dictate her movements was one of Callie's favorite things about ballet. Similar to writing, where the characters decided the direction the story would go, so too did music direct the dancers. She'd wait for the right moment to plié or her favorite: perform a grand jeté. Dancing freed her from having to think. It was a wonderful feeling to be able to let go and not worry, since that was one of her biggest personality traits.

Sweat trickled down her spine as she sipped her bottled water. It didn't matter what she was doing or what she had in her mind; dancing always seemed to clear it. Performing was the best outlet she had for stress. It was as though her worries flowed out of her fingertips with every extension and toe-spin. There wasn't much else that made her as happy. Well, except for sharing it with the next generation of dancers.

She glided over to her pink duffel bag, wiped her brow with a small towel, and tossed the towel aside. Chatter and the sounds of slipper-clad feet filled the room. Looking up at the mirror, she smiled when she saw her class start to file in, and she turned to wave at them.

Hailey ran up to her. "Hi, Miss Callie!" Her high-pitched, excited voice echoed in the room.

"Hello there, Hailey. Have you been practicing?"

"Uh-huh. I practiced in my basement. I call it my dance room. You'd love it. I'm getting a barre; you should come over and make sure it's right."

"You're getting a barre in your basement? That sounds wonderful."

"Yes, my daddy's doing it for me. Well, Daddy and Uncle Hudson. He's the bestest and says Daddy doesn't know a hammer from a hole in the wall." Her giggle made Callie laugh. "Not sure what that means, but Uncle Hudson thought it was funny. Isn't he fun? When he watches me, we play house. You'd laugh. I bet you could help them. You should come over too."

Confused, Callie cocked her head to the side, not sure what to say. Thankfully, Hailey's mother walked up to them. "Okay, go get ready for class," Isabelle said, tugging on Hailey's high ponytail. The ladies watched her scurry off to the side, where her classmates were all chatting. "Sorry about that. Hailey gets a bit excited. She loves her uncle."

Callie looked at Isabelle, wondering how she never noticed the resemblance before. They both had the same honey-brown hair. Except Isabelle's had more blonde highlights running through it, where Hudson's was more neutral. Now that she knew the relation, Callie even saw a bit of Hudson in Hailey.

"I can see that. Look, I don't want you to think you need to add me to your guest list for your anniversary party. Hudson and I haven't been seeing each other very long. I'd hate to intrude on a family event." *Family. She really needed to call Tommy.*

When Hudson first mentioned the party, she'd been thankful that he'd agreed for her not to go. But after what happened in Hudson's office, it seemed that had all flown out the window. Callie couldn't imagine meeting all his family. Nor could she imagine lying to everyone.

Isabelle waved her hand back and forth. "Nonsense. You must come. It will be fun. I'm so happy that my brother found someone. To be honest, I didn't even know he wanted a girlfriend." A pang of guilt slammed against Callie's rib cage. She felt the corners of her lips turn down. It'd be so easy to come clean and explain, but she couldn't do that. Not when Hudson wasn't there to tell his side. "I don't mean any offense by that. I'm thrilled for both of you."

The BOOK BOYFRIEND

"Thank you."

"I wish I would have thought of it… of you two together. I see it now, of course. You balance each other."

Callie smiled, and the alarm on her fitness watch beeped. "Thanks. I better get class started or I may have a mutiny on my hands."

Isabelle let out a sweet laugh. "Yes, go on. Sorry, I just get so excited thinking about everything. I'll see you in an hour. Oh, and if you want to come over with Hudson, that's fine. Just no making out on the couch until after Hailey goes to bed."

Still confused, but not enough for her face to flame red, she just nodded. As soon as the double door closed behind Isabelle with a clank, Callie let out a breath and walked to the front of the room.

She clapped three times. "Okay, kids. Today we'll be running through our dance for the recital." Squeals and cheers made Callie laugh. "But first, we need to stretch." Ten little groans echoing off the wood floors replaced their jubilation. Callie couldn't help the glee that spread across her face and filled her heart, remembering she used to feel the same way.

For the next sixty minutes, the only thing Callie focused on were the tiny dancers she hoped would one day love dancing as much as she did.

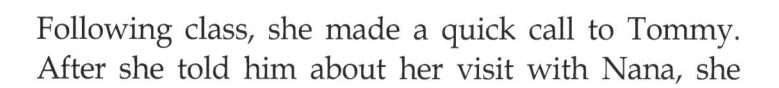

Following class, she made a quick call to Tommy. After she told him about her visit with Nana, she mentioned Hudson just in case one of Gretchen's friends had seen the interview. Callie satisfied all of them as best as she could. He let her know he was happy for her. She headed home and sat at her computer. Words flowed from her fingertips at a faster pace than they had at her last attempt. Three chapters in, she stopped and stretched her hands above her head, feeling each ache release one tendon at a time. Deciding she needed a break, she tossed her glasses onto her keyboard and went to grab a snack, only to find a message from Hudson waiting for her.

It didn't matter that she knew the difference between the Hudson she'd written about and the one who'd just written her; Callie still had to remind herself that they weren't one and the same. And when she read his text, it was difficult to separate the two.

> *Hi. Did you see the latest airing of Pop Entertainment?*

She had to think about what he was talking about. Picturing Hudson watching a pop-culture television show was comical. Then again, if he had, then what was so intriguing?

A bit nervous, she typed back.

> *No, did you?*

She watched three dots dance, stop, and then begin moving again.

> *I caught a piece of it earlier. You may want to search for it online. We went national.*
>
> *WHAT?!!!!*

Callie's heart began frantically beating. National? Their relationship was national? Channeling Gina, she grabbed her phone, and sure enough, there were more sales. Callie could picture her best friend preening at the spike on the chart and the golden banner that sat prettily next to her book title. *Was this real life?* Everything began to blur.

Ignoring her text with Hudson, she tapped on Gina's name. If anyone knew what to do, it would be her.

"Hi! I was just going to call you." Her jubilant friend's voice prompted Callie to let out a huff. "What's wrong?"

"G, I don't even know where to start. Hudson just told me about *Pop Entertainment*."

"Isn't it wonderful? Everyone is loving the story, and by the way, it's the truth: you met because of the book, hit it off, and are now dating. It's seriously the cutest and most romantic story."

"And fake."

"Meh, to-may-to, to-mah-to."

You'd think Gina's cavalier attitude would lessen Callie's nerves, but it might have been too late for that. And why wasn't Hudson upset? Why didn't he send an angry or confused face emoji with his text? Even the guy she met at his office said Hudson was high-strung. Yet, like Gina, right at that moment, he seemed to be the opposite.

Her phone beeped with an incoming call. Maybe it was a blessing because, in Callie's opinion, Gina had started to lose it.

"G, I have another call coming in. I'll call you back."

"I have a date tonight, so I'll talk to you tomorrow. Bye, Cal."

After she pulled the phone away from her face, she stared at the name Book Boyfriend. *Great.*

"Hi, look, I had no idea it was going to go national. Gina is on it."

"Hello to you, too, and I'm not worried about that. Being national fodder works better for me. Yesterday, Keira got something from Portland."

"Maine?"

"Oregon."

"Oh." Callie rubbed her left temple. "What's up?"

"I'm calling because I have a question." When Callie remained silent, he continued, "Did you tell Hailey and Izzy that you were helping me tonight?"

All she could do was blink and play back the high-spirited conversation she'd had with the sweet girl and her mother earlier in the day. *You should come over tonight. Uncle Hudson is helping.*

"No, we were talking about her basement. And how you were putting a barre in…" Callie looked toward the ceiling, searching for a clue that she had committed to going there. Then it dawned on her. When Hailey said, *I bet you could help them,* Callie had replied with, *You're getting a barre in your basement? That sounds wonderful.* "Oh, she misunderstood."

"Yeah, she has a way of doing that. I'm pretty sure that's how she gets grown-ups to do things.

I'm telling you my niece should be an attorney or in the CIA."

Callie laughed.

"So, I'll pick you up at six?" he asked.

Wait. "What? Six? For what?"

"Ballet-barre installation, and then Izzy and Dwight are going out for dinner. I'm hanging with Hailey. She's expecting you. And she also said something about bringing your slippers. Not sure if you're supposed to bring your pajamas too."

Despite him not being able to see her, she shook her head. "She calls ballet shoes *slippers*."

Hudson's chuckle sent a wave of tingles down her spine. "That makes more sense."

Not wanting to disappoint Hailey, and a bit intrigued to see Hudson on uncle duty, Callie said, "Okay, I'll see you then."

She pressed the red button and dragged herself into the bathroom to get ready for another night with her boyfriend and his niece. Then a memory rang in her ears: *No making out on the couch until Hailey is asleep.* "Shoot me," she said to her reflection before turning on the shower.

Maybe the warm water would ebb her nerves. Nah, who was she kidding? It didn't matter what the temperature was. With each day that passed, the web they weaved got gnarlier. She just hoped when they parted as friends, it would somehow untangle itself.

CHAPTER 12

Hudson knocked on Callie's door, half expecting her not to answer. He knew that if it weren't for Hailey, she most likely would have turned him down flat. What surprised him more than that was his reaction to the turn of events. When Izzy called to tell him that Hailey had invited Callie over, he wasn't exactly shocked. That being said, he *was* shocked that he wasn't upset about it.

Maybe it had been the jubilation in Hailey's voice, or maybe it was because the last thing in this world Hudson would want to do was disappoint his adorable niece. He knew that Callie didn't want that, either, but he also knew that she wouldn't want to upset her after they parted ways.

The door whipped open, and a grin cracked Hudson's face. "Hi. No green today?"

Her brows frowned; then she raised her hand to her cheek, and Callie teasingly narrowed her eyes. "Funny, and no. Come on in. I need to grab my bag."

Hudson let his eyes roam up and down Callie's body. She had on pale-blue loose-fitting jogger-style pants and an orange shirt that crisscrossed between her shoulder blades. The evening sun streaming through her window brought out the gold in her hair. Little by little, Hudson started to notice things about Callie that he hadn't before.

When they first met, he'd observed her perfect posture, but now knowing she danced, it made sense. Her graceful carriage stemmed from her slim waist to her elegant neck. They might have been in a fake relationship, but he was a man, after all, and the response his body had toward her wasn't surprising.

She flicked on the lamp next to the couch and looked at Hudson. "You're staring."

"Am I?" He let out a laugh. "Sorry." Pointing to her small desk with a laptop and colored highlighters on it, he couldn't help but ask, "Did you write today?"

"I did. You know, you should be nice to me. Haven't you ever heard the saying, 'Don't make a writer mad, you may end up in one of her books'?"

"But I'm already in one of your books."

"Yes, but you're currently breathing."

She giggled, and Hudson couldn't help but laugh too. "And what would end up being my demise?"

"Hmm…" She tapped her index finger on her chin.

"Okay, okay, let's go before you get any grand ideas."

"If I didn't know I'd have a mutiny on my hands, I'd kill you off."

"Not very romantic."

"I know," she said breezily. "I guess you'll live another day."

"Lucky me."

Callie rolled her eyes as Hudson walked by where she stood in the doorway. Their bodies innocently rubbed up against each other, but for some reason this woman who'd upended his life turned him on in a way he hadn't expected her to — his heart pound faster and a charge ran up and down his spine. Ignoring his urge to stand there a beat longer, he moved toward the sidewalk, hearing the click of the door behind her.

He opened the passenger door of his midsize pickup truck and held out a hand to help her in.

Taking it, she placed her right foot on the chrome running bar and lifted herself into the cab, setting her bag onto the floor in front of her. Once Callie was settled, he closed the door, walked to his side, and hopped in.

"I never pictured you as a truck guy."

Hudson pushed the start button. The deep rumble vibrated the bench seat. "No? What did you picture?"

Callie shrugged, and her cheeks pinkened. "I don't know, really. I suppose, seeing you now in jeans and a T-shirt, that maybe I was wrong. When I first met you, I figured you for a luxury car. Since you are all business and everything."

"Well, I shouldn't need to tell you not to judge a book by its cover."

"No, I suppose not."

They pulled out of her neighborhood and onto the highway toward the west side of town. "Tell me about Dwight."

"Ahh, well, he will tell you that he's the best brother-in-law ever."

"Is he?"

"So far, so good." He chuckled. "He's a great husband and father, so that's all I really care about."

"Hailey said you were both working on the basement. But her father didn't know a hammer from a hole in the wall."

Hudson stopped at the red light and snapped his head toward Callie. Rather than dispute his niece's recollection and retelling, he smirked. Once again, Callie rolled her eyes.

"What? It's true. Just ask him."

This time Callie was the one laughing. "Maybe I will."

By the joy-filled gleam in her eye, he had a feeling she might just do that.

As soon as Hudson turned into his sister and brother-in-law's driveway, Callie leaned forward.

Her eyes widened as he stopped in front of the grand farmhouse-style home. He loved everything about their house, and by the look of awe on Callie's face, so did she.

"Wow, this is beautiful. I love the different shades of white with the deep-charcoal accents. It's so different. Modern, but not. The lines are so… I don't know what the word is. Elegant maybe? I love the angles in the roof. And even the garage doors are amazing. Reminds me of stables. What's that style called?"

Hudson loved hearing her describe the home. She hadn't been wrong—each window, roofline, and accent were thoughtfully placed. "They're carriage style."

"Right, I think I saw them on a home show once."

He hopped out of the truck, and before he could get to Callie's side, she had opened her door. Just as when she'd gotten in, he reached out his hand to help her down. Her foot missed the small step, and she fell into him. His hands went to her waist, and her bag swung around and almost hit him in the head.

When she had both feet firmly planted on the ground, he slowly released her. "You okay?"

"Yes, thank you. I never understood why trucks need to be so high. It almost needs a ladder, and I'm not short."

"You'll get used to it." He hadn't thought about what he was saying, but when she remained silent, he didn't bother to delve into any sort of rationalization. Nor did she seek one out.

They walked up the stone path flanked with azalea bushes and pressed the doorbell. Knowing Hailey was home, and that he wouldn't be walking in on his sister and husband—as he'd done one fateful night, though thankfully his sister had been fully clothed—he pushed open the door and stepped inside, with Callie behind him.

"Hey, anyone home?" he called out. The pounding of tiny feet sounded against the hardwood flooring. Hailey sprinted toward him, dressed in a black leotard and purple tutu that flittered up and down with each of her hurried steps. "Hey, squirt."

She jumped into his arms and squeezed his neck. After a peck on the cheek, she loosened her grasp and pivoted toward Callie.

"Hi, Hailey."

"Hi, Miss Callie." Hailey looked at the bag. "Did you bring your slippers so we can show Uncle Hudson my dance?"

"I did, but I didn't know that's what you wanted to do."

Her pigtails bounced with each nod of her head. Before Callie could agree, Izzy came around the corner. They exchanged hellos, and Hudson set Callie down.

"Your home is beautiful," Callie said, admiring the impressive family room that boasted a floor-to-ceiling see-through fireplace acting as a window, allowing the view of the rolling hills behind their house.

"Thank you. Hudson designed it."

Callie flicked her eyes in his direction. "You designed this? I didn't know you were an architect. I thought you were in business."

Talking about why he wasn't doing what he always wanted to do, and rather what his father thought he should do, hadn't been on his agenda. Thankfully, Dwight walked in and unknowingly saved him.

"There he is. Your tools are still downstairs, and the barre is ready to be put up."

Hailey squealed. "Come on, Miss Callie. I can't wait to show you."

Hudson watched his young niece take Callie by the hand and tug her toward the small personal dance studio. Izzy turned and looked at him. "I like her a lot, Hudson, and she's pretty too. Don't you think so?"

He'd been down this road with Izzy before. There had been no doubt in his mind that Hailey had learned all her cute investigative tactics from her mother. Rather than answer her, he simply grinned and headed downstairs, all while thinking that Callie wasn't just pretty—she was stunning.

CHAPTER 13

With each step she took into the home, the more Callie fell in love with it. To think that Hudson designed it shocked her. He seemed so set in his business life, yet she knew that when it came to the creative side of someone's mind, order sometimes fell to the wayside. Still, the angled ceiling in the family room, the warm wood beams that matched the mantel, and the built-in bookshelves housing pictures and books all had Hudson written all over them… order and all.

Hailey's pigtails and tutu bounced as she bounded down the stairs. Callie gasped as soon as she turned the corner. It was a scaled-back version of the family room she'd just left. Callie didn't realize she hadn't moved until a small hand wrapped around hers.

"My dance room is this way."

Heavier steps echoed behind her. Hudson laughed, and thanks to the reflection in the mirror, it must have been at Dwight's expense, since he was the only one wearing a scowl. They acted more like brothers than they did in-laws, which she thought was special.

Callie's heart fluttered at the mere sight of Hudson. It didn't seem to matter that she'd seen him a moment before. The combination of his casual style and his carefree laugh had her lady parts tingling. She knew it wasn't just her that he had that effect on. Callie had witnessed it firsthand, from Annie the barista to Gina, who if it weren't for being her best friend most likely would have jumped on the Hudson express… literally.

When this all started, it was a means to an end. For him to stop getting gifts, marriage proposals, and God knows what else. It was a shame, really. Callie couldn't help but wonder if they would have been drawn to one another in other circumstances. If they had met on the street or at a bar, would the air have crackled? Would there have been that magnetic pull? Would her spine have shivered when he was near? Because if she were being honest, she did feel a pull, and she did feel a shudder race up and down her spine each time she laid eyes on him.

It had to be nerves; that had to be the reason. And especially now that his family was involved, it was something neither of them had bargained for.

Of course, they knew Isabelle would most likely see the morning show, but sweet Hailey, who all but had Callie and Hudson married, would be the hardest one to explain it all to.

Hailey stopped at glass-paned french doors, and when they swung open, she couldn't believe how stunning the small studio was. Callie would have traded all her other toys for a room like this one when she was a little girl. Pale-pink paint decorated three of the walls, and the one in front of her was all mirrors. Black and white pictures of dancers and one of worn toe-shoes made Callie smile. It reminded her of the one that hung in the studio where she studied.

Small white speakers were tucked away in the corners of the room. Of course there was the barre. But rather than it being on the wall, it was lying on the floor, waiting to be set up. She hopped up and down before turning toward Hudson, who stood in the doorway with Hailey's parents.

Callie bounced on the balls of her feet, noticing the way it absorbed the shock. "Is this a sprung floor?"

"It is," Hudson said, pride lacing his words. "Only the best for my niece."

Callie was a bit surprised that one had been installed. Then again, this was Hudson they were talking about.

She suddenly thought she needed a mantra. That being, *Don't fall for him.*

For the next thirty minutes, Hudson and Dwight worked the barre and stand that stretched from one end of the mirror to the other. Meanwhile, Hailey sat on the floor, playing with two of her dolls, making them dance together. Callie could see so much of herself in the little girl.

She remembered doing the same in her grandmother's living room. Her sweet nana would sit on the couch for however long it took for Callie to complete her routine. Even back then, Callie enjoyed making up her own dances. Joy filled her heart when she was able to watch her students with the same jubilance that she had. Granted, not all of them were like Hailey. Some were there because their mom wanted their daughter or son to dance. Callie understood them too. Doing something that wasn't in your heart made you feel as though you were trudging through mud rather than dancing on air.

"He's special." Izzy's voice interrupted her trip down memory lane.

When Callie brought her gaze to Hudson, his arms flexed, pulling the cotton fabric of his T-shirt tight around his biceps. It wasn't as though she hadn't noticed his broad back or how beautiful his physique was. She'd need blinders on to miss any of that. However, Callie had done her best to ignore it all. The only problem was, when she sat at her desk to pen book number two, the man in front of her had become her muse.

"And handsome," slipped out of Callie's mouth. The corners of Izzy's lips tipped up. "Sorry, probably not something a sister wants to hear about her brother." Or something Callie had expected to say.

The BOOK BOYFRIEND

She cleared the air with her hand. "Believe me, all of my friends thought so. It's not lost on me that my brother's looks rival that of some movie stars." She paused before asking, "Have you read the book?"

Callie almost asked which book to buy her some time, but instead she nodded and ignored the slight tension in her eye. "I'm familiar with it."

"I'm so shocked I haven't heard more about it. Although many of my friends aren't huge readers. Most have small kids, and by the time they're ready to settle in with a book, they're asleep. I don't think I'll be able to read it. I have this fear of picturing my brother as the hero." She shimmied her shoulders as though an icy chill had run up her spine. "I am glad you two are together. And what a small world that you're Hailey's teacher."

That was an understatement. "Yes, I was a bit surprised. Your daughter is a sweetheart and one of my best students. Some kids at that age just want to spin around or hang on the barre. But your little ballerina gets a sparkle in her eyes when the music starts. It's as though she can feel it in her bones."

Izzy nodded and looked at her daughter, who was now in her father's arms, watching her uncle put in the last screw to secure the barre onto the stand. Hudson tossed the tool into the box and turned toward Hailey. "Okay, squirt, you're all set."

"On that note, we should be going, honey," Izzy said to Dwight, who kissed Hailey before setting her on the ground.

"Miss Callie, you're going to stay, right?"

Callie looked at Hudson, who answered for her: "Of course she is."

Hailey made a fist and pulled it toward her waist. "Yes! I'm going to go get my ballet slippers. You go get yours, too, Miss Callie."

"Okay, bye. We won't be too late. The pizza should be here in about thirty minutes. Help yourselves to whatever else you'd like." As though they were being chased, Izzy and Dwight hustled out of the room and up the stairs.

"Can we show Uncle Hudson my routine now?"

"I'd love to see it," he said with a gleam in his eye. Callie hadn't danced in front of anyone in years. Naturally, she'd demonstrate moves to her class, but that was the extent of it.

"Are the speakers Bluetooth so I can connect my phone to the song?" When Hudson told her he could pair it for her, she plucked her cell out of her bag, unlocked it, and handed it to Hudson. "It's track two on my recital playlist."

While Hudson worked on connecting the music, Callie went through her warm-up with Hailey. She loved watching the concentration on the sweet girl's face switching from first to second position and then into a demi plié.

"Okay, I got it. Are you two ready?" Callie looked down at a beaming Hailey, and Hudson chuckled. "Here we go."

Rather than take the position of teacher, Callie stood next to her student. When they locked eyes,

Callie winked, eliciting a precious smile. As soon as the piano version of "Twinkle, Twinkle, Little Star" started bellowing through the speakers, Hailey lifted her arms in second position at the same time Callie did.

The pair moved through their steps, from different positions to the one she knew was a student favorite, a two-footed relevé with arms in fifth position. After the last bar of music played, they both turned on their toes until they faced forward and ended in reverence as a thank-you to the parents or guardians in the audience.

Hudson stood and clapped. "Bravo! Bravo!" he shouted. Hailey giggled when he swooped her up into his arms. "Amazing. You were great." He locked eyes with Callie. "You both were."

Warmth swept through Callie. She was so proud of her class. Even before she had a connection to Hailey, the little girl had been a standout. She soaked up direction and choreography as if she were a wet sponge in a tub full of water.

Back on two feet, Hailey gave Callie a hug at the same time her eyes once again met Hudson's. Suddenly, everything felt very real. Breaking her connection with him, she looked down at Hailey. "You did so well."

"You're the best, Miss Callie. And you too, Uncle Hudson. Maybe next time you can learn too. You can get a pair of tights."

"Who's hungry? The pizza should be here soon. And the bill is all taken care of," Hudson said, immediately changing the subject, forcing Callie to clamp down on her bottom lip to stifle a laugh of her own. "Sweetie, why don't you run upstairs and pick out a movie for us to watch."

Hailey ran out of the room before she spun around, sending her tutu fluttering around her little legs. "Can we eat on the couch?"

Callie loved the interaction between the pair. He brought his finger to his lips and made a zipping motion. "Our secret, yes?"

She giggled her way up the steps.

"Boy, that girl has you wrapped around her finger." Callie slipped off her ballet shoes and put her sandals back on. When she looked up, Hudson was staring at her. Heat flowed through Callie's body in an awareness she hadn't been used to. One she hadn't felt in… well… forever. It was a shame relationships weren't her thing. Except, she reminded herself, this one wasn't real.

Callie wasn't sure then why it felt that way.

CHAPTER 14

Hudson was in uncharted territory. He watched his niece practically float up the stairs after dancing her heart out, and the woman he was *dating* was the reason for it. Never had he expected the feelings that burst inside him. This wasn't supposed to be real. Dating Callie was a means to an end. To get his life back in order.

Except something told him the opposite was happening.

The doorbell ringing brought him out of his thoughts. Realizing the girls were upstairs, he hurried up the steps, headed into the family room, and saw Callie carrying two boxes.

"Here, let me take those." Hudson took the pizzas and set them down on the island next to the paper plates and napkins that Izzy must have left out for them.

"I want cheese, please." Hailey rushed to the counter and slid to a stop.

Once everyone had a bottle of water and a slice — or in Hudson's case, two slices on their plates, they went and sat on the couch, Hailey announcing that she was sitting in the middle.

Hudson grabbed the remote, and just like the last time he watched his niece, he fiddled with the remote until Buzz and Woody came on the screen. Hailey's purple-socked feet, which barely reached the end of the cushion, mimicked a pendulum swaying in time to the theme song, "You've Got a Friend in Me." Between chews, she sang along, bringing a smile to both Callie's and Hudson's faces.

It didn't take long for them to finish eating. He put the plates on the coffee table, and they continued to watch the movie. Hudson had lost track of how often he'd seen it. His niece had most, if not all, of the lines memorized, and she made sure they knew it.

"Who's your favorite character, Miss Callie?"

She curled her lips to the side and cocked her head. "In this one, I think I'd have to go with Woody or maybe Hamm. I think he's funny. What about you?"

"I like Woody, too, and Buzz. I think it would be cool to have wings… and a laser beam." She turned toward Hudson. "What about you, Uncle Hudson?"

The BOOK BOYFRIEND

"Hmm…" Using his thumb and forefinger, he rubbed his chin. "Let's see… I think I'd have to go with Bo Peep." He waggled his eyebrows, and Callie shook her head and laughed.

"You're so weird, Uncle Hudson." Hailey snapped her gaze toward Callie. "Isn't he weird?"

"Sooo weird," Callie said conspiratorially.

"Hey…" He started tickling his niece, who squirmed until she almost landed on Callie's lap. Her sweet giggles filled the room. "Take it back." He stopped tickling Hailey, and she sat up, her pigtails now askew. "Are you done picking on me now?" he teased.

The girls laughed once more, and then both shrugged. Hudson looked at Callie over Hailey's head, and it dawned on him that whatever was going on between him and Callie had shifted. He wasn't sure how, when, or even what — he just felt an invisible tether pulling them together, and for once he didn't want to cut it.

"Are all boys weird, Miss Callie? You know, there are going to be boys in my kindergarten class. My neighbor Erin's mom is a teacher, and she said that there are going to be twelve boys in my class. I hope they're cute."

Callie laughed and Hudson scowled. "What do you know about cute boys? How about you just worry about making all sorts of friends and not just the boys."

"I will, silly. Miss Callie, do you think my uncle's cute?"

Hudson angled his body toward the girls, waiting for a reply. Both Hailey's and Hudson's eyes were focused on her.

Callie looked at Hudson. "Yes, I think your uncle is cute."

Hailey giggled, and Hudson gently rubbed his fist on her head *noogie* style. They all laughed, but when Hudson looked at Callie, she gave him a shy grin, then returned her focus to Woody and friends on the screen.

Halfway through the second movie, a soft snore could be heard during a lull in dialogue. "She's out," Callie whispered over Hailey's head, which was currently resting on Callie's upper arm. At some point during the movie, his niece had inched her way closer to Callie and made herself comfortable.

Hudson pushed himself up, paused the movie, and whispered, "I'll take her to bed." Callie nodded, trying not to move too much. He scooped his niece up, his hand grazing Callie's thigh. Their eyes met, and he wondered if she'd just felt the same zing of electricity he had.

He straightened himself. Hailey's head fell to his chest, and her little socked feet dangled over his arms. After mouthing, "Be right back," he carried his niece upstairs.

Hailey's room looked as though it belonged to a princess. When he laid her down, she stirred a bit, and her bright-blue eyes fluttered open.

"Good night, squirt."

"Good night," she whispered. He stood to leave and she said, "Tell Miss Callie I said bye."

"I will."

"I like her." Hailey's eyes fluttered closed, and Hudson whispered back, "So do I."

He left her door ajar and headed downstairs to find Callie cleaning up the water bottles and tossing the paper plates and napkins into the trash.

"Hey, you don't need to do that," he said, doing his best not to wrap her up in his arms.

"I don't mind. Is Hailey still out?"

"Yes, but she woke up long enough to say that she wanted me to tell you bye for her. And that she likes you."

"I like her too. She's a sweet girl and definitely loves you."

His heart swelled. Not because Callie told him something that he didn't already know, but because every time he thought about his niece, it made him happy. "I couldn't love her more if she were my own."

Callie nodded. "Do you want kids one day?"

His eyes widened.

"Never mind, you don't need to answer that. It's really none of my business."

Except at that moment he wanted it to be her business. "I haven't thought about it too much, but yeah, I'd like to be a father."

She smiled. "You know, you can toss your orderly life out the window when that happens."

Hudson chuckled. "I suppose you're right."

The way things were going, his orderly life had already been disrupted. Oddly, it didn't bother him as much as it normally did. They both remained silent, the air heavy as though the proverbial elephant had just sat down and made itself comfortable. Callie put the leftover pizza on a plate and put it in the refrigerator.

Suddenly he found himself asking, "What about you? Do you want kids?"

"I—"

"We're home." The front door opened, and in walked his sister and brother-in-law. He swore he saw Callie flush with relief. He didn't want to make her uncomfortable, nor did he intend on getting too personal with her. She was the one who'd asked him first.

Izzy walked into the kitchen with Dwight by her side. "Hi, you two. How was our angel?"

"Perfect," Hudson replied.

She rolled her eyes. "You always say that."

Hudson nodded. "Because she is."

"Right." She looked at Callie. "Get my daughter and brother in a room together and no one else exists."

He thought about that and then thought about how she gravitated toward Callie. Apparently, that was no longer the truth.

"Well, we're going to get going."

They said their goodbyes and headed out. Once settled in his truck, he turned on the radio and pulled out into the road.

"Thank you for coming with me tonight."

Out of the corner of his eye, he saw a bright smile spread across her face. "I had fun. I love your family. I feel so badly lying to them."

He nodded. "I know. I'm not that big of a fan of doing it either." Fact of the matter was that his family wasn't supposed to be this involved. It had just happened.

They remained silent for the rest of the drive until they pulled up in front of Callie's complex. He put the truck into park, automatically unlocking the doors. She grasped the handle and opened it.

"Thanks for everything," Callie said, picking up her bag from the floor in front of her.

"I'll talk to you later."

She hopped out of the truck, gave him a quick wave, and shut the door. Hudson watched Callie head inside before he drove away, knowing he'd started to have *real* feelings for the pretty author.

CHAPTER 15

What am I doing? she thought, lying in bed and staring at her ceiling. How she wished she understood the emotions swirling within her. What was fake, her relationship with Hudson, felt real, and what was real, her recent success, felt fake. Being able to recognize the validity of either started to feel impossible.

All night long, she tossed and turned, hoping for something to come to her. Even a spark that made her want to get up and write, but nothing came. At one point around 3:00 a.m., she grabbed a notebook out of her nightstand and her favorite pen in hopes something would spring to mind and find itself on the lined paper… it hadn't.

Around five o'clock, she'd had enough. Tossing the covers off her, she padded into her kitchen and flicked on the light, cursing at the way her pupils rejected it, before preparing her coffeepot. While that brewed, she decided to take a shower, still hoping an idea for her book would come to life.

She stripped out of her clothes, regulated the water, and stepped inside the stall. The only thing that came to her mind was Hudson. The real one. The way he was with his niece, how kind he was to his family. And his talent for architecture made him even sexier.

Callie closed her eyes, letting the water stream down her face. His back and biceps in that T-shirt... and his butt in his jeans. The man could wear anything and look like something out of a dream. And then there were his lips, like soft pillows that seemed to know hers.

After she let out a sigh, realizing the only thing the shower was doing was confusing her, she quickly washed and rinsed before she flipped the faucet's handle, turning the water cold to cool her off.

"I'm losing my mind," she said, wrapping a towel around her body. Taking a tissue, she wiped the steam off the small mirror above her sink. Even her reflection shook its head at her. Callie sighed, went through her morning routine, and tossed on comfy clothes.

The smell of freshly brewed coffee was calling to her. Definitely needing caffeine, she went and poured herself a cup and grabbed her cell off the charger. A red circle on the texting icon caught her attention. She grabbed a pair of her reading glasses off the counter, slid them on, and tapped her screen.

Hudson.

12:01 a.m.

I hope this doesn't wake you. I just wanted you to know that I had fun tonight.

Callie stared at the message. She didn't bother replying, since it was so early, but she'd remember to later. She did have a good time—a great one, in fact. One that had her laughing, dancing, and feeling confused.

She sat on her sofa, sipping coffee and scrolling through her phone. One thing she tried not to do every hour was check her sales. Realizing it had been a good day, she first clicked on her book, only to see that it had fallen out of the top one hundred. *Meh.* She shrugged. It had a good run. Then she clicked over to her account, and she couldn't believe the amount of zeros at the end of the number that would be deposited into her bank account.

Maybe she could one day quit her job at the club. Then again, how could she when she couldn't even think about how to end Hudson's story? Callie decided she needed a break. She took her coffee and poured it into a to-go cup, deciding to hop in her car and go for a drive.

"Let's think about this," Gina said, rubbing the sleep out of her eyes.

Callie hadn't intended on driving to Gina's apartment, and thankfully she was alone and not entertaining anyone.

"Do you not want to write the sequel, because you don't need to? As a reader, would I want you to? Yes, definitely. But honey, if you can't find the words, then you can't find the words. Move on. Maybe start something else, and Hudson will yell at you."

Callie's brows pulled together.

"Not your Hudson, the fake one."

Gina was pretty much saying exactly how Callie had been feeling, and Callie shook her head. "That's the problem. I'm finding it difficult to separate the two. I almost feel as though I'm in my book. How bizarre does that sound?"

"Not going to lie, it's a little bizarre. But, sweetie, use your muse as inspiration. Even if he was just in your imagination before. You basically brought him to life. Use that to fuel you. I know I'd use it on a multitude of levels."

Callie laughed. "You're incorrigible."

"And you're blind and stubborn. The man is sex on legs, and you're all ho-hum about it. Fake relationship or not, he's a real man. You're a real woman. Do I need to continue?"

She shook her head. "Please don't."

"Then you're good?"

"Um... sure, I guess. Why?" A toilet flushed.

"Who's here? I thought you were alone."

"Jordan"

"I'm sorry, you should have told me." Gina nonchalantly shrugged. "Well, at least one of us is having fun." She kissed her best friend on the cheek.

"You could be, too, just remember that."

"Yeah, yeah. I'll talk to you later."

Just before Callie walked out, a cute guy she assumed was Jordan walked into the kitchen. Although good looking, he didn't hold a candle to Hudson.

Once again realizing… that no man probably would. Back in her car, she finally replied to his text.

I had fun too.

CHAPTER 16

Hudson stepped into the café for the first time since his life turned upside down. He stopped himself from inhaling the rich scent of roasted coffee beans and fresh-baked goods. When Annie's eyes rolled up over the cash register and made contact with his, she gave him a tight grin. "Good morning, Mr. Newman. Your usual?" When he cocked a brow, she added, "Large black dark roast?"

"Yes, thank you, Annie."

She nodded and skirted around Jen, the other barista, who gave a quick glance to Hudson before scooting out from behind the counter to clear off a couple of tables.

Annie set the coffee down, and Hudson pulled out his wallet. "I'm really sorry about the last time you were here, Mr. Newman. It was wrong of me to act the way I did. Believe me, my manager told me as much. It's just that I read that book and I knew you, well, I—"

He put his hand up. "No apologies."

After he walked out, he took a sip and savored the taste. Aside from the cup that Callie brought, he'd missed his morning ritual. Finally, things were starting to come together. He strolled into his office building, waved to Michael, who was on the phone, headed into the elevator, and waited for the illuminated numbers to reach his floor.

Keira met him as soon as the brass doors slid open and rattled off the meetings he had on his morning agenda. And she added that the appointment he'd blocked out his afternoon for had been canceled due to a travel delay. Frustrating, because he and Jack had been working on a contract for that client for over a month.

Once in his office, he fired up his laptop. While he waited for it to boot, a picture he had on his desk of himself and Hailey at the zoo last summer caught his attention. An immediate smile spread across his face. God, did he love her. Then he realized he didn't have a picture of him and Callie, as most couples would. He clicked an app on his phone, finding one of the images that was taken at his house.

He stared at one of them kissing. Feelings began to whirl inside of him. He wanted to know more about her. More than just knowing she liked to write and dance. He thought that maybe he would get to know more about her the night they watched Hailey, but his sister and brother-in-law had walked in.

Hudson was a man who knew that once something started to gnaw at him, he needed to resolve it. The *something* now was Callie. He needed to find out why thoughts of her were consuming his mind. There was only one way to find out the answers.

Feel like playing hooky this afternoon?

Hudson waited, and as soon as he saw that Callie had read the text, tiny dots started to bounce on the screen.

I wish. I have a meeting at 2. Why?

My afternoon appointments were canceled. Figured I'd spend it with my "girlfriend." Can you reschedule your meeting?

Dots once again appeared, then vanished three times before another text from Callie popped in.

OK.

OK? You'll play hooky with me?

Yes.

Can you be home and ready by 1?

Sure.

I'll pick you up at your place. Dress casual. And lunch is on me.

A thumbs-up emoji had been her response. Hudson chuckled and tossed his phone onto his desk.

It was a perfect summer afternoon. Low humidity, no clouds obscuring the blue sky, temperature in the low eighties, and light traffic. Thanks to his buddy Josh at Prism, he had the perfect picnic lunch packed, less the basket. But when he went home to change, he did remember to pack a blanket and grab a bottle of wine and two glasses. Well, red plastic cups, since he didn't have anything else that wouldn't break.

When he pulled up to Callie's, she was standing outside in a white sleeveless dress that hit midthigh, showing off her toned legs. The strappy flat sandals she wore suited her perfectly, as did her casual ponytail. She raised her hand and waved at him before strolling toward the edge of the sidewalk.

"Hi, thanks for playing hooky with me." He opened the passenger-side door.

"Thank you for being a bad influence... on a Monday, no less." Callie laughed and sighed when she looked at his truck.

"What?"

"I may end up flashing my neighbors trying to get into this thing. I'd hate it if Mr. Rogers saw me. He's eighty."

The Book Boyfriend

Hudson would have laughed, but for some reason anyone seeing her, regardless of their age, didn't sit well with him. Reacting in the moment, he swooped her into his arms and placed her in his truck. Callie gasped and then giggled. "Um, thank you. That was very chivalrous of you. May need to put that in my book."

He nodded and glanced around before rounding the hood and getting behind the wheel.

"Wait, your neighbor's name is Mr. Rogers?"

"Yup. No cardigan sweater or polyester pants, though. This Mr. Rogers prefers leather. He was in some biker club. If it weren't for Mrs. Rogers, he'd still be driving his motorcycle. It's cute, really. They just celebrated their fifty-eighth anniversary. Can you even imagine?"

Hudson almost replied, *Yes, I can*. But since he had no idea where that came from, he simply said, "Wow."

"So, where are we going?"

"How does a picnic sound?"

"Really? I've never been on a picnic."

He stared at her. How could it be that she'd never been on a picnic? It wasn't as though he'd been on several, but he had thought that with her loving romance and all that she would have at least been on one. "Well, then let me be your first."

A blush crept up her face when she replied, "I'd like that."

All types of scenarios flew into his brain. So many questions he wanted answers to, but the first one was to himself. Why? Why did he want—no, need—to know all about the gorgeous woman sitting beside him? The one whose lavender perfume would linger in the cab of his truck long after she got out. The one who'd disrupted his life. And the one he couldn't get out of his head.

Callie stared out the window as they drove down tree-lined streets. The more they drove, the more rural the landscape became. Rolling green fields with split rail fences were in abundance. There were some areas that seemed to fade into the horizon. Those were Hudson's favorites. On a clear day, like this one, it felt as though you were in a picture book.

As if she read his mind, Callie said, "Wow, this would be a wonderful place to write. It's so peaceful."

"I love it out here."

They came upon a gravel driveway, one that he'd been down more and more lately. He turned in and drove until it turned into grass. Hudson stopped the truck, put it in park, and killed the engine.

"This is where we're going to have a picnic?"

"It is."

"Do you know the owner?"

"I do." Hudson had never brought anyone to his property. His family didn't even know about it, but he wanted to show Callie. Maybe it was because of how she loved Izzy's house. Or because she seemed to understand the creative part of him.

"It's you, isn't it?"

He nodded, and a bright smile lit up her face. Hudson was sure he had a similar one on his. "Yes, it is. Come on, I'll show you my favorite spot."

He hopped out of the truck, hurried over to her side, and helped her down. Her dress's skirt flew up in the light country breeze, but she just laughed. "Oops."

Hudson had to do everything in his power not to act on his primal instincts. After all, it had been a while since he'd been with a woman in the most natural sense of the word. He wasn't one to sleep around, but he had his moments.

Things were different with Callie. Their relationship being a means to an end was one thing. The other thing was he didn't want to have a one-night stand with her. Or in this case a one-afternoon stand. He wasn't sure what he wanted. All he knew was that the order in his life hadn't been restored. Mainly because the gorgeous woman whose green eyes sparkled like diamonds, and who had a smile that could outshine the sun, confused him. She had him wanting to do things he otherwise wouldn't have done.

She righted her dress, and when their eyes locked, he watched her neck work down a swallow. Instinctively, his right hand rose and cupped her cheek. Her strong pulse thumped against his pinky. She licked her pink-tinted lips, and he all but lost it.

Rather than act impulsively, he opened the back door and grabbed his blanket, the shopping bag with Prism's logo on it, and a cooler containing the wine and some water.

"Fancy picnic."

Hudson chuckled. "Come on, let's go eat before it gets cold."

She took the blanket from him, and the two walked down the path to Hudson's favorite spot. When they reached the flat plateau that overlooked rolling hills and a lake off in the distance, Callie gasped. That had been a similar reaction to his when the Realtor had showed him this property.

Callie unfolded the blanket and laid it on the plush grass. They both kneeled, and while Hudson unpacked the bag, Callie went to work on the cooler, taking out two bottles of water and a bottle of white wine. She laughed when she saw the red cups.

Hudson shrugged. "I know, but it's all I had." He uncorked the bottle and poured each of them a few fingers' worth.

"Well, I for one think they're perfect. As is this place. Thank you, Hudson. This is the best picnic I've ever been on."

"It's the only picnic you've been on."

"True, but I'm sure all others would have paled in comparison."

He lifted his cup. "To firsts," Hudson said, looking into Callie's eyes.

"Firsts," she repeated.

They each took a sip, and before she could say anything else, he leaned over the Caesar salad and kissed her.

CHAPTER 17

*C*onfused thoughts swirled in Callie's head like a hurricane forming over the Gulf. Heat rose in her body as she got lost in the moment. His soft lips, tasting of aged grapes, were on hers, and all she could do was close her eyes and kiss him back, not thinking too much about what it all meant.

After a few seconds, he broke their connection, and the smile that spread across his face rivaled that of the afternoon sun. Neither said anything, allowing the birds flying overhead to provide the ambient noise.

Finally, after the brief sonata flew off into the distance, Hudson said, "I like you, Callie."

"I like you too," easily breezed out of her.

Another smile appeared before he began doling out salad on paper plates that Josh had the foresight to pack. He also uncovered the rest of their meal, which consisted of mozzarella-filled arancini with a side of marinara sauce for dipping, tomato crostini, and, of course, perfectly delicious macarons baked by his pastry chef.

"Can I ask you something?" he asked right after she took a bite of her crostini.

Rather than answer and risk spraying crumbs all over, she nodded.

"Why are you single?"

She took a sip of her wine, trying to buy time, but she knew the answer, since it was a question asked of her often. Callie didn't want to say because she never had a great example of how a man should treat a woman. Yes, Tommy treated his wife like a queen, but he always said that he'd do it differently than their father, and he did.

Still, Callie had yet to meet the one to sweep her off her feet. Gina said she was too picky. Callie didn't think she was picky enough. Did she have a lot of boyfriends? No. Lately, what she had were more first dates than second ones. And even that number was low. Then there was marriage, which, unlike with a lot of women, had never crossed her mind. She didn't put a pillowcase on her head and pretend it was a veil or dream of the type of dress she'd wear. Gina did, though. Just goes to show you how different two people, even best friends, could be.

Then again, one would need to go out to meet someone. Thanks to her book, she could blame her manuscript as a reason for not having the time to do so. Oddly, thanks to that same manuscript, she was staring at a man that dreams were made of.

Maybe that was why she opted for fiction. Being able to dictate how a person would act and feel became an outlet for her. Something that she needed more than she realized. It wasn't until Callie typed *The End* that she let her tears fall, knowing she'd left her heart in the fictional Hudson's hands.

"Callie?"

Blinking a few times, she cleared her head. "I could deflect and ask the same of you, but the simple answer is, I'm not sure. At times I feel as though I'm too old-fashioned. But it's something I picked up from spending time with my grandmother. I want the iconic relationship that Joanne Woodward and Paul Newman had. I want to be the Doris Day to a Rock Hudson… you know, like in their movies."

Hudson shook his head. "I actually don't."

"What? How has this never come up before? Are you telling me you've never watched a Rock Hudson and Doris Day movie? I don't even know if we can be friends, much less anything else," she taunted.

"No, sorry. I did see *The Hustler.* You know, for the other part of your character. Oh, and *The Color of Money.*"

All Callie could do was stare at him and blink.

"What? Come on… Fast Eddie Felson? He's a legend."

"But you know who Rock Hudson is, right?" When his lips quirked up in the corners, Callie shook her head. "We will rectify this, Mr. Newman." He laughed again, but she'd been serious. "Anyway, that's why I'm single."

"I'm not even sure you answered my question."

Callie laughed. "Now you. What's your story? And don't give me that you need order, because that excuse is getting old."

"The short of it is, since we moved a lot, I didn't have time to build a relationship or have a high school sweetheart. I had a girlfriend in college, but she ran off with my roommate shortly after graduation. They're married now. But that's not why I don't have one now or why I don't date. I just haven't found someone who interests me… for a long period of time."

Right, more than one night. Jealousy began to rear its ugly head. *Do I even have the right to feel that way?* She wasn't sure but still couldn't deny that the green monster had paid a visit.

Hudson's eyes caught the sunlight enhancing his already pretty blue irises. "You do, though."

She tipped her head to the side. "I do what?"

"Interest me, Callie. I'm not sure if it's because I watched you with Hailey or what the reason is. Maybe there is no reason."

Warmth, and not from the summer heat, flourished inside her.

"Do you know I've never brought anyone to this spot?"

The Book Boyfriend

She shook her head. That had been something she never contemplated. It was such a serene, beautiful place. Leaf-filled trees created the shady spots perfect to take a break from the warmth of the summer sun. Callie didn't even need to close her eyes to imagine herself leaning against the large trunk, reading a book. Despite the fear of not liking the answer, she still asked, "Why not?"

"Because it's where I want to build my forever house. One that I've been working on for years, but something has been holding me back from pulling the trigger. Then when I saw your reaction to Izzy and Dwight's home, all of my desire to do it came flooding back. Could be I'm feeding off *your* creativity."

That was not what she'd expected him to say. Knowing no one had been there made her feel more special than she ever had. "If it's anything like your sister's house, I'm sure it will be amazing."

Hudson raked his fingers through his hair, leaving it with that sexily messy look—one he wore very well. That, blended with the navy T-shirt and tan twill shorts, made her mouth water more than the arancini did.

"I'm not doing this very well."

"Believe me, this is all amazing."

"No. I mean, thank you. Yes, the picnic is great, but that's not what I'm talking about." He took her hand in his and laced their fingers together. "Callie, when we met, my approach was based on annoyance." She rolled her lips between her teeth to stifle a chuckle. "Now, it's based on something else. Call it admiration or maybe curiosity, but I want to see where this goes. Take it one day at a time. No deadlines. No pretenses. Just us. I realize I'm doing a one-eighty and throwing this at you out of the blue, but it doesn't feel fake."

She gazed out over the horizon before looking back at him. "Umm." *Good retort, Callie.* "I didn't expect you to say that."

"Neither did I. It still doesn't make it less true. I don't want to put a deadline on us…"

Callie stared at the gorgeous man. Could she do that? Would she want to? She thought about Gina and could almost feel her hands on her shoulder blades, nudging her toward Hudson. She wasn't sure what to say. His eyes held hers. They had agreed on one month. Now, he was asking for more. "No deadlines. No more threats about delisting my book."

"No deadlines. No threats. And while we're at it, no killing off Hudson Newman in your next novel."

She relaxed a little, laughed, and said, "No promises."

"How does your book end, anyway?"

Callie shrugged. "I'm not sure yet."

That was the truth. She knew it would end in a happily ever after, but how he got there was still yet to be seen.

"Does he have a love interest?"

"He's in the process of finding one." The irony wasn't lost on her. Life imitates art after all, or was it the other way around? She didn't know and had never bothered to analyze it before. Something told her the more time she spent with Hudson, the more likely she'd find out that answer.

"I don't get it," Hudson said, popping a few pieces of popcorn into his mouth. He'd been asking questions ever since she started playing the DVD of *Pillow Talk*. Thanks to devouring each morsel prepared by the award-winning chef a couple of hours earlier, they'd skipped dinner and gone straight for the salty and butter-coated snack.

Callie rolled her eyes. "What's there to get? Back then they shared a phone line with strangers." Something she couldn't fathom in this day and age. People freaked out when they didn't have a strong signal. Anarchy would ensue if they couldn't call someone or have someone call them when they wanted to.

"I mean, she's a total babe," Hudson teased. "If you haven't noticed, I have a thing for blondes." She had noticed, because despite Gina's beauty, he never gave her a second glance or looked at her with desire in his eyes the way he did when he was with her. "He's not very nice. He lied to her and he's a total player. Then she trashed his apartment. How is this a romance?"

"Technically, she decorated it. And he might have been a player, but not after he met her. And he's so dreamy," Callie breathed. The couch cushion shifted, and when she looked to her right, an incredulous Hudson was gaping at her. She waved her hand back and forth before reaching in the bowl for a few buttery kernels. "Fine, he's not the best in the beginning to her. But she fought him too. They're complete opposites."

Hudson stared at her as though she'd grown three heads. His odd expression caught her so off guard that she was happy she'd swallowed her snack, because a snort-laugh ripped out of her.

"What in the world was that sound? And what's so funny?" *Again, three heads.*

A case of the church giggles attacked her. They were the ones that hit you at the worst possible times. Like when you're sitting in a pew next to your nana, listening to the priest recite the sermon, and your brother picks that exact time to tell you a joke. Callie could remember the back of the wooden bench pressing up against each bump in her spine as she tried to hold it in. The way her grandmother tapped her with her elbow, which only spurred her on more.

Callie wiped the tears of laughter that formed beneath her eyes. "Can you imagine if you had to share a phone line with someone? I could only guess the schedule you'd have printed in triplicate and, if I had to guess, laminated. The disorder that would cause in your life would be unheard of. I mean, you lost it when you weren't given the right coffee."

"That was your fault."

A familiar song came on the screen, ceasing her hysteria. "Ooh, ooh!" She pointed at the television. "Shh, this is my favorite part." For the next several minutes, they watched Doris and Rock realize that they belonged together. Callie sighed as soon as the credits started to roll. "So good."

Hudson looked at her. "Okay, now it's my turn to pick a movie."

"Fine, what are we watching now?"

"What else? Fast Eddie." Hudson winked, and despite what she might have led him to believe, that happened to be one of her favorite movies too.

CHAPTER 18

"Callie," Hudson whispered, gently rubbing her shoulder. "We need to get up."

Up. That one word almost made him laugh, considering he couldn't feel his legs. When Callie had fallen asleep last night only a little over an hour into the movie, Hudson hadn't had the heart to wake her. He also hadn't thought she'd stay asleep all night, but she had. Now, with her head on his lap, her knees pulled to her chest, and her ponytail pressed up against his *natural* morning alarm, she needed to move—or he was going to have a problem.

For the past thirty minutes he'd been trying to gently nudge her awake. The sun crept in through the living room windows, but it wasn't bright enough to jostle her out of her slumber. Thankfully, beeping came from the small table next to him, where she had plugged in her phone before they'd settled in for the second movie. He pushed the side button, silencing her alarm.

She stirred on his lap, and her hand went to his knee first, then slowly glided up his thigh. She sighed and held on to him tighter. Tiny pinpricks from the sleep that had taken over his nerve endings forced him to sit up straighter.

"Callie," he said a bit louder.

"Hmm…" Her hand had resumed its trek when she must have realized what she was touching… or in this case… who.

Callie sprang up and looked at him with horror in her eyes. Strands of blonde escapees framed her heart-shaped face, and aside from the faint black smudges under her eyes, no other makeup was visible. Not that she needed it. Rubbing the sleep away with her fingertips, she looked at Hudson.

"Oh my God. Why are you sitting on my couch?" She looked down, and her hand went to the sweatshirt she'd changed into after Doris and Rock had gotten their happily ever after. "Right… the movie," she drawled out in a yawn as the memories had most likely started to make an appearance. "I fell asleep?"

Hudson grimaced before forcing a grin. Each cell in his body felt stiff. He shook out his feet and rubbed them on the carpet in front of the couch.

"Yeah," he groaned, arching his back, trying to work some circulation into his body.

"And you sat here all night while I slept on you? What time is it?"

"Guilty. I'm not sure. What time is your alarm set for?"

"Six."

"Then it's a few minutes past six." On an exhale, he pushed himself up, using the rolled arm of the couch for support. "You missed the end of the movie."

Callie began to fold the blanket that he had pulled off the back of the couch once he realized she was out for the count. "It's fine. I've seen it a dozen times."

His eyebrows pulled together. "You've seen it? Why did you say you hadn't?"

Her teeth clamped down on her bottom lip before explaining, "Sorry, technically, I didn't say that. Plus, it seems that I enjoy giving you a hard time, I guess."

"Do you now?" He narrowed his eyes, grabbed her, tossed her on the couch, and began to tickle her. She writhed beneath his quick-moving fingers.

"Okay, okay, I'm sorry. Won't happen again," she rasped out between giggles.

Hudson pulled her up and teased, "It better not."

Shaking her hands out to the side, she seemed to regain her composure. "I need to get ready for work. I'm sure you do, too, after you took yesterday off. I can make you a quick breakfast if you'd like."

"No, thank you. I need to get to the gym."

Her eyes roamed up and down his body. "You must go there a lot."

The BOOK BOYFRIEND

Hudson knew he was in good shape. He did his best to make sure he didn't get complacent since his days were spent in a chair behind a desk. Although more and more lately, he'd started to wonder if that may change in the not-so-distant future.

"How about dinner tonight?"

Callie nodded. "Okay, but I can't make it a late night. I need to write when I get home. I'll also need to meet you there. I have a meeting with a few women from the ladies' golf association." Her lips quirked to the side.

"What's that look for?"

"They're just so… stodgy. They're very old-school when it comes to certain things. Anytime I make a suggestion, they shoot it down. Especially Constance. She's the president, and her grandfather was one of the original founders. She's also on the board and won't let anyone forget it." Callie cleared her throat, and in the worst British accent, she said, "Callie, dear, we mustn't encourage those who don't take club rules seriously. There's etiquette involved… a standard we don't deviate from. The members are the heart of Shadow Oaks." Callie rolled her eyes.

"Maybe she needs your book."

Callie laughed again. "Are you kidding? My book would send her on a completely different tangent. She also is in charge of preparing girls for their debutant events. The proper way for a young lady to act. I'm sure a character heading to a club and engaging in debauchery isn't part of her curriculum."

"How do you do it?"

"What, not want to reach across the conference room table and slap her?"

Now Hudson was the one laughing. "No, a full- and part-time job, plus your novel. It's no wonder you fell asleep on my lap." Not that he was complaining.

A blush graced her cheeks. She shrugged. "I just do. Plus, I only teach one dance class on Saturday mornings, so that's no big deal. My job pays the bills. When it comes to writing, I never really thought about it as a job. And although I'm so thankful for everything, there are some days I'm completely stressed out and can't figure out one word to type. I do horrible under pressure."

"Sounds rough."

"It's fine. I'll figure it out. But I do need to get moving."

"Right," he said. "If you'll excuse me one moment." He walked down her hall to take care of business, and after he used her bathroom, including her mouthwash, he walked out to find her sitting at the kitchen island. She stood, and they both crossed the room to get to the front door. "I'll text you the restaurant's address. Will seven work?"

"Okay and yes. Thanks again for yesterday and for being my pillow. I had a great time."

"Me too. Thank you for introducing me to Rock and Doris." A cute giggle filled the otherwise silent room.

"My pleasure."

The BOOK BOYFRIEND

Using his signature move, he cupped her cheek and kissed her.

When he finally broke their connection, Callie fisted her hips. "That's not fair. You're minty fresh, while I'm—"

"Don't care." He pecked at her lips once more before walking out. "See you later."

The door clicked closed behind him. Hudson hopped into his truck and went home to change, grab his clothes, and head for the gym.

Less than thirty minutes later, Hudson stood behind the weight bench, spotting his friend. The smell of sweat and antiseptic filled the stale air. "Let me get this straight," Jack said, lifting the weighted bar over his head before lowering it to his chest. "You're really dating now?" He exhaled and pushed the bar until his arms were straight, then bent them again.

"Yeah, she's different. I want to get to know her better."

"I get that," he grunted, moving the bar to the holder before sitting up. Hudson handed him a small white towel. "You don't need to be off the market, though. Don't get me wrong. I'm happy for you, but I've just never imagined you'd fall for her. I figured you'd break things off or call it quits after life calmed down. From what I've heard, only a few packages have come to the office. And you've clearly been getting your coffee, since your mood isn't as foul."

Hudson had thought that, too, and it had been

his intention, but things had changed. "I like her. There's something very intriguing about Callie. And *fall* is a strong word. We're getting to know each other."

He had said the same thing to her. Out of all the people he'd met throughout his life, only a few knew about his love of drawing and architecture. Yet, after knowing her for only a short period of time, Callie knew. Not only did she know, but she encouraged him. Other than Izzy, no one had pushed him to pursue that dream.

Bringing her to his prized possession, the one where he wanted to build his forever home, shocked even him. It seemed several things that revolved around Callie surprised him. Maybe it was because their relationship started off that way. When he'd gone to her office, the last thing he intended to do was give her an ultimatum. He tried to stay ornery, but she didn't let him get under her skin. Ironically, and in no time at all, she'd gotten under his.

CHAPTER 19

"Let me get this straight..." Gina's voice boomed through Callie's car speakers. "You're dating for real now? How did that happen? Please don't misunderstand. I'm happy for you, and it's about time a man appreciated you for you, but I'm just shocked. In a good way," she amended. "This is very un-Callie-like."

Callie brought her car to a stop at a traffic light, cursing the number of cars on the road. At this rate, she'd be lucky to get to the restaurant by seven thirty. She went on to explain the picnic, less the part about where they were. She knew that was important to Hudson and something he didn't want broadcast.

She also neglected to tell Gina about falling asleep on his lap. Lord only knows where her friend would take that conversation. No, she knew exactly where that would be… straight into her bedroom. Callie shifted in her seat at the mere thought of it. Although it would have been much more comfortable than her sofa.

When she'd woken up this morning, the feeling of warm fabric against her cheek hadn't registered at first. Then her hand had decided to go on a little trip up and down his bare leg. Callie had felt a smattering of hair, along with his muscles tensing beneath her palm. Even half-awake, she'd wanted to continue exploring. It had felt as though she were in a dreamlike state and didn't want to wake up. Almost afraid to open her eyes, but when she had, and she'd looked at him, it had taken every ounce of willpower not to lie back down.

The poor man must have been as stiff as a board when he unfolded his six-foot-plus frame and pushed himself off the couch. Yet, aside from a few moans, he hadn't complained. Score one for chivalry. She kept meaning to ask him about the emails he'd been receiving. Callie knew that the gifts had slowed down considerably, and any that did come in were getting sent back.

Order. She'd never forget that word and how important it was to Hudson. Then to go and take an impromptu picnic? Where was the order there? She'd never seen quite a spread like that, even in movies.

"Yes, it is. He's nice and so is his family. You're the one always telling me to step out of my box.

The BOOK BOYFRIEND

Except the last time I listened to you created this circumstance."

"You're welcome."

Callie wasn't sure she exactly meant that as a thank-you. When Gina said all of this was very "un-Callie like," she wasn't exaggerating. She didn't really *do* boyfriends. She didn't really do anything. All she knew about romance came from old-fashioned movies. Her grandfather passed away before she witnessed their love. Her parents were definitely not in love or a part of her life. And although she could see it all around her, she never felt a part of it. Callie needed to navigate uncharted waters.

The light changed, and she drove a couple of more miles until the robotic voice coming from her car told her she'd reached her destination.

"Hey, I'm here. I'll talk to you tomorrow."

"Sounds good, and let yourself have some fun, Cal."

"Yes, Mom."

"Whatever. I'll talk to you later."

Once parked, Callie looked at the clock on her dash. "Twenty minutes late. Great, Callie," she grumbled, killing the engine. She should have cut the meeting off when they started talking about their book club. Except she was interested in what they were reading. Naturally, it was a nonfiction book written by a former First Lady. She laughed, picturing Constance Granger reading romance. Then again, she'd be the type who would keep that under wraps... etiquette and all. God forbid she read about a woman receiving pleasure—or giving it, for that matter. Callie rolled her eyes and got out of her car, hoping that Hudson had run late too.

She hustled in and was instantly greeted by a nice young man at the host station. "Welcome to Vidalia's."

"Hi, I'm meeting Mr. Newman here. Do you know if he's arrived yet?"

"Yes, let me get someone to take you to him."

A large group of people noisily walked in behind her, taking the host's attention for a brief moment.

"It's okay. If you just point me in the right direction, I'm sure I'll find him."

"Thank you, sorry. We're a little short-staffed tonight. If you walk straight toward the back of the restaurant, Mr. Newman is seated at the last table before you get to the hallway leading to the private rooms."

Callie thanked him and was a bit surprised to see that a lot of the tables were full. Then again, she was there on a weeknight, too, so who was she to judge anyone? A few people looked at her with curiosity. Ever since her picture was shown on the morning show, every once in a while someone would quizzically look at her. At one point she started to feel paranoid. Then she remembered it also promoted her book.

Maybe it was a good thing that she was out in public with Hudson. And then again, maybe it wasn't. Callie stopped dead in her tracks when she

The BOOK BOYFRIEND

spotted him flanked by two very pretty women standing on either side of his chair. They were all smiles and giggles, and they batted their eyes as though something had flown into them.

When she brought her attention to Hudson, there was no mistaking his discomfort. He raked one through his hair. That move caused the woman on his left to sway. Seriously? It had been clear they knew who he was, and if that was in fact the case, then they proved her right—some women were not deterred if a man was taken. Instead, some felt it was more of a conquest or coup to be the one to steal him away.

Well, she thought, *no stealing would be happening tonight.* With her chin held high, Callie strolled toward the trio. Hudson must have sensed her, because she was still ten feet away from the table when he blessed her with his glorious smile.

"Hi, honey," she said, nudging the brunette to the side. Hudson stood, cupped her face with his hands, and kissed her for all to see. Callie had intended on greeting him with a kiss of her own, but in her mind, it would have been a quick, PDA-approved peck. Clearly, Hudson had a different idea, because the way his lips moved against hers hadn't been quick nor PDA approved.

Her eyes slid shut, and her blood hummed in her veins. It didn't take long to get lost in the sensation. Public be damned, she circled his neck with her arms, lifted onto her toes in a relevé, and melted into him.

Their own private dance could have gone on for who knows how long if someone hadn't cleared their throat. Callie almost didn't hear her through the thrumming of her pulse in her ears, but Hudson must have, because he left her panting a little when he broke their connection.

Rather than look at where the sound had come from, they kept their focus on one another. From a bystander's point of view, they looked to be a couple madly in love rather than one trying to figure it out. Still, Callie couldn't knock that kiss. She knew no matter what life brought her, no man would ever be able to top it.

"So, you are real?" came from the redhead standing to Hudson's left.

"I am. And you are?" Callie knew she hadn't told her what her name was, but that didn't mean she wasn't curious about hers.

"I'm Michaela, and this here is Chelsea." She lifted her hand in a cute wave.

"Well, I'm his girlfriend, and considering you knew that, I suggest you take your little party back to your own table."

Michaela tsk'd and rolled her eyes. Ignoring Callie, she placed her hand on Hudson's shoulder. "Call me if you get bored."

Callie's lip curled into a snarl. and she gritted her teeth to keep her jaw from dropping open. But she couldn't prevent her eyebrows drawing taut, highlighting her glare.

The pair walked away, and both Callie and Hudson sat down.

"Sorry, I told them to leave more than once."

"I'm sure you did. What did I say about a girlfriend not being a deterrent? I bet your mail clerk at the office has sent back more gifts than you know about."

"That may be so, but I'm with you."

"Yes, well, if there was any doubt, I'm thinking it may have been obliterated with that kiss." She could still feel the tingle in her lips, the taste of the whiskey he'd been sipping, and the force with which he wanted to prove a point.

"I didn't kiss you because of them."

"Why did you kiss me then?"

"I kissed you because of you."

Okay, Rock, she felt like saying. *Way to make a woman turn into a pile of goo.* Needing to change the subject, she opened the menu. "What's good here?"

"Everything." She nodded and placed her menu down. "How was the rest of your day?"

"Interesting. I talked to Gina and brought her up to speed. She's thrilled, by the way."

Hudson beamed. "I'm sure she is, and is it safe to assume a bit surprised?"

"Yes and no." Callie waved her hand back and forth, dismissing Gina's *meant-to-be* attitude. "And you'll be happy to know that, although tempting, I didn't slap Constance during the meeting."

His chuckle reverberated around the room. "I still say you should give her your book. Who knows, maybe it'll lighten her up."

"Or give her a heart attack. Maybe the day I quit my job and announce that I'm Lily, I'll send her a signed copy."

"Well, if she's married, her husband will thank you."

Callie's face heated with embarrassment. She had to be one of the most reserved romance authors. Yes, she talked a good game, but she wouldn't do half the things her characters did. Hudson, on the other hand, probably already had and was great at them.

"Did I say something wrong?"

"No, not at all. Anyway, it was probably good that your *fans* saw us out in public. Although, you must admit I was right."

"About?"

"Knowing you had a girlfriend didn't deter them. The kiss, on the other hand… Constance most certainly wouldn't have approved of such a display."

His deep laugh caught the attention of a few neighboring tables. "Then I must have done it right."

Yes, well, she most certainly couldn't dispute that.

CHAPTER 20

Soft music filtered into the hallway just outside of the ballroom. Dwight had gone all out preparing for his and Isabelle's anniversary party. Hudson knew his brother-in-law wanted to make sure that everything was perfect, just as it was the day they became husband and wife.

"Wow," Callie said, looking at the small room decorated in soft summer hues. "This is beautiful."

Hudson nodded and turned to look at her. "So are you. That dress... you're lucky this isn't their actual wedding, because a guest isn't supposed to take the attention away from the bride. I love my sister, but you truly are beautiful."

He wasn't exaggerating, nor was that a line. When he went to pick her up and she opened the door, he hadn't been able to form a coherent sentence. Instead, he kissed her. The silky deep-pink fabric hugged each of her curves. It didn't have any straps, and Hudson had never noticed how sexy a woman's collarbones could be. Then again, this was Callie. Every inch of her was sexy. Gown aside, the woman was a walking dream.

"Well, thank you very much." She rocked up onto the balls of her feet and gave him a chaste kiss. "You look very handsome yourself."

"The fact that my brother-in-law made this a black-tie affair is a bit much."

"What would you have done?"

A clear-as-day image popped into his head. Him standing next to Callie on the spot where they'd picnicked. The guests would be in casual clothing, and nature would provide all the other decor. Leaving out the sappy part of her being by his side, he shrugged. "Not sure, what about you?"

"Oh, well, I don't necessarily see myself in that scenario, but if I had to pick a place, I'd pick your property."

Hudson kissed the top of her head, ignoring that she'd dismissed the future, and agreed with her. "Yes, that would be an amazing location."

"Uncle Hudson! Miss Callie!" Hailey squealed, running in shiny black shoes, white socks trimmed in a ruffle of lace, and a purple-and-white frilly dress. Her ponytail whipped around as she weaved through guests to get to them.

"Hey, squirt," Hudson said as she catapulted into his arms.

"I'm so glad you're here. Mommy said that I can stay for one dance. Will you dance with me?"

Hudson's heart doubled in size. "Of course I will."

"Miss Callie, your dress is so pretty."

"Thank you. I like yours too. The bottom looks like a tutu."

She shimmied out of Hudson's arms and spun around. The skirt lifted and she giggled. "That's why I like it."

Over the speakers came an announcement that dinner was going to be served. "Come on, we're all sitting together. Wait until you see Grandma's dress. It looks like a garden."

When Callie didn't move, Hudson told Hailey to run ahead and they'd catch up. He turned toward his date, and her eyes were darting all around the room. "Hey, what's wrong?"

"I didn't even think about your parents being here. I mean, of course they would be, but maybe it's not the best idea for me to be. I can always slip out. No one would miss me."

Hudson hadn't put much thought into his parents being there either. Or having to introduce his girlfriend to them. There was zero doubt they hadn't heard about her. No way did his sister not call their mother immediately to tell them about Callie.

Taking her by the hand, he walked them back to where they had just come in from. He brought her hand to his lips and kissed the back of it. "Everything will be fine. At least we're not lying now. Do you trust me?" She nodded. "Okay then." He pecked her glossy pink lips and laced their fingers together. "And by the way, I would miss you. Let's go."

"Wait." She lifted her free hand and ran her thumb beneath his lower lip. "You had some of me on you." He groaned and she felt it everywhere. "Okay. We can go now."

"Sure, easy for you to say." She giggled once more, and they headed inside.

Guests were sitting at round tables, sipping wine and eating their salads. More than a few pairs of eyes watched them walk in. Hudson knew most of them, but some he assumed were friends of Dwight and Izzy's from work. Rather than stop at each table to say hi, he waved or nodded.

Giving Callie's hand a gentle squeeze, he walked with her up to the table where his family was sitting along with Dwight's parents and brother.

"Well, there they are," Izzy said, standing to hug him and then Callie. "You're late," she whispered in his ear.

"You look beautiful, sis. Happy anniversary, you two," he said to the happy couple. Then he tugged Callie a bit closer.

"Fine, you're forgiven." She smacked him on the arm. "Hi, Callie. I'm so glad you could come." Izzy hugged her, and he could see the tension in Callie's shoulders dissipate. The ladies released one another, and Izzy added, "I'll let Hudson do the rest of the intros."

With Callie in tow, he walked around the table, gave his mother a kiss, and shook his father's hand. "This is Callie. Callie, these are my parents, Hank and Kerrie Newman."

"Hi, it's a pleasure to meet you. I was so shocked when Hailey told us that Hudson had a girlfriend," his mother said to Callie. "Then to find out you're her ballet teacher, what a lovely coincidence."

"Yes," his father said, giving Callie a warm smile.

He then introduced Callie to Dwight's parents and quickly introduced Callie to Hailey's other uncle, Zack, who he thought let his eyes linger on her a bit too long. They were close in age, and he couldn't really fault Zack for appreciating her looks—except she was his.

After the salads were cleared, they waited for their main course.

"Mommy, can I go and get some juice?" Hailey asked, sliding off her chair.

"I'll go with her," Zack said, earning himself a huge smile from their niece. They watched her skip away.

"Callie is such a pretty name," his mother said, kicking off the conversation.

"Thank you. My grandmother picked it. Lilies are her favorite flower."

Hudson didn't get the connection, but his mother did when she nodded.

"Calla lilies are very pretty. She made a great choice."

"I agree," he said, giving her hand a squeeze.

"So tell me, how did you two meet?" his father asked.

"Well, it's a funny story, actually," Hudson said, while he felt Callie's knee pressing against his under the table.

His mother took a sip of her champagne. "Hudson, Isabelle said something about a romance novel, and you went on TV? You know you should tell me these things."

Callie's hand trembled as she reached for her glass of water. He knew she had to be nervous, but he wanted to assure her that everything would be fine. Deciding truth was the best way to go, that was what he opted for... well, a version of it, anyway.

"It's a bit of a funny story, actually. Coincidentally, a romance author used the name Hudson Newman in her book. The book took off and became quite popular. Some readers got a bit overzealous and looked up the character's name, only to find my picture thanks to an online business article that my office published. I started to receive gifts and emails." Hudson chuckled, trying to make light of it, despite how annoying it all was in the beginning.

"You were one of those fans?" His father's almost disapproving tone had Callie's perfect posture sagging.

Hudson had opened his mouth to defend her when she did it for herself.

The BOOK BOYFRIEND

"No, actually, I'm the author."

Despite the light chatter in the room, the sounds of flatware pinging against china, and the soft music, everything went silent at their table.

Hudson's head snapped to his right, and he watched Callie give him a tight grin.

"You're Lily May?" Isabelle asked. "How come you didn't say anything? I'm confused. I thought you met at a coffee shop?"

Callie shook her head. "No, we met after the fact. I didn't know your brother until after I released the book."

"Sorry, Iz," Hudson said to his sister.

Callie continued, "I'm sorry too. What he said about some readers was true. To be honest, I was flattered that they took such an interest in my book and character. Unfortunately, it brought a bit of chaos to your brother's life." Her eyes shifted to his father. "Something he doesn't do well with." He nodded. "Anyway, to make a long story a bit shorter, his assistant found out my real name and where I worked. Then one day he came to my office—"

"And I asked her out," Hudson interjected. "How could I not? And the rest you know." No way did he want his family—or anyone, for that matter—to know that their relationship had started out the way it had. Not only would his mother string him up by his fingernails for the ultimatum he'd issued, but it wouldn't be fair to Callie either. And what he said wasn't a lie. He did ask her out… just not maybe as conventionally as others would have.

"What a wonderful story," his mother said.

"I agree. Don't worry about your fib. This is so romantic," Izzy added.

"Yes, well, if you could all keep it to yourself, Callie's pen name is important to her."

They all agreed, and Callie leaned across him to tap Izzy's arm. "Again, I'm sorry I didn't tell you. I was afraid of the other moms knowing. Hudson kept the secret for me. Please don't be upset with him"

She placed her hand on Callie's, completely unfazed that her bracelet was dangling on his bread plate. "Don't you worry about the moms. I know a few of them who have read the book. Just this morning Bridget's mom mentioned that her book club was reading it. Believe me, if they knew you were the author, the only thing you would need to worry about would be how many signed copies to bring to class. And trust me, my brother is no angel. He knows it would take a lot more than this for me to be upset with him. I'm just happy you two found one another."

A genuine smile blossomed on Callie's face. "Thank you."

"Great." Hudson picked up his glass. "Now that we have the details of my relationship cleared up, how about we toast the happy couple?"

Zack and Hailey had returned, and they all followed Hudson's lead, lifted their glasses, and congratulated Dwight and Izzy.

CHAPTER 21

The plates were cleared, Dwight made a tear-jerking speech about his wonderful wife, and Callie found herself amid pure romance and loving every minute of it.

The DJ started to play music, and Hailey didn't hesitate to grab her uncle Hudson's hand and tug him up. He gave Callie a smile that made her insides flutter, and she watched as he escorted his cute niece onto the dance floor, where they swayed next to the happy couple. Hailey looked so tiny next to him, but he held her hands in the formal position, and befitting the little ballerina she was, regardless of her head being craned back to look at her uncle with admiration, her posture was immaculate.

"Care to dance?" Zack asked, catching her off guard. She almost forgot that he was sitting there.

Considering they were the only ones at the table, she felt weird saying no. Plus, he was Dwight's brother.

"Sure." She removed the napkin from her lap, placed it on the table, and got up. As soon as his hand went to her back, Hudson looked over with narrowed eyes. Callie almost laughed, but instead she puckered her lips and kissed the air in his direction. That seemed to appease him for a bit, but the flash of jealousy warmed her insides.

Zack was a handsome man, dark hair a bit longer and shaggier than Hudson's, warm brown eyes, and a carefree demeanor that made you want to be friends with him. He stood a few inches taller than her but maybe one or two shorter than Hudson, though he had a similar build.

He took her right hand in his and placed his other on her hip as they began to move to the music. "So, a writer? That sounds exciting."

His statement didn't register with the look of boredom on his face. "Does it really?"

He chuckled. "No, it sounds awful."

Callie tossed her head back and they both laughed. "What do you do?"

"I'm a bio-engineer."

"Impressive."

"Do you know what that is?"

She shook her head. "No, not a clue."

Once again, they found each other funny, and their laughs mingled with the music. When the song changed, he spun her away from him and right into a familiar broad chest. Arms circled her waist, and hers went around his neck. Over her head, Hudson said, "I'm cutting in."

Zack walked by them and nodded. "Thanks for the dance, Callie."

She was about to say, *My pleasure,* but Hudson moved them away.

"Possessive much?"

"I have no idea what you're talking about." He leaned down and kissed her lips first, then her neck, then the soft spot behind her ear, creating a shiver that coursed through her before he whispered, "I was getting lonely."

"Well, we can't have that now, can we?" she managed to say, trying not to sound too affected by his soft kisses.

"Nope."

The music switched to something fast, and rather than continue dancing, Hudson took her hand and walked her off the parquet-square floor.

As the night wore on, they spoke to a few more family members, had dessert, and then said their goodbyes. Hudson's parents, who left early with Hailey, were nothing like she had pictured. For some reason, she imagined his father rigid and stiff, but he was the opposite. Callie could see some of Hudson in him, but aside from his stature, he actually favored his mother more. They both had the prettiest blue eyes, and lucky for her, she had the same natural highlights in her hair — at least she believed them to be natural.

She felt a bit envious when she saw how tight-knit their family was. Yes, she knew that Hudson and his sister were close, but to see him with his parents was something completely different. Callie felt bad feeling that way, since she did have Tommy and Nana, but seeing a three-generation bond had Callie wishing things could have been different for her.

Thankfully, they'd driven her car to the party, since there was no way she'd be able to get in or out of his truck without needing to hike her dress up to her waist. Seeing him in her little sedan was comical. Even before he got in, he moved the seat all the way back. Now all Callie wanted to do was take off her shoes and change into her favorite pajama-short set.

He took her hand in his and placed them on her knee, sending a tingle up her leg. "Did you have fun tonight?"

"Yes, I did. Thank you. Your parents are very nice. So is the rest of your family."

"Thank you. Everyone adored you. I still can't believe you announced you were Lily May."

Callie couldn't believe it either. "I couldn't lie or have you lie. It just didn't feel right."

"Well, thank you. I know that couldn't have been easy."

She shrugged. "Honestly, it was easier than I thought it would be. I don't know why it freaks me out so much. It's not that I'm embarrassed by it. Especially after what Isabelle said about the other moms. I feel so much better now."

The BOOK BOYFRIEND

Hudson lifted her hand and kissed it. Something she could definitely get used to. "I'm glad."

The stars were out in full force. Summer was her favorite season, and clear nights where the moon lit the sky were special. Even the air was still. So many people complained about humidity, but at least it kept the nights warm.

They made a turn onto Callie's street, and Hudson's truck came into view. "Would you like to come in for a bit?"

He pulled her car behind his truck and killed the engine. "If you're too tired, I don't need to."

"I'm fine, really. I promise not to fall asleep on you."

His eyes met hers and he said, "That's a promise I don't hope you keep."

Flutters came to life inside her. For someone who didn't watch romance movies and clearly didn't read romance books, he had it down in spades. Then again, remembering how his parents would steal a kiss or share a knowing glance with one another, it started to make sense.

Same with Isabelle and Dwight—they acted as though they had just gotten married rather than celebrating ten years together. In truth, Callie's mind had whirled all night with different scenarios and future book plots. Maybe she was turning into a writer after all.

Crediting all the love she felt at the party and the make-out session on her couch before Hudson went home as the catalysts, Callie couldn't sleep for more than a few hours. Rather than fight it and potentially forget the ideas that swirled in her head, Callie got up, made herself a cup of coffee, and sat at her desk.

After opening her document, she closed her eyes, forcing herself to become one with the characters, and began to type. One hour, then three passed. Callie read the last passage over before starting the next chapter.

Hudson strolled toward the young woman standing at the end of the dock. Her hair lifted with the ocean breeze while seagulls soared up ahead. With each step he took toward her, his heart beat faster.

Nerves, maybe. Excitement, probably. Need, definitely.

She wasn't a stranger or an ex-lover. No, the woman who sparked his interest was his best friend, Reese. The one he felt the most comfortable with. The one who had no idea he'd caught feelings for. And despite being able to discuss just about anything with her, telling her his feelings had changed had to be the most terrifying thing ever.

The wood plank creaked beneath his feet. Hope spun, her eyes wide, but the gorgeous smile she graced him with settled his nerves.

"Hi, what are you doing here?"

"Came to see you," he said.

Reese nodded but looked a bit confused. "Everything okay?"

The BOOK BOYFRIEND

Hudson took another step toward her. "I was wondering if you'd like to go out with me?"

"Sure, where?" she was quick to reply.

He wanted to smack himself in the head. Naturally, she'd agree. They'd been hanging out together for years. There was no way on God's green earth that she'd assume he meant as a date and not two friends hanging out together.

"I thought I'd take you to dinner. Maybe a movie... as a date."

Reese's eyes flew open. "You want to take me out on a date?"

Hudson nodded. "Yes, what do you think?"

A knock on her door startled her. She picked up her phone, noticed that it was after 9:00 a.m., and couldn't believe she hadn't noticed the bright sun streaming through her window.

Shoot, I'm supposed to be at Nana's in an hour.

Callie got up and went to see who was at the door. Pulling it open, she was surprised to see Hudson standing outside, the smell of blueberries wafting in the morning breeze.

"Good morning." He kissed her on the cheek and held up a coffee holder with two cups in it and a white pastry bag. "Brought you breakfast. I tried calling, but you didn't answer. Did I wake you?"

"What? Oh, no. Sorry, I was writing. Please come in."

"Well, then I won't overstay my visit. I wouldn't want to interrupt your creativity."

Callie stood and stared at him. The more she knew him, the more he did seem like the epitome of a book boyfriend. Throwing his order to the wayside, she started to realize that when it came to people he cared about, that order wasn't as important. And right now, he cared about her.

Ignoring that his hands were full, she roped her arms around his neck, rolled up on her toes, and kissed him.

"Thank you for bringing me breakfast. I need to jump in the shower, though, because I'm going to visit Nana."

His face softened. "Would you like some company?" When she didn't reply right away, he added, "I don't need to come in, but I'd be happy to drive you there."

"Sure, okay. Thank you. That'd be great. I'm just going to go get ready. Make yourself at home."

Before she headed into her bathroom, she saved her manuscript and closed her laptop. When she glanced over her shoulder, Hudson was looking at her with an arched brow.

"Habit," she gave as an explanation. "You'll be happy to know that fictional Hudson has found his love interest. He's falling for his friend."

"Ahh, the safe way to go."

"What do you mean?"

He shook his head. "Nothing, it's just there's less chance of getting hurt. Sure, if the friend doesn't want that type of relationship, then albeit a bit awkward, eventually, they'll have their friendship to fall back on. Less chance of being alone. Whereas if they fall for someone new, that may not be the case."

"Hmm. I guess I never thought of it that way. So what you're saying is, I shouldn't fall for you?"

His smile immediately fell away.

"Okay, well, have it your way. I'll be in the shower."

He gave her that playful look, and she couldn't stop the giggles when she darted away, and he followed.

CHAPTER 22

Hudson held Callie's hand as they drove to see her grandmother. After chasing her into her bedroom, and forcing her to retract her statement by tickling her until she cried, it took every ounce of willpower to stop himself from following her into the shower.

He knew how important seeing her grandmother was to her. The bond they shared was evident in the stories Callie had told him. Hudson's heartstrings tugged each time she spoke of her grandmother. Still, he could tell that she needed it. Almost as though it was therapeutic.

"Tell me more about her."

"My grandmother was one of a kind. Because she was a teacher, she loved history and books. Or maybe she always did, and that's why she went

The BOOK BOYFRIEND

into that profession... I'm not sure. Until she needed more care, I'd never been without her or vice versa. I honestly don't have many memories without her in them. She made the best oatmeal raisin cookies, loved cooking vegetables from her garden, and she always had fresh flowers on the dining room table."

"She never wanted to remarry?"

"No. When I was about sixteen, we were talking about dating. Tommy had his baseball groupies that followed him around, and I was just getting my feet wet — so to speak. I was a bit dorky at times."

Hudson couldn't believe that, but he remained silent and let her continue.

"I asked her about dating. She's such a wonderful woman with so much love to give. I didn't want her to be alone."

"What did she say?"

"She said she wasn't alone, because my grandfather was in her heart." Callie sniffled, and Hudson was almost sorry he'd asked. "I can't imagine loving someone like that. To give your heart and soul for someone to hold, and then to lose them. Each time she spoke of him, I could feel her pain through her smiles."

They stopped at a light, and he looked over at Callie, who appeared a bit flushed. "I'm glad she loved that hard, or you wouldn't be here."

She flashed him a tight grin that didn't meet her eyes. "She used to say the same. Don't get me wrong. I'm glad, too, obviously, but that still doesn't take away her pain. I think that although she doesn't always remember things, she'll always remember him."

If the red light hadn't changed, he would have pulled her into his arms. The urge to wrap her up and help her keep it together was fierce. Instead, he had to move along with the traffic. Callie's focus returned to the passing trees lining the two-lane road. A large driveway with BIRCHWOOD ASSISTED LIVING CENTER engraved on a white sign came into view.

"We're here," she said, pointing to the parking lot on the right.

He turned in and parked in a visitor's spot. Callie took a deep breath while he got out to open her door, and then he took her hand as she climbed out.

"I'll be here waiting. Take as much time as you need." She nodded and gave him a tight grin right before she glanced up at the sun. The air was a bit humid, but Callie shivered.

"Are you okay?" he asked.

"Yes, I just never know what I'm going to walk into. She might remember me; she might not. Or she may think I'm someone completely different. Then there are times when she can remember things that I can't, and she'll seem completely fine."

Hudson pulled Callie into his arms and held her. She relaxed into his embrace, and for the first time in a very long time, he didn't know what to say. This was uncharted territory for him. What he did know was he wanted to protect her from whatever made her sad. Except in this case, there was no way he could.

Callie arched her back to look up at him. Their eyes held, and Hudson kissed her forehead. "I wish I had something eloquent to say."

"You don't need to say anything, but thank you. Would you like to come in with me? Maybe she'll be having a good day. The nurse at the desk will know if that's the case or not."

"I'd be happy to go with you." Hudson closed her door, and after the double beep sounded, he took her hand in his and kissed it.

Walking into the facility, he found it different from what he had expected. Somewhere in his head, he had pictured it more hospital-like, but it was homey.

"Hi there, Miss Callie."

"Hi, Monica. This is my friend Hudson. How's my grandmother today?"

"She had a bit of an episode late last night."

Callie's head dipped a bit.

"But you know how tenacious Priscilla is," Monica continued. "This morning, she seemed a bit tired, but better. I'm sure seeing you will brighten her day… and your handsome friend."

When Callie laughed, Hudson felt the tension that had coiled up in him release. Callie signed them in, they each got a badge with a big *V* on it, and they started down the hall and up the stairs until they got to her room.

A white-haired woman sitting in a wheelchair, watching television, turned to look at them.

"Hi, Nana." Callie released his hand, walked farther into the room, kissed her grandmother's cheek, and sat in the chair next to her.

"My sweet girl." Her grandmother looked at Hudson, who smiled. "Did you bring me a present?"

Callie giggled and Hudson laughed. "It's nice to meet you, ma'am. I'm Hudson Newman, Callie's friend."

"Well, aren't you a looker. And honey, if he's your *friend*, then I didn't teach you well."

"No, Nana, you taught me well."

She patted Callie's hand. "That's my girl."

Hudson put a fist over his mouth to stifle a chuckle, and Callie rolled her eyes, smiling the entire time.

Wanting to give them some time alone, he told her grandmother that it was nice meeting her, and when he met Callie's eyes, he pointed to the hallway. She gave him a small nod and mouthed, "Thank you."

As soon as he was out the door, he heard Nana say, "Nice butt too."

That time his chuckle wasn't stifled. He turned in his badge and told Monica that Callie was having a nice visit.

"You're that guy," a girl in pink scrubs said. Monica looked blankly at her. "You don't see the morning show because you work, but he's the book boyfriend guy."

"I'm sorry. Please excuse Becky. She just started here."

"It's fine," Hudson said. "I get it all the time."

Monica gave him a kind smile, and he had a feeling she knew exactly what Becky was talking about but was professional enough not to say anything. Without further explanation or hanging around to chat, he said goodbye and headed out to his truck to wait for Callie.

Their conversation rattled around in his head. Hudson would never forget the sallow look on her face or the way her eyes glistened when she spoke about the love her grandparents shared. He thought of Dwight and Izzy and how much they loved one another. Not to mention his parents. Still, he had no profound words to say other than he was glad she was born.

When Callie walked out fifteen minutes later, practically skipping toward him, he let out a breath, and thanks to the evident joy on her face, he couldn't have been happier.

Between the sun hitting her golden hair and her bright smile, she looked more beautiful than she ever had. He was so entranced he forgot to open her door for her. Once inside the cab of his truck, she leaned across the seat and kissed him.

"Thank you so much. Nana likes you."

"Yes, and my butt."

Callie shook her head and laughed. "She was so good today. I wish I could explain how this makes me feel. My heart is just so full. Thank you, Hudson."

"No need to thank me. Where to?"

"Do you mind if you take me home? I feel energized, and Hudson won't shut up."

He furrowed his brows.

"Not you, *fictional* Hudson. He's talking. I know that sounds a bit nuts, but I need to write."

"Who am I to stand in the way of creativity?"

She bounced in her seat and looked straight out the front window before turning to look at him. "You're not such a bad guy, Hudson Newman."

"You're not so bad yourself."

CHAPTER 23

*C*allie spent the majority of her week working and writing. It had been a few days since she'd seen Hudson, and she started to miss him. They'd talk on the phone at night, but they were both so tired at the end of their days that getting together hadn't been an option.

After their visit with her nana, Callie had fallen a little more for Hudson. When she explained about what it was like growing up, he didn't place judgment, nor did he lie and say he understood, because he didn't—he couldn't. The only thing he would be able to relate to was being brought up in a loving home, because as nontraditional as Callie's was, it had love in spades.

Nana had told her that she had a video chat with Tommy, which Monica confirmed, and Callie couldn't have been more pleased. It was important for their grandmother to see both of them, and thanks to technology, she did.

Thinking of her brother, she decided to take a break. Callie removed her glasses, placed them next to her keyboard, grabbed her phone, and told Gwen she was stepping outside. As soon as she walked out to the patio overlooking the ninth green, the bright sun attacked her pupils, and she cursed herself for not remembering her sunglasses.

Callie turned her back to the yellow orb heating the air, dialed her brother's number, and waited.

"Hey, Cal," he said after the second ring.

"Hi, Tommy. Am I catching you at a bad time?"

"No. I always have time for my little sister. What's up?"

Callie couldn't help the happiness she felt when she spoke to her brother. He was the one person who could relate to everything she'd been through, because he had been there with her. Granted, he had a better social life thanks to sports, he had gone on to college, and he was married, but who was keeping track? Plus, Callie was thrilled for her brother.

"Just calling to say hi. Nana said you spoke to her."

"I did. She's still the same fiery woman." He chuckled. "We had a good conversation. She even asked me when Gretchen and I were going to have a family. And before you ask, too, we're thinking about trying next year."

"That's wonderful. I'd love to be an aunt." Her mind immediately went to Hudson and how cute he was with Hailey. "I can't wait," she added.

"Well, you'll be the first to know when it happens. Then Nana asked me how many strikeouts I threw in today's game."

Callie's lips turned down. She knew what those conversations were like. It was as though someone had flipped a switch and a time warp happened. In some cases, her brightness dimmed, and those were the worst times. "What did you tell her?"

"That I pitched a no-hitter. I figure, why not give her the best news, even though—"

"I know. Even though it wasn't the truth. I saw her on Sunday." Callie hesitated and then said, "I brought Hudson with me. He wasn't going to come in at first, but I wanted him to meet her."

"Really? I'm glad. How did she react?"

Callie giggled. "She said he had a nice butt."

"I did not need to know that," he said with a groan. "I'm happy for you, Cal. Hey, I gotta run. Let's talk soon. I miss you. Maybe a video chat so I can meet that guy of yours and threaten him within an inch of his life if he does anything to my sister."

She thought about Tommy going head-to-head with Hudson. The truth was, they'd get along great. Most likely form a bromance and cut her out of the picture. "Okay, sounds good. Love you, and tell Gretchen I said hi."

"Will do. Love you too."

They ended the call, and before Callie walked

inside, she heard a familiar chuckle. Today happened to be guest day, so Callie had set up a few membership perks to try to either poach members from other clubs or entice guests to become members. Shadow Oaks was a little under full capacity, and until they got there, Callie needed to be on her toes.

A foursome stood on the perfectly manicured green, sizing up the slopes, bends in the grass, and whatever else they did to ensure their ball would drop into the four-and-a-quarter-inch-diameter cup.

Callie lifted her hand to shield her eyes from the sun's glare. One man looked a bit older and used his club to help him up from a crouching position; the others seemed younger. The man next to him lined up his shot, only to have his ball veer to the right and about a foot past the hole. Two of them had their backs to Callie. Both wore baseball caps, and by their physique and stance, she assumed they were younger.

Once they all hit their shots in, they meandered over to their carts to get ready for the next part of the course. She took a step onto the grass next to the path and smiled at the two gentlemen she knew to be Mr. Lopez and his guest, Mr. McAfee. Then the other cart pulled up behind them, and Callie's breath hitched.

The driver was Jack, Hudson's colleague and friend, and sitting next to him was Hudson. Jack elbowed him, and when her eyes met his, Hudson grinned, slid out of the cart, and shocked her. Since she was at work, Callie never thought he'd rope his arms around her waist and kiss her as though his next breath depended on it.

Per usual when she was around him, she allowed herself to get swept away. Her body molded to his, their lips moved in complete synchronization, and Callie wished she were anywhere but outside her office.

Her office.

She placed her hand over the logo of a horse on his chest and gently pushed him back. Their connection broke, and Hudson gave her the make-your-knees-weak smile that, indeed, did what it set out to do.

"Hi, Callie," Jack said before Hudson even uttered a word. "I'll be back. Need the men's room." He disappeared into the pro shop.

Hudson cupped her cheek with his right hand and put his left one on her hip. "Yes, hi, Callie."

"Funny. What are you doing here?"

He laughed. "Golfing."

She shook her head and wanted to smack him. "No, I mean, I know that. I'm just surprised to see you."

"We were at work, and Jack's dad called him and said he was playing a round of golf today and two guys had bailed. He asked if I wanted to play. My schedule was clear, so here I am. I wanted to surprise you when we were done. But lucky for me, here you are."

"Wait, Jack's dad?"

"That would be me," Mr. McAfee said, extending his hand to Callie. "You can call me John. I understand you're the membership coordinator here."

"Callie Richardson," she replied, taking his hand and giving it a quick pump. "It's nice to meet you, and yes, I am."

Dread filled Callie. The last thing she should be doing is making out with a guest at the club. Thankfully, Mr. McAfee didn't see it or didn't care that he had. That still didn't make Callie not want to smack Hudson. Speaking of, what happened to Mr. *I Need Order in My Life?*

"Hi, Callie." Mr. Lopez walked up to the group and greeted her.

"Good afternoon, Mr. Lopez. It's nice to see you. I hope you're all enjoying the day."

"We are, thank you. You know what they say: a bad day on the golf course is better than a great one at the office." The guys chuckled and Callie smiled, having heard that saying quite a few times. "If it wouldn't be too much trouble, could you please put together a packet for Mr. McAfee?"

She nodded. "Yes, it would be my pleasure." Little did they know, she had already planned on giving him one at the end of the round. Callie had checked the reservation list and knew they'd be in the members' room after they finished.

"Fantastic, thank you, and nice seeing you again."

Jack walked out with a bounce in his step. "What'd I miss?"

Hudson winked at her. "I'll see you after we're done."

"Okay, and no more kissing me at work, Mr. Newman."

"Sorry, you tend to be irresistible."

Callie felt her face flush as the guys got into their cart and drove off to the tenth tee. When they were out of sight, she turned to head back into her office and found Constance glaring at her with pursed lips.

"Miss Richardson, did I just see you *kissing* that man?"

Great. "I'm on my break," she said, as though that would appease her.

It didn't.

"Break or not, you are on Shadow Oaks' time. There will be none of that while on the clock."

Callie wanted to tell her to go shove a putter where the sun didn't shine, but she refrained. "Yes, ma'am."

Her agreement didn't appease the stodgy woman. "Members are the heart of Shadow Oaks. They keep this club going. It's the same place that hired a girl without a degree or experience. I don't think I need to tell you that."

Nothing like tossing a bucket of ice water on what would have been a wonderful memory. "No, ma'am."

"Very well. See it doesn't happen again."

She spun on her prissy Mary Jane heel, adjusted her designer bag under her arm, and strode away. Callie would have tried to defend herself a bit more, but Constance wasn't wrong. Employees weren't allowed to have relations with members. Technically, Hudson wasn't a member, but Constance would look at him as a potential one.

"Whatever," she grumbled.

Callie walked into the club, and the AC felt a bit cooler this time. When Gwen saw her, she said, "I saw. I'd tell you to ignore her, but she's vile. I swear if she gets any more face filler, no one will be able to tell if she's smiling or ready to burst into tears."

"Yes, well, it's over with."

She went back into her office and decided to send Hudson a text.

> *You got me into trouble.*
>
> *The old lady with the scowl?*
>
> *Yes. That was Constance.*
>
> *Oh! Sorry. You're just too irresistible and so far the best part of my day.*

Flutters came to life inside her. She placed two fingers on her lips, remembering how good his kiss felt.

> *Not golfing well?*
>
> *Actually, I'm under par. Round of my life so far.*

Hudson always seemed to know how to make her feel better.

The BOOK BOYFRIEND

Fine. You're forgiven. But please don't do that again.

No promises.

Rather than volley it back to him, she tossed her phone on her desk and tried to get back to work. Except the only thing she could think about was the man who once again turned her day upside down. Not that any warm-blooded woman would blame her. Seeing Hudson in a suit or jeans was hot, but just like at their picnic, seeing him in twill shorts kick-started her heart. Long, toned legs with a smattering of hair, and a golf shirt that molded across his pecs, made her mouth water. It was no surprise that when those strong arms of his wrapped around her waist, she lost her mind.

Consequences be damned—if he wanted to kiss her again, no one, not even threats from the uppity Constance Granger, would stop her.

CHAPTER 24

Hudson felt bad for putting Callie in a difficult position. In his defense, he hadn't seen Constance until after they'd kissed; nor did he know who she was. Still, he should have warned her rather than let her turn and face what he guessed was a one-woman firing squad.

He tended to lose his head a bit when Callie was around. There she stood, looking all professional in a formfitting black dress, heels that made her toned calves look sleeker than they already were, and those glasses that turned him on. When she smiled, he couldn't help himself. Kissing her had been the only option. Fine, maybe not the only one, but one that he couldn't resist.

If it weren't for them being at her place of employment, he would have kept their connection going. The woman tasted like candy and felt like heaven. That was the only explanation for his reaction to her.

For the next nine holes he had been energized. He shot the round of his life, and even Jack gave Callie credit. Well, he gave the kiss credit. Although he didn't see it, he saw the remnants of her pink-tinted lip gloss on Hudson's mouth. Jack told him he should kiss someone every time they played a round of golf. Although Hudson chuckled along with the other guys, it dawned on him that the only woman he wanted to kiss was Callie.

That thought should have sent his mind spiraling, but instead it only made him anxious to see her again.

The foursome headed inside the clubhouse to grab a drink. He spotted Callie speaking to one of the bartenders. She laughed, and he immediately felt relieved, in hopes her day had turned around.

"You're whipped," Jack said, standing next to him. "Don't get me wrong. She's gorgeous, and I'm sure she's nice, but for as long as I've known you, and that's a long time, you've never been so lax."

Hudson's head snapped to his right, and Jack's hands immediately went up in defense mode.

"I'm not knocking it," Jack said. "It's just an observation. What happened to you needing order?"

Hudson thought about that, but he still had order. Yes, since starting his relationship with Callie, some things had shifted, but he still followed a plan of sorts. It was just being with her made him want things he hadn't thought of before.

In his past, women came and went. As he had told her, none intrigued him. Not until her. And now he began to think beyond that. He began to want what his parents and sister had. A notion that wasn't as foreign a feeling as he thought it would be. Izzy had told him after she met Dwight that once you found the one, you'd know it. All he remembered was wanting to warn the man his sister had fallen in love with not to hurt her. Much as Gina had warned him.

If Jack wanted to say he was whipped, then fine, he wasn't going to dispute it. "We're taking it one day at a time. Getting to know one another." The truth was, their relationship had moved quickly. She'd met his family, he'd met her grandmother, and things had just clicked. Maybe that was what Izzy had meant. He wasn't in love with Callie... yet, but for the first time, he didn't dismiss the idea of it.

"Well, I'm happy for you." Jack clapped him on the back. "I'm going to go and grab a drink. Can I get you anything?"

"No, thanks. I have a call to make."

He had an idea and wanted to get the ball rolling. As soon as he stepped outside, he bumped into someone looking down at her phone. Dark hair hung like a curtain, hiding her face from him. After she let out an "Oomph," Hudson put his hand on her arm. "Are you okay?"

She tossed her head back. Gina. "Oh, hi. Sorry, I shouldn't text and walk." Then her brows pulled together. "Wait, why are you here?"

He wanted to laugh, because why would he be there dressed in shorts and a golf shirt if not to play golf? Her reaction was the same as Callie's. She must have realized the answer on her own when she waved her hand back and forth. "Never mind. Have you seen Cal? Gwen said she was meeting the bartender, Trace."

"Yes, she's inside."

"Great. Sorry I crashed into you."

She disappeared through the doors, and rather than follow her to see what was going on, he headed toward the parking lot to make his call.

Ever since their picnic Hudson had wanted more time with her... and for them. He knew that she'd sneaked away from work once — doing it again may be a stretch. Especially since crotchety Constance saw their kiss. When she said she got into trouble, he wanted to run to her defense, but it was her place of work, so he thought it was better to stay out of it.

After their movie night at her apartment, he decided to see what other Rock and Doris movies he needed to familiarize himself with. That was when he stumbled upon an outdoor film festival, just outside of Virginia, featuring classic movies. When he scanned the list, he noticed the title of the movie they'd already watched and then a couple of others that starred her favorite couple. He also knew exactly where to stay, if she agreed to go with him.

He scrolled through his contacts until he got to the one he wanted. Izzy's house hadn't been the only home he'd designed. A friend of Dwight's had a plot of land just as you crossed into West Virginia. It was beautiful there. Mountain views for days, hiking trails, and the perfect setting to escape.

After Hudson tapped the name on his phone, Dave answered on the second ring: "Hudson Newman."

He chuckled. "Hi, Dave. How are you?"

"Good, good. Getting ready to retire and move into my mountain house permanently."

"That's great. I'm happy for you. I have a question: Is the house available next week? I need it for two or three nights."

"Just let me know the dates you'll be there, and it's yours. Another small group is coming the following week."

Hudson was happy to hear the property was getting a lot of use. "Busy place. That's great. I just need to check on a few things and get back to you."

"It is busy because it's beautiful. You know, I have had people ask me who designed it. Per your request, I haven't given them your name. Son, I know you're a successful businessman, but your talent isn't going unnoticed."

Each time Hudson spoke to Dave he'd tell him the same thing. Except Hudson knew that architecture was a hobby. He'd design his own home and then that would be it.

"Thank you."

"You're welcome. Let me know what you decide."

"Thanks, will do."

They disconnected the call, and now all Hudson needed to do was to convince Callie to go with him.

Hudson headed back into the clubhouse to thank Mr. Lopez and say goodbye to Jack and his dad, who were sitting at the bar, having a drink. But there was no sign of Callie.

His eyes scanned the room, searching for the beautiful blonde.

"She left with her friend a few minutes ago," Jack said, knowing exactly whom he was looking for.

"Thanks."

Rather than go to her office and risk someone spotting him, he sent her a text.

> *I have a surprise for you.*

It took her a moment to text back, but when those dots started to bubble up on his screen, it pleased him.

> *I think I've had enough surprises for one day.*

Was it what Gina wanted to talk to her about? The smile that had been on his face faltered.

> *Are you okay? Is it Constance? I saw Gina. Did she have bad news?*

Then it dawned on him. He'd surprised her.

> *Is it me?*

Dots danced. Stopped. Started again.

No it's not you. You're the best part of my day. I have to stay late and afterward, I just want to go home though. Would you mind coming over later? Let's say 8? Will that ruin your surprise?

Not at all. I'll see you then.

Thanks, Hudson. By the way, that was the best kiss ever.

He couldn't help puffing his chest out a bit.

You ain't seen nothing yet.

CHAPTER 25

*C*allie could still feel her lips tingling from Hudson's kiss. So often she had replayed their kisses in her head, but although memories were wonderful, there was nothing like the real thing. He just did it for her. Now he wanted to surprise her. *Romantic.* That would be the only word to describe him… well, not the only one.

The way he'd approached her today made it impossible to contain her smile. Even though she was at work, when their lips met, it was as if she'd fallen under a spell that immobilized her. She couldn't help but close her eyes and remember how Hudson's soft lips felt against hers. Cupping her cheeks, taking control with his palms, which he loved to do so often, sent a wave of trepidation down to her toes.

Never in her life had she felt so much for someone in such a short amount of time. That thought sounded cliché even to her own ears. Definitely not love at first sight for either of them. More like annoyance. The thing was, it was more than the kisses; it was their conversations, time with family, in an odd way, and understanding one another. Hudson truly wanted to get to know her and vice versa. Aside from talks with Tommy and Gina, she never spoke of her parents or lack thereof, and no way would she have ever thought to take someone to visit her grandmother. The man was just different. That was the only explanation for it.

She sat at her desk, determined to secure another member and prove to Constance that she was good at her job. That notion alone irritated her. Callie knew she was great at her job, and feeling as though she had to prove it bothered her more than the snarky woman herself.

Not taking her eyes off her screen, she heard a knock on the door. She turned, and Gwen stood there with a large vase filled with an array of flowers, from roses to tulips to hydrangeas, peonies, and calla lilies. Her heart beat faster. Callie had never seen anything more beautiful. It looked as though a summer garden had been artfully arranged, probably because it had been.

"These just arrived for you." For a moment Callie had thought the flowers might be Gwen's and she was taking them home, since it was past five o'clock. Her assistant lowered her nose to them and inhaled. "They smell so good." She set them on her desk. "There's a card, but I'm sure you know who they're from." Callie still hadn't said anything. "Well, I'm going to head out unless you need me."

Finally out of her floral-induced stupor, she shook her head. "No, thank you. I'm all set. See you tomorrow."

Gwen left, and Callie took the small envelope from the plastic holder. She pulled out the card and read the handwritten note.

Callie,

I'm not going to apologize for kissing you. I just hope everything is okay at work. Also, you never told me what your favorite flower was, so I had to take the easy way out.

See you soon.

Yours,

Hudson

Callie stared at the arrangement. There had to be three dozen blooms in the large crystal vase. The colors alone were beautiful: white, blue, pink, yellow, and then a red rose tucked in here and there. She couldn't get over their beauty. Callie grabbed her phone and snapped a couple of pictures at different angles, knowing nothing would do them justice.

She sent a quick text to Hudson.

*Thank you so much for the flowers.
They're beautiful.*

Before she set her phone down, it vibrated in her hand.

Just like you.

Sweet talker.

Truth teller.

Callie giggled and set the phone down. The sooner she was finished, the sooner she could leave. All she needed to do was ignore the fact that a gorgeous man would be waiting for her.

She had one thing left to tell him.

Peonies are my favorite.

Are they in there?

She let out a laugh. `Yes`.

Phew. Okay. Go back to work. Do you want me to grab dinner?

No. I have something here. Thank you though.

For the next two and a half hours, Callie composed and sent follow-up emails to potential members she had already met with or who had inquired about joining Shadow Oaks. Once the last swish sounded from her laptop speaker, she took off her glasses, set them on her desk, and rubbed her tired eyes.

The flowers sat prominently on the corner of her desk. She wished she could take them home with her, but short of trying to buckle them into the front

The BOOK BOYFRIEND

seat, that wouldn't happen. So she'd leave them in her office to enjoy tomorrow. At least she'd have them to look forward to.

All evening she half expected Constance to pop her head into her office, but thankfully that didn't happen. Not wanting to stay there a second longer, Callie rolled her chair back, got up, and arched her back to work out the kinks from sitting and not moving for the past couple of hours.

She was about to close her laptop when a notification chimed. When she saw it was from Mr. McAfee, she was a bit surprised. Her eyes scanned the email, and she couldn't prevent the smile that grew across her face. Shadow Oaks had a new member. All he needed to do was fill out the application, have it approved by the board, which wouldn't be a problem thanks to Mr. Lopez, and then pay the initiation fee.

Take that, Constance.

With a bit more pep to her step, she grabbed her purse—as well as a peony out of the vase—turned off her lights, and went to go meet her boyfriend.

Hudson's truck couldn't be missed when Callie turned into her complex. Nor could the man leaning against it. His casual stance, arms crossed over his chest, legs leisurely crossed at the ankle, and his scruff-covered face looked even more handsome as dusk started to settle in.

She pulled in next to him, and before she could do it herself, Hudson opened her door and offered his hand to her.

"Hi," she said before reaching into her car to get her purse and flower.

"I was getting worried."

"Sorry, I stayed later than I thought." She twirled the flower's stem between her thumb and forefinger before bringing it to her nose and inhaling. "This is a peony, and you're the greatest boyfriend ever."

Callie leaned forward, roped her arms around him, and kissed him. She realized she had never initiated a kiss before. His hands went to her hips, the warmth of his palms seeping through the thin cotton material of her dress. He pulled her closer and deepened the kiss.

She relinquished control and melted into him. Once again, out in public for anyone to see, and after the day she'd had, Callie couldn't have cared less.

When they broke apart, Hudson ran his thumb over her cheekbone. "That's quite a greeting."

"Well, you know what they say, what's good for the goose…"

He chuckled. "Right. Well, feel free to do that anytime you want."

"Okay, I'll remember that."

He took her hand, laced their fingers together, and walked with her to her door. Once inside, she kicked off her shoes and set her purse down, never letting go of the flower.

"I can't tell you how surprised I was when Gwen brought in the vase. Come to think of it, how did you have them delivered so quickly?"

"Easy, it's who you know."

"Oh, I see. You have florists in your back pocket?" she teased. "I bet all of your girlfriends appreciated that."

His eyes softened, and she thought she might have offended him. "I did it." When she didn't say anything, he added, "I delivered them. After I left the club, I felt bad for what happened in front of Constance. Although she needs to lighten up. Anyway, I made a call, they arranged them, then I got it and left it with the receptionist."

"Why didn't you come to my office?"

"And risk getting caught again?"

"True. Well, thank you. That was the second great thing to happen. Was that your surprise?"

"Nope, not even close. Wait, what was the first great thing?"

"Your kiss."

With an extra bounce to her step and a bit of a fuller heart, she scurried into her room. After she tossed on a pair of her practice pants, which felt like air on her body, and a T-shirt, she tossed her hair into a ponytail and went to see what the gorgeous man in her living room had in store for her.

CHAPTER 26

Hudson had hoped he hadn't built up his idea too much. Despite him being excited to whisk Callie away for a few days, he could only hope she'd feel the same. So many ideas raced around his head of things they could do once they got there.

While waiting for Callie, he walked around the apartment. A picture of her and her grandmother sat on her desk next to her laptop. Beside it was a picture of a couple getting married. He picked it up and realized that it must be her brother. Setting the frame down, he glanced to his left to see a notebook that had passages she'd written highlighted and some crossed out. It was tempting to pick up and read, but although he saw his name a few times, he knew it wasn't about him.

She came out of her room, looking absolutely

The BOOK BOYFRIEND

adorable, until her face fell when she saw where he was standing. Moving away from her desk, he sauntered up to her, cupped her cheeks, and gave her lips a soft kiss.

"I didn't read anything. The pictures caught my eye."

"It's fine. There honestly isn't much for you to see, since I have no clue what I'm doing. The first book was so much easier to write. I had an idea, no preconceived notions or wondering what people would think. I just wrote it because I had a story I wanted to tell. Now I feel so much pressure that a huge brick wall keeps popping up, preventing me from consistently putting anything down on paper or otherwise that makes sense. It's frustrating. I have spurts of clarity and then nothing." She let out a sigh. "Sorry, I'm just tired."

"No apologies necessary. What if I said I may have a solution?"

"Are you going to write it for me?"

He laughed. "Not unless you want your editor to charge you double for having to rewrite it."

Callie smiled.

"No," he continued. "I want to take you away." When he saw her lips turn down, he took her hands in his. "Just a couple of days. Bring your laptop; maybe you'll be inspired to write."

She blinked a few times and let out a deep breath.

"It'll be fun, I promise." All she did was stare at him in a trance-like state. "Callie?"

She shook her head. "Sorry, I was lost in thought. Where?"

"It's a home just outside of Virginia. You'll love it there. It's serene, and you'll be able to relax. I know you have work, but I also know you can't go away on the weekends because you teach and you see your grandmother."

Her eyes softened.

"What do you say?"

"I shouldn't because I already played hooky with my unpredictable boyfriend." She playfully narrowed her eyes before winking. "But I do have a few vacation days left. I can ask—"

Hudson wrapped his arms around her and pulled her into an embrace and kissed her. Callie giggled against his lips before relaxing in his arms. He was falling hard and fast for the woman pressed against his body. If he didn't step away from her, she'd see just how much he felt for her. Jack was 100 percent right… he was whipped.

"Now, how about we relax for a bit and you can tell me about your day."

"Do I have to?"

He chuckled and kissed the top of her head. "No, how about a foot rub?"

"Yeah, now you're speaking my language."

They moved to her couch, and once they sat down, he pulled her bare feet onto his lap. Her pink-tipped toes wiggled as he began to rub the arch of her foot with his thumb. Callie moaned and laid her head back on the arm of the sofa.

He didn't like that she'd had a bad day while he was enjoying himself. All he could think about after he left the club was how he could make it better. Granted, she looked pleased after the kiss, but that was short-lived. Then the flower sitting on the side table caught his eye.

"Why did you bring home only one flower?"

Keeping her eyes closed, she brought her nose to the bloom before looking at him. "All of the flowers were spectacular. My office has never smelled better. I couldn't manage to bring them all home, so I brought that one. It's perfect. They all were, really. Thanks again."

"You're welcome."

"Constance may think I'm a hoochie." She laughed. "Maybe she thinks that's how I get members to join."

His hands stilled and she laughed. "Just kidding, I don't do that… not all the time, anyway, and just with the cute ones."

Hudson knew she was playing around, but she must have noticed the spark in his eye. "Let me rephrase. Only you. But I don't want you to join."

He continued to rub her feet from the bottom of her arch to her toes. Moving from one to the other would elicit a small moan from her each time.

"Why?"

"Because then I can't date you," she said through a yawn.

Then no way would he join. After a few more minutes, Hudson felt the tension in her feet relax beneath his fingers. He knew it wasn't because he was a masterful masseuse, but because she'd fallen asleep. Very carefully, he moved her legs off his, pushed himself off the soft cushion, and, rather than leave her to sleep on the couch, gently scooped her up into his arms.

Much as his niece did, Callie rested her head against his chest, and his heart swelled. He carried her to her room and looked at her unmade bed. He laid her down, then was lowering himself to kiss her cheek when her lashes fluttered open.

"I'm going to go. We'll talk tomorrow."

Callie wrapped her hand around his wrist. "Stay with me."

When their eyes met, there was nothing he wanted more than to hold her all night. Hudson whispered, "I'll be right back."

He went into the family room and locked up. When he stepped into her room, Callie was curled into the fetal position, hands under her cheek, and her blonde hair, which she must have taken out of the elastic holder, was fanned out behind her.

Hudson covered her, and then forgoing his own comfort, he left his jeans and T-shirt on and lay down behind her. Callie scooched her body toward his, and when his arm wrapped around her midsection, she held on to it.

"Good night, Callie," he whispered into her hair. Her only reply was a sigh.

Soft kisses and the smell of lavender and mint jostled him awake. Lips on his forehead, cheek, chin, tip of his nose—then those lips started once more along the same path. Gentle fingers played with his hair. Hudson should have opened his eyes, but he happened to be enjoying his wake-up call and, quite frankly, didn't want it to stop.

Except he knew they both needed to get to work. He let her circle his face once more with her lips before opening his eyes. Sun poked through the slats of the window blinds, throwing small streams of light into the room and creating an almost halo effect around Callie.

"Wake up, sleepyhead," Callie said with a bright smile. If he ever wondered if she was a morning person, he just got his answer. "Do you want to shower here?"

"Are you going to join me?" he rasped in his morning voice. Callie's chest rose and fell with the deep breath she'd just taken. He didn't want to rush anything, but that didn't mean he didn't crave intimacy with her. Or want to feel her skin pressed up against his. It was something they hadn't talked about.

Yet, ever since he'd read her book, he wondered how much of it was true. Did she want an adventurous lover, the romantic, or a combination of both? What he did know was she loved old-fashioned romance, and that was something he would be more than happy to give her.

"I'm already showered," she said, not giving any indication if it would have been a yes or no.

"Shame," he murmured, bringing his lips to the pulse point on her neck and kissing it.

"It is." *And there's my answer.* "I hate to break this to you, but it's six forty."

Hudson couldn't believe he'd slept in. He knew her alarm went off at six, but she hadn't woken him. Instead, she'd taken a shower and was ready to go. His eyebrows shot to his hairline.

"I did try to wake you, but you didn't move. So I decided to get ready and try again."

She moved over so he could sit up. He scrubbed his face with his hands, sparking a bit of circulation. Hudson couldn't remember when he had slept so long. After lying down with Callie, it hadn't taken long for slumber to take him away.

"I'd oversleep every day if it meant waking up to your kisses."

Callie rolled her eyes, grabbed his hand, and pulled him up. "Okay, Romeo. We both need to go to work. Would you like some coffee?"

Hudson chuckled. "No, I'll grab some on the way to the office. Do you feel better this morning?" Despite her cheery a.m. demeanor, he hadn't forgotten that she'd had a rough day yesterday. All the more reason he was ready to sweep her off her feet and take her away.

"Yes, much better. If Constance wants to come at me today, let her. I can't worry about what is already done."

Guilt still hit him square in the chest. "I'm—"

She put her index finger on his lips. "Don't say it. I'm glad you kissed me."

He nodded. "It's become one of my favorite pastimes."

And he was going to do everything in his power to make it stay that way.

CHAPTER 27

Hudson wanted to tie up loose ends before heading to West Virginia with Callie. More and more his fingers itched to get back to drawing. Meanwhile, he sat in his office, taking in all that he had amassed in a short period of time. Granted, he'd done it along with his coworkers, especially Jack, and their success had been a true team effort.

He looked at the crystal orb that he had won for most accounts accrued during a single fiscal year. There were similar ones next to it on his bookshelf. Some engraved with only his name, others with his and Jack's. If someone would have told him that he'd be contemplating switching his career goal, he would have scoffed at the idea. Then again, if someone had told him that he'd be falling for a woman, he would have brushed that off just as quickly.

Regardless of the accolades, money, and relationships he'd built internally and externally while working for Logan Enterprises, the only one that concerned him was Jack. The only thing going in his favor was that first and foremost they were friends. He also knew that Keira wouldn't be affected either.

As though her ears were ringing, his assistant stepped inside his office, holding a box. "Oh no," Hudson immediately said. The gifts had slowed down considerably, and for all intents and purposes, he hoped they would stop altogether. Except by the look on Keira's face, that wasn't the case.

"Do I want to know?" he asked, rounding his desk and sitting in his large leather chair.

"I know, I'm sorry. I peeked inside, of course, but this one contains alcohol, and I didn't think it would be appropriate for the shelter."

"Finally," he said, reaching into the box and pulling out a bottle of Macallan. "Remind me to thank Lily May for giving her character good taste."

Keira laughed. "If you don't mind me saying so, I like this side of you."

"Which side would that be?"

She shrugged. "The one who smiles more."

"I didn't smile before?"

Keira shook her head. "Not really. Maybe after you and Jack signed a client or had a good meeting, but ever since you started to date Callie, you seem happier. It's nice to see."

He contemplated what Keira had said. Hudson

knew he was serious; it was one of the things that had driven him to confront Callie about her book. And in the past, he'd almost be proud that he had been so focused that he didn't have the time to feel anything. Except looking at Keira, he realized how wrong that was.

"Thank you. I am happier. Actually, I'm taking a few days off." Her eyes widened. "I know. I just took some time not too long ago."

Keira couldn't hide her happiness from him. "I'll clear your schedule."

"Thank you. And could you send Jack in, please?"

"Yes, sir." She turned to leave.

"Wait, does your husband like good scotch?"

"Um, I really don't know."

Hudson picked up the bottle that he'd just received and handed it to her. "Here, enjoy."

"Wow, thank you. I'll call Mr. McAfee and let him know you'd like to see him."

She walked out, and Hudson sent Callie a text confirming they were still on for their getaway.

Did you get the time off?

Gwen put it on my calendar.

Great. I'll confirm.

What are you confirming?

Hudson chuckled.

Nice try. Surprise, remember.

Callie sent a rolling-eye emoji. He laughed once more and Jack walked in.

"Hi. Keira said you wanted to see me."

"Yes, I'm taking a couple of days off to take Callie to West Virginia."

Jack stared at him for a moment before the corner of his lips quirked up. "Doing anything special there?"

"Yes, actually. Which brings me to something else I want to discuss with you."

"What's that?"

"I'm considering putting in my resignation."

Hudson couldn't believe how easy that line was to say. Even Jack didn't look surprised. Instead he said, "It's about time. Despite how good you are at this job, your talents lie elsewhere. I'm happy for you."

"Thanks, Jack, and if you could keep it to yourself, that'd be great."

"Keep what to myself?" The men shared a look. "Was that it?"

"Yes."

Before walking out, Jack said, "Oh, and if your fans send you another bottle of Macallan, I call dibs."

Hudson chuckled. "Fine, it's yours."

On a nod, Jack opened the door and left.

A sudden whoosh of relief washed over Hudson. For the rest of the day, he found himself tying up loose ends and wrapping up a couple of proposals. When the day was over, he closed his laptop and headed to the store to pick up a few things for their trip.

The week dragged, but it was finally time for his vacation with Callie. They sat in the cab of his truck. Every few minutes she'd slyly probe for clues, like, "I hope I packed the right clothes," and "I wasn't sure if I needed anything fancy," or "Will there be stores just in case I forgot something? Like a pair of shoes?"

Hudson gave her one-word answers when he could and remained vague on the others. Then she started in with the signs. "Hmm, we're heading west, and we've been on the road for about an hour."

"Were you like this as a child?" he asked, clicking on his turn signal and getting off at the exit on their right.

"Like what? Adorable?"

"No, annoying."

"Well, Mr. Newman, that's not nice. I tell my class that if you don't have anything nice to say, you shouldn't say anything."

He rolled up to a stoplight and placed his right hand over his heart. "I'm sorry. I'm also sorry that I don't have one of the blindfolds I got as a *Ready to Fall* gift."

Callie's cheeks turned pink. "You got a blindfold?"

"No, I got more than one."

She dropped her head in her hands. "I'm so sorry."

Thankfully, she missed the sign as he turned onto the main road in town. Old colonial-style homes and oak trees older than him lined the streets, creating the perfect summer canopy for the rest of their drive.

"Wow, this is stunning." Callie rolled down the window, letting the warm summer breeze pick up her hair. "It's so peaceful," she said into the wind.

They came upon a sign for Andrews Lane, and Hudson turned down the private winding drive. He couldn't help the joy that broke out in his chest at seeing the first design he'd sold come to life. A quintessential country cottage with a minimalist yet elegant feel came into view. Callie gasped, and once again Hudson beamed.

She remained silent as he put his truck into park and turned off the ignition. Callie didn't bother to wait. She grabbed her purse and hopped out of his truck, closing the door behind her. The gravel driveway crunched below her sandaled feet.

Still not saying a word, she craned her head back to take the front facade in. The simple honey maple gables added a unique aesthetic to the angles of the otherwise dark roofline. Another favorite of his was the front porch, which spanned the width of the house. Dave had added rocking chairs, a small round table, and a hammock at the south end. Beams in the same oak as the gables supported the roof over the porch.

Hudson moved to stand beside her. She shielded her eyes from the sun. "This is yours, isn't it?" When he didn't answer, she added, "Design, I mean. Did you design this?"

"Yes, how did you know?"

"There's something about it that reminds me of Izzy and Dwight's." She stepped back. "It just looks like your style. Beautiful. Simply beautiful."

He laced his fingers with hers. "Come on, I'll show you around and come back for our bags."

She nodded, and he led her up the porch steps. He lifted up a faux gray rock, flipped it over, and opened a little door, exposing the key inside. Once he slipped it into the lock, he turned the knob and swung the door open.

It had been a while since Hudson had been in that house. He remembered how proud he was of it when it was completed. The designer Dave hired had done a spectacular job. Rich navies and white, with the occasional jewel tone, brought the country house to life. Minimalist elegance. That was what she called it, and she was right.

"You're doing the wrong job," Callie said, not even realizing he thought the same thing. They walked around the house, Callie stopping every once in a while to compliment him. When the tour was over, he felt as though he were walking on air rather than a wood-planked floor.

"I've been thinking about making a switch."

Not even balking at his declaration, she simply nodded. "Good, because you should."

"There's one other room I want to show you." He once again took her hand and led her down a hallway. Hudson opened the door. Callie sucked in a breath when she saw the old-fashioned desk situated in front of a picture window, facing the back of the home.

"Wow."

"Use it while you're here. Maybe you'll be inspired."

Callie rolled up on her toes, circled her arms around his neck, and kissed him.

Yeah, she definitely likes the house.

They went outside, and he grabbed their bags out of the bed of the truck. After they returned inside, he asked her which room she would like. There were four bedrooms: the primary and three guest suites.

She looked at him and said, "Whichever one you'll be in."

"You know, I didn't bring you here to get you into bed."

"Considering you've already been in my bed..."

She didn't need to tell him twice. Without further hesitation, he brought their things to the largest room, set them down, and looked at her.

"Now what?" she asked.

"Well, I can think of a few things, but we have plans tonight."

"What sort of plans?"

"It's a surprise."

"How many surprises are there going to be?"

Hudson shrugged, and Callie let out a huff. "Come on, I'll show you the property, and then we'll head out. I promise you'll love it."

She turned and looked at him. "I'm sure I will."

CHAPTER 28

Hudson made good on his threat and used one of his shirts to blindfold her. During the drive, he pulled over and secured the cotton fabric so it covered her eyes. She joked around and told him she might get carsick, but he hadn't fallen for it. Instead, he ignored her and said that if she didn't play twenty questions each time he tried to surprise her, he wouldn't have had to go to such extremes. She considered rolling her eyes, but what would be the point?

After what felt like hours, but was most likely twenty or so minutes, the truck slowed to a stop, and then she heard the engine shut off.

"Stay put," he said. She felt the cab move a little when he got out of the truck. Her door opened, and with his hands on her hips, he helped her out. His warm palms cupped her cheeks as he brought his lips to hers. Maybe it was the loss of sight, but a surge of pleasure mixed with the unknown ran through her body.

The silky fabric around her head loosened. Callie blinked a few times, thankful that the sun had started to set, and let her pupils adjust. Callie wasn't sure what she was seeing or where they were. The gravel parking lot hosted several cars. People carrying coolers, blankets, and folding chairs milled about. Hudson reached into the bed of his truck and pulled out a blanket and a small cooler of his own before taking her hand in his.

"Come on, let's go."

She wanted to ask, "Where?" and "What's going on?" but his "twenty questions" comment had her zipping her lips. Considering they seemed to be at a park and he had a blanket in his hands, she assumed he had another picnic planned. Except there were so many people around. No, it had to be something else.

They walked up a dirt path and ducked under a couple of branches until they came to a large clearing. "What is this?" she couldn't help but ask. Three large movie screens were set at least one hundred yards apart at different angles—one facing to the left, one to the right, and one facing center. Couples and families set down blankets or had foldable outdoor chairs. "Are we at a concert?"

Still silent, Hudson continued walking to the screen that faced left. As they got closer, she noticed speakers on stands reminiscent of a drive-in theater without cars. They found a spot, and Hudson unfolded the blanket and set down the cooler.

Her eyes scanned the large area. The plush green lawn was bare in spots, and trees dotted the space, yet behind the screens the trees were in abundance, creating a beautiful emerald backdrop. Hudson uncorked a bottle of wine and poured her a glass.

"Thank you." She couldn't help but peek into the cooler. He'd brought fruit and what looked like a small charcuterie board laden with meat and cheese covered in plastic wrap. "When did you do all of this?"

"I have my ways." He winked, and she melted a bit. Over the next several minutes, they sipped their wine and snacked as the sky became darker. The speaker crackled, and a bright smile grew across Hudson's face.

Callie's confusion vanished when the screen lit up. "Welcome to the classic movie festival…" She didn't bother reading the rest of it; her head snapped to look at Hudson with now tear-filled eyes.

"This is amazing," she said with emotion hitching her breath.

"You don't even know what movie it is. Could be an old-fashioned Western."

"I don't care." And she didn't. The fact that he had done all of this, knowing how much it was a part of her childhood, warmed her to her core. "Thank you, Hudson."

The BOOK BOYFRIEND

Familiar music sounded, and she couldn't contain her glee when she realized that *Send Me No Flowers,* starring her favorite movie couple, was about to begin.

Callie felt like a kid, except for the wine, of course. She crossed her legs and got lost in the movie. When it was around the halfway mark, she repositioned herself between Hudson's outstretched legs and used his chest as back support.

The beat of his heart thumped against her spine, and she couldn't help but melt a bit more into him. Hudson wrapped his arms around her and held her as they both watched the rest of the film. She looked up at him and kissed his scruff-covered jaw. A smile cracked his face as he looked down at her with a softness in his eyes. He gave her a look similar to the one his brother-in-law gave his sister, and she'd be lying if she said that didn't scare her.

Relationships weren't her thing. Her longest relationship had lasted six months, and that was a few years ago. It wasn't that she didn't appreciate the company of a man, because she did, but beyond that was an anomaly. A fluke of sorts. Sure she may write about it, but to her, anything beyond dating felt like fiction.

Applause rang out when the credits began to roll. Callie sat up, instantly missing the feel of Hudson's arms around her. They stood and gathered their cups and plates, which they packed away in the cooler. He grabbed the blanket and draped it over her arm.

"They're playing movies all night. Did you want to stay and watch another one?"

Without knowing what other movies would be playing, she shook her head. "No, this was wonderful. I'd rather go back to the house. Unless you want to stay."

"Nope, I'm good. Let's go."

Callie's thoughts bounced all over the place, thinking about how wonderful a boyfriend Hudson was and how lucky *she was* that he was hers.

Back at the house, they put their movie provisions away and headed up the stairs. She was exhausted and couldn't wait to get ready for bed. It was weird knowing they'd be sharing a room. Technically, it would be the third time they'd slept together, but the first two times were different, considering she'd been asleep and was half out of it. This time, although exhausted, she was awake.

Callie reached into her bag, grabbed a pair of pajamas and her toiletry bag, and headed into the bathroom to change. After taking care of her nighttime routine, she put her toothbrush back in its portable holder and opened the door.

Her pulse soared up to her ears when she saw a bare-chested Hudson standing in his boxers, waiting to trade places with her. *Toned* didn't even begin to describe his body. No, it was more like a work of art. It was a good thing she hadn't tried to

The BOOK BOYFRIEND

imagine what he looked like, because no way would she have been remotely close.

Rounded shoulders, taut pecs, and abs that seemed to be carved into his body were flanked by the delectable vee that made some women lose their minds. And now she knew why—firsthand. Callie forced herself not to let her eyes trail even lower for fear she'd make a fool of herself.

When her gaze traveled north, his playful eyes met hers. "Can I help you?" he asked, clearly knowing the effect he'd had on her.

"No, um... I'm fine. The bathroom is all yours."

An all-knowing smirk that said, *I saw you check me out,* spread across his face. "Okay, thanks." He purposely brushed his body against hers as he walked into the bathroom and closed the door.

A bit frazzled, Callie stowed away her toiletries, turned the cover down on the left side of the bed, and climbed in. Nerves laced with wonder pricked every inch of her skin as she prayed that the cool cotton sheets would lower her body temperature, which she was sure spiked after laying eyes on her masterpiece of a boyfriend.

Then the door opened, and when he appeared, the light streaming in from the night sky, mixed with the soft light on the ceiling, made him look even sexier.

Hudson hit the switch, leaving the moon to do its job, and climbed into bed. Her nerves vanished when they lay on their sides and faced one another.

"I had a great time tonight, Hudson. The movie

festival had to be one of the coolest things I've ever been to. I must say, you're turning out to be a great boyfriend."

He reached his hand to her cheek and tucked a few strands of her hair behind her ear. "You deserve all of that and more." Hudson opened his mouth to say something else, but a sudden surge of fear of what that might be hit her square in the chest.

Callie knew only one way to prevent that from happening, so she closed the gap and kissed him.

CHAPTER 29

After making love to Callie, drifting off to sleep should have been easy, but it wasn't. So much had shifted in their relationship in a short amount of time. It didn't matter that he was living it; Hudson still wasn't sure how any of it was possible. Yes, he could chalk it up to fate or kismet, whatever anyone was into, but pre-Callie, that wasn't his life. The question was: Why wasn't he freaked out about it?

Morning loomed outside the window shade, allowing golden light to filter into the room, and he still didn't have any answers as to why Callie was the one who made him want more. He took a moment to appreciate her beauty: a heart-shaped face, faint highlights in her hair that seemed to have gotten lighter over the past few weeks, and a delicate nose that sat right above the rosy lips he enjoyed kissing so much.

Callie stirred beside him. Her lashes fluttered, and then the eyes he'd never tire of staring at appeared. "Good morning."

He tipped his head forward and gave her a quick kiss on the lips. "Good morning, yourself. Did you sleep well?"

"Mm-hmm." She stretched, and the sheet fell, exposing the top of her chest. "Did you?"

"How could I not, with you beside me?" A pretty smile appeared, spurring on one of his own.

"Charming even before coffee. Lucky me," she chided.

Hudson studied her, thinking about the effortless relationship between his parents and also between Dwight and Izzy. Could it be that easy? Would she even want that? Did he? Questions swirled, creating a tsunami of doubts, wonder, and hope. Rather than delve into those thoughts, he said, "I'm always charming."

Callie sighed into her pillow. "Right, how could I forget?"

As much as he wanted to spend the day in bed with her, one of the reasons he'd brought her there was so she could be inspired to write. "How about some coffee and breakfast?"

"Sounds perfect."

He begrudgingly rolled out of bed, slid on his boxers and a pair of shorts, and grabbed a T-shirt out of his bag. The wood flooring creaked below his steps as he made his way toward the door. When he looked back, Callie's eyes were slowly roaming up and down his body. Appraising him. That was when he knew *he* was the lucky one.

"You know," he said, tugging the shirt on. "If you keep looking at me that way, we're not going to be leaving this room."

"Could be worse, I suppose." The corners of her pretty lips kicked up. She fiddled with the cotton secured around her body until she released it and let it fall to her waist.

Without hesitation, he whipped his shirt off and stalked toward her. Her eyes sparkled in the now brighter sun, amplifying her beauty. The mattress dipped beneath his knees as he crawled toward her until their faces were mere inches apart.

Hudson brought his lips a breath away from hers, and before he kissed her, he hoped she could see how he felt for her when their eyes met. He paused and said, "I'm falling for you."

"Wh—what?"

A jackhammer replaced his heart in the core of his chest. Not hesitating, he repeated, "I'm falling for you, Callie. Is it quick? Yes. I know it is. Except you make me feel things that I've never even considered letting myself feel. Want things I didn't know I wanted. I can see a future with you." The color in her face drained, and she shimmied up toward the headboard, resting her back against it, once again covering herself. Hudson sat back on his heels. "I'm screwing this up," he said with an insincere chuckle.

That was what happened when a plan wasn't put into place—things could go awry. He could see the unraveling begin before his eyes. Never had he done something that hadn't been thought through. That wasn't true. The last time he acted impulsively it was when he found himself with a fake girlfriend. It seemed he lost his head around her. Even when he changed his goals from architecture to business... despite itching to go back to it thanks to the woman currently staring at him as though he'd struck her.

"Callie, all I'm trying to say is, I'm starting to want it all... with you. I see how you are with my family, with Hailey. What a wonderful friend you are and your creativity; although it brought chaos to my life, it also brought us together. You ignite something in me." She adjusted the sheet, almost bringing it to her collar bone and fisting it so it didn't slip.

"I'm going to go make breakfast. We can talk about this some more or not. I just wanted you to know you're very important to me."

Hudson leaned forward, kissed her forehead before putting his shirt back on, and walked out the door, clicking it closed behind him.

He lowered his head and wondered what Callie was thinking. Except if he had to guess, it wasn't good.

Despite waking up hungry, Hudson's appetite diminished after his declaration to Callie. He didn't even know who he was right now. Never had he confessed anything to a woman after being intimate with them. Much less telling them that he'd fallen for them. Hudson flipped a pancake and shook his head. "Of course you've never said that, because you never felt that way before," he said out loud for only him to hear.

Dumb. That was what he was. He didn't know what had come over him. He suddenly felt like a lovestruck teenager. Love. Did he love her? No, he couldn't. Then again, if he didn't, why had he said all that he did to her? Hudson let out a huff and took a sip of his coffee before tending to the meal he was preparing, not knowing if it was going to be enjoyed.

He'd never forget the look on Callie's face. Fear. Shock. Confusion. Pick one, any one, and that pretty much summed it up. He heard the stairs creak, and when he turned, Callie was dressed and, by the look of her damp hair, showered.

She slowly walked toward him. "Smells good," she said in a quiet voice.

"Thanks. It will be done soon. I made coffee and took out a mug for you."

She nodded and gave him a tight grin.

Hudson took the last of the bacon out of the pan and flipped the last pancake onto a plate. "Let's eat." *Eat.* His stomach had a proverbial rock in it. He'd be lucky if he could finish his coffee. Callie sat across from him. "Please help yourself."

On the table were their place settings, orange juice, warm maple syrup, and scrambled eggs he hoped weren't cold.

"This all looks great. You made a lot in twenty minutes."

It had been closer to forty-five, but he wasn't going to point that out. He had to do something, because with each minute that passed, he wanted to run back upstairs and fix what he'd messed up. The caveat to that was, he meant it. He was falling for her.

Their eyes met and both said, "I'm sorry," in unison.

When she looked at him, he took the reins. "I shouldn't have sprung that on you like that. If it's any consolation, I didn't even know I was going to say it. Once again proving that when it comes to you, there's zero order in my life. That doesn't mean I didn't mean it."

Her head slowly bobbed forward as her fork mindlessly pushed eggs around her plate. "I like you, Hudson." She paused, and he could see her fighting back tears. "A lot, in fact."

"But…"

"But I didn't expect this. I didn't expect to meet a guy that could make me angry and swoon at the same time. I didn't expect to have a fake relationship that turned real. I didn't expect to meet his family or for him to meet mine. I didn't expect… you. And the joke of it is, you're perfect. In every way. Yes, your original delivery could have been

The BOOK BOYFRIEND

better, but if I were to write a man, a book boyfriend, you'd be it." She stopped to laugh. "Which as you know I did, but even he wasn't as great as you are. Except I'm not the heroine in the story. I can't be."

He had absolutely no idea what she was talking about. Hudson got up, moved to where she sat across from him, and crouched next to her. "We write our own story, Callie. There's no reason why you can't be the heroine in *our* story, especially if I'm the dashing hero." Hudson tried to add some levity, but all he got was a short-lived grin. "And why can't you be? Are you secretly married?"

She shook her head.

"I know you're not a nun, so that's not it."

She rolled her eyes and blushed.

"Talk to me."

Callie stood, and he followed her into the living room. "What it comes down to is we want different things. You can't fall for me."

Hudson's chuckle died on his lips when he saw the resolve on her face. "I'm not exactly sure that's your choice."

"But it's *my* choice. I'm not cut out for love and marriage, Hudson. And I know that isn't what you said, but before you do, you need to know that. I've never pictured myself with a family. I've seen you with Hailey. The way your eyes light up when she looks at you and the love you two share. You deserve that and more. Plus, love leads to loss, and I just can't."

His brows furrowed as it all started coming together. Callie didn't want kids? Or to fall in love for fear of losing that person? Then he remembered what she'd said in the car when they went to visit her grandmother: *I can't imagine loving someone like that. To give your heart and soul for someone to hold, and then to lose them.*

Doing his best to be understanding, he said, "I've seen you with my niece, too, and you're wonderful with her. I'm sure you're that way with all of your students. You might not see it, but I do." Callie shook her head slightly. He felt as though he were in a losing battle. "Loss is inevitable. But when it comes to love, you can't think that way. You can't not love something because you're afraid to lose it, Callie." She raised her chin, almost challenging him. Something clicked, and maybe he shouldn't have continued, but he did. "Is that why you decided to write romance? That way you can experience it without putting your heart on the line?"

Callie turned away from him. She dropped her head, and he watched her back rise and fall. "You don't think that I didn't put my heart on the line by writing that book? That I'm a coward because I write about love because that way I won't get hurt?" Her lip quivered, and all he wanted was to take her into his arms, but he stopped himself.

After a pregnant pause, she looked at him with glassy eyes. "Maybe you're right and that's exactly what I did." She shrugged, and he swore he saw a mask slide over her face as she rolled her shoulders back. "But you know what, Hudson, regardless of why, at least I did it. You have an amazing talent, but your" — Callie lifted her hands and made air quotes — "*order* has prevented you from pursuing what you really love. I bet your father doesn't even know about your designs. So what does that make you?" Their gazes locked. "If you'll excuse me, I'm going to go pack."

She put her uneaten breakfast on the counter next to the sink and turned to head upstairs.

"So that's it?"

Callie turned her head to look at him. "You're great, Hudson. Truly. And this getaway, the picnic, was perfect. And last night… I'll never forget our time together." Her fingers flexed on the stair's banister. "I'm sorry, but I think it's best that we stop seeing one another."

Hudson took a deep breath, looking at the gorgeous soul in front of him. He made her happy; he knew that he did. She all but said so. Last night was beyond anything he imagined. No woman made his heart beat as hard and with as much purpose as Callie did. But seeing the resolve on her face fueled his frustration. "Just like that? You confess that we had a great time, we shared something special, but now it's over?"

Callie nodded. "We want different things. Eventually, you'd resent me. That would hurt more than what you just said." Silence filled the room, and what had been a fun romantic getaway turned into the opposite.

He couldn't figure out a way to salvage it, so he said the only thing he could. "I didn't mean to hurt you." She solemnly nodded and continued up the stairs. Maybe he should have followed her, or try to convince her they were perfect for each other. But how could he when the woman that he had indeed fallen in love with had just slammed the door closed on her heart?

The answer was, he couldn't.

CHAPTER 30

One hour and thirty-seven minutes of deafening silence. If it weren't for the humming of his truck's engine or the tires rolling over countless seams in the road, Callie would have thought she had lost her hearing.

It wasn't that she expected the ride home from West Virginia to be upbeat and full of laughter, but aside from Hudson asking Callie if she needed anything when they passed a rest stop, they hadn't said a word to each other. About twenty minutes in, Hudson turned on the radio, but each song, commercial, and DJ interruption sounded like white noise.

A couple of times she wanted to say something. It was silly not to, except no words sounded even a fraction as important. All she kept thinking about was what Hudson had said to her. How she wished she were the type who could have just wrapped her arms around him and said, "Me too!" But how could she? Despite having strong feelings for him, she still thought it best for them to move on from one another.

One day, he'd thank her.

One day, he'd find someone who wasn't afraid. Who wasn't scared to love and be called *Mom*. One day, he'd ask that woman to marry him, and she'd be the luckiest woman on the planet. And she'd be happy for him because regardless of how infuriating Hudson could be, he was also one of the most magnanimous people she knew.

Her apartment came into view, and Hudson turned the truck into the lot and parked. The engine ran idle, the silence even worse now that they were stopped. Not able to take it anymore, Callie opened her door and hopped out. She needed to wait for him to get her bags out of the bed of the truck, but once he did, he held on to them.

"I can take those," Callie said, reaching out her hand.

"I don't mind carrying them."

Not wanting to say no once again, she simply nodded. The door opened, and Mr. Rogers walked out. "Hi, Callie. Haven't seen you in a while."

"Hi, Mr. Rogers. I've been busy. How's Mrs. Rogers?"

She hadn't intended on making small talk, but it did feel good to see him.

"You know how she is." He chuckled. "Gets tired of hearing me talk about Tessa."

The BOOK BOYFRIEND

Callie laughed and looked at Hudson. "Tessa was his Harley."

"Real beaut too. Sure she gave me a bit of trouble sometimes, but what woman doesn't, right?"

Callie nodded, and Hudson gave what looked like a forced smile.

Mr. Rogers looked between Callie and Hudson. Then it dawned on her that she hadn't introduced them. "Oh, sorry, Hudson, this is my neighbor, Mr. Rogers. Mr. Rogers, this is Hudson."

She watched Hudson's Adam's apple bob as he held his hand out. "Nice to meet you, sir."

"You too. Do you have a bike?"

"No, sir. I've never been one for motorcycles. Love the look and the sound of them, but never thought to buy one."

"Well, they're not for everyone. Mrs. Rogers doesn't like them, either, but then again, I don't like knitting." He chuckled again. "Probably what keeps us together. She can go her way, I can go mine, but in the end, we end up in the same place. Well, I better get on to the market before she comes out here and hurls one of her needles at me."

"It was good seeing you," Callie said to her sweet neighbor.

"You too. And don't be a stranger. It's almost cobbler season."

Callie nodded.

"Good meeting you, Hudson. Be kind to this one. She's special."

"Yes, sir," Hudson said as her older neighbor walked toward his car. "Nice guy."

"Yes, he's a riot." Callie went up a few steps, put the key into her lock, and opened the door. Hudson walked past her and set the bags down.

Her pulse charged up to her ears. Was this what it felt like when a broken heart still beat? Was it forcing her to hear it? To take note that she was walking away from a great guy? No, she said to herself and to the little angel or devil that was prodding her.

Callie set her keys on the side table and turned to him. "Would you like something to drink?"

"No, I'm good. Thanks." The tension-filled air hung between them. Hudson turned to walk out, and she didn't know what to do. How to act. What to say.

She took a step toward the door, and when he looked at her, Callie couldn't help but drink him in. She felt as though she were wandering in a desert and had just come upon a natural spring. The urge to want to take a sip taunted her, because it may be forever until she saw water again.

"Thank you for everything." He bobbed his head forward in acknowledgment. "I'm very sorry, Hudson."

"Don't, Callie. Don't tell me that you're sorry."

Tears pricked the back of her eyes. "Okay."

"See you around."

She watched the white six-paneled door close behind him, and she finally let her tears fall.

The BOOK BOYFRIEND

Gina and Callie decided to head out for cocktails. Although Gina wanted to check out Prism, there was no way Callie would go there. Instead, they picked a bar near Gina's apartment so they could walk home if they needed to... and the way Callie felt, that just might be a reality.

Their server placed a dirty martini in front of Gina and a glass of pinot grigio in front of Callie. When he walked away, Callie did her best to explain her breakup with Hudson. As much as she didn't want to talk about it, when Callie called Gina to go out, it was because her apartment felt as though the walls were closing in on her.

"Now that we're here, tell me what is going on, because the last time I talked to you, Hudson was whisking you away. Did you not end up going?"

"No, we went." Callie mindlessly ran her finger along the rim of her glass and stared at the pale clear liquid.

"And... ," Gina prodded.

"And we broke up." She glanced up and looked at her best friend. If there was one person who would understand, it would be her.

"Okay, why? Was the getaway that awful?"

"No, actually, it was wonderful." Callie could still smell the freshly cut lawn at the park and hear the birds and chatter of the other festivalgoers. She could remember the spicy taste of the salami and the creamy bite of the havarti cheese, only two of the items on the charcuterie board. Then her favorite couple appeared on the screen, and Hudson held Callie as they watched, laughed, cuddled with each other, and had the best time. Then they spent the night together. No man had ever or would probably ever again make Callie feel as though she were floating.

Callie explained everything, leaving out a few intimate details, then everything that led to them breaking up.

Gina held her hand up. "Hold on a second. It's a little noisy in here. I swear you said that he surprised you by not telling you where you were going, then took you to a beautiful part of West Virginia. Then created the most romantic moment at a film festival that happened to be showing one of your favorite movies."

Callie nodded, shrugging a shoulder to her ear.

"Then you spent the night together, which I'm very proud of you by the way..."

Callie arched a brow.

"We both know it's been a while. Then the next morning, he tells you he's falling for you, and you panic?"

"I didn't panic. I don't want that, Gina. Relationships, love, it's not who I am."

"Says the romance author."

Heat began to rise beneath Callie's skin. "He tossed that in my face too." She went on to explain what Hudson had said.

"Look, I know that you don't do relationships. Maybe that's why I wasn't upset when you started this thing with Hudson. But, sweetie, I know you care about him, and him you… obviously."

It didn't matter, and that was what she told Gina. "Can you be on my side, please?"

"I'm always on your side, Cal. Let's talk about something else. Not knowing what you were going to tell me, I took it upon myself to voir dire a readers' group about the second book."

"Voir dire?" Callie laughed for the first time that day. "Are you channeling *My Cousin Vinny?*"

Gina laughed. "I did watch that movie last week. So good."

Callie giggled along with her friend. "And what was the verdict? Do I want to know?"

"They want it. You need a preorder this time."

"First, I need to finish the book. I'm stuck."

"Art imitating life?"

"Ha ha. Look, I was happy before Hudson; I'll be happy after him."

Callie said the words but highly doubted Gina believed her, since she didn't believe herself. A woman's giggle caught both of their attention. They looked toward the bar. Callie's heart plummeted when she saw a gorgeous brunette draped over a man. She couldn't help but stare. When the man finally turned, and she realized it wasn't Hudson, she let out a breath.

Gina stirred her drink with the tiny plastic sword before lifting it to her mouth and pulling the olive off it. "Tell me," she said, using the little spear as a pointer. "What are you going to do when you run into Hudson and he's with someone else?"

She shrugged. "Be happy for him."

"Exactly what I thought you'd say." Gina sighed. "How about we ditch this place and have a slumber party?"

Callie nodded. "Sounds perfect. My place or yours?"

They both laughed, and Callie had never been more thankful for her best friend.

CHAPTER 31

For the past few days, Hudson had gone through the motions: gym, coffee, work, repeat. Each day seemed to drag longer than necessary. Acquisitions seemed lackluster when in the past they'd acted like fuel to a carburetor. He was taking care of business and trying to get back on track of how things used to be.

Except he knew that wouldn't happen. Even the absence of emails from the fictional Hudson's eager fans didn't lift his spirits. They were his connection to Callie, and as much as he hated to admit it, her words rattled around in his head. Not because they annoyed him but because they were true.

But at least I did it.

He took a look around his house, one that he hadn't designed and one that he had been renting.

When they did the photo shoot there, he didn't tell Callie that he picked that house to see if he could live in a quiet setting and if dealing with traffic would be a nightmare. Hudson realized he loved the serene beauty and being away from it all. That was when he'd decided to buy the piece of property where they'd picnicked. The land that, other than what nature had built, was empty.

But at least I did it.

Those six words, said in the voice he missed hearing, ping-ponged around his head. He walked into one of the spare rooms he used as an office, flipped the light on, and decided it was time. Time to do what he always wanted.

For the next several hours, Hudson sat at his drafting table and worked on the blueprint he'd started years ago. He made a few major tweaks and a couple of minor ones. After spending time with Callie there, he'd had the idea to create a dual office. Something he never would have thought of before. And something that may never be put to use if he couldn't win her back.

Because that was his plan. He missed her. Plain and simple, she was his heart, and he wouldn't rest until he convinced her of such.

After a few more shifts of his ruler, a couple of angles adjusted, he sat back and couldn't believe what he'd created. Hudson stood and arched his back, his spine groaning at the time he'd spent in his chair. He hadn't even realized that in a few hours the sun would be dawning. Hudson clicked off the desk lamp and called it a night.

Hudson walked into his room, sat on his bed, and put his phone on the bedside table. He stripped out of his clothes and lay in bed, hoping he'd be able to sleep. In the morning, he would start putting his plan in place. And that meant a call to the one person he needed to talk to—his father. It didn't matter that Hudson was an adult; he still relied on and valued his dad's opinion.

Then when the time was right, he would go get his girl back. He thought long and hard about everything that Callie had said to him. Still, despite her fear, he just hoped by then it wouldn't be too late.

The cloudless sky cast the perfect light on the lake beyond his property. Hudson had decided to stake out where he wanted his home, which he planned to do while he waited for his father to arrive. When he'd called and told him where to meet him, his dad didn't even ask why, just said he'd be there. Meanwhile, sweat darkened his blue T-shirt as he continued to pound stakes into the ground.

Of course it wasn't in detail. All he wanted was to see the positioning and size. He tossed the sledgehammer on the ground and picked up the roll of pink surveyor tape and began stringing it between the stakes.

"What do we have here?"

He hadn't even heard his father's car.

"Hi, Dad," Hudson said, setting the roll down. He wiped his hand on his shirt and shook his dad's hand. "Didn't hear your car."

"Well, it looks like your mind was elsewhere."

Hudson nodded. "Yeah, guess so." He picked up the hem of his shirt and wiped his brow. "Let me show you around." Without any questions from his dad, Hudson lifted an end of a ribbon off one of the stakes and said, "Come on in."

They both turned and looked out at what would be the back of the property. "This view is spectacular," his father said.

"Yes, it is. That's why I wanted it to be my backyard."

"It's about time," his father said, shocking him.

Hudson turned and looked at his father with arched brows.

"I wondered when you were going to finally tell your old man that he was wrong."

Hudson shook his head in disbelief. "Wait… what?"

"Son, I'm sorry. I know it's my fault. I swayed you into taking the business route when"—he swung his arm out in front of him—"you were meant to do something else. I hope you can forgive me."

"Nothing to forgive. Come on, I'll show you my plan." Hudson reached into his back pocket and pulled out a small copy of his blueprint. He unrolled it and started showing his father the layout. "It will be around five thousand square feet, four bedrooms, three and a half bathrooms."

Pride swelled within him with each second his father stared at the drawing. He lifted his finger and pointed. "What's this room?"

"An office."

"Wow, it's big."

Hudson nodded. "Yes, it's meant for two people. There will be barn doors installed, so if someone needs a bit more quiet, the doors can be closed."

"I see. Someone like a writer?" Their gazes met. "I notice you haven't mentioned her. Izzy said Callie was very quiet after Hailey's class. Your sister has been itching to call you. We, well, your mother told her that maybe you needed space."

Right, ballet class. It had been one of those things that he forced himself not to think about. "We broke up."

"I'm sorry. Then what is all of this?"

"This is my promise to her and to myself." He faced his dad. "I'm putting in my resignation. I've already filed for an LLC for my architectural business. In truth, going to business school may have been beneficial, since I'll be owning one of my own. I know that it will be tough at first, but I'm covered. All I really need is Callie; everything else is just a bonus."

His father placed his hand on Hudson's shoulder. "I'm proud of you, son. When are you breaking ground?"

Still a bit stunned, he happily replied, "I had inspections done a while ago. I have one other adjustment to make. Then if all goes well, they should break ground next week. I have a general contractor in place, and once they have the paperwork, they'll start."

"And Callie? What are you going to do?"

"All I can do… get her back."

"That's my boy. Can I do anything in the meantime?"

"Yeah, wish me luck."

"Son, can I give you a piece of advice?"

Hudson nodded.

"I don't know what happened, and it's none of my business. But the woman we met at your sister's anniversary party looked at you the way your mother looks at me. And don't think we didn't notice the way you looked at her. It doesn't matter how you got together or how long you've known one another. When your heart meets its other half, it knows."

Hudson nodded, then shook his head. "I never thought my father, a marine, would be so sappy."

A boisterous chuckle echoed in the still air. "Son, I may be sappy, but I can still kick your butt. And soldiers have a lot of time to think about things when they're keeping post. When I was away from your mother, even if it was a short stateside deployment, I missed her more than I thought I'd ever miss anyone. If that makes me sappy, then so be it. My point is, like your dream of being an architect, don't give up on her. You're a planner, I know. But sometimes the best things in life are unexpected, even if it takes a bit of time to get there."

They spent another hour together, taking a walk along the property that his father thought was the perfect place to build a home and raise a family. Something that Hudson now wanted more than anything. That was, if Callie was by his side. All he had to do was take his time… even though that would kill him, he would do it if it meant getting her back.

CHAPTER 32

For the past couple of weeks, Callie had felt the void he left in her life... one that she forced upon herself. When she arrived at the studio, she walked into the larger room and began to set up the chairs for the parents and guests. Recital days were always nerve-racking, but assuming Hudson would be there to watch his niece made it all the more so.

Gina tried to pick up her spirits, but that didn't work. Sadly, her last visit with her grandmother ended up going back in time. As far as her nana knew, Ronald Reagan was president, and it was the first time since Kennedy that she appreciated watching the president speak. They took a stroll through the courtyard; then she got tired. Callie brought her back to her room, and she promised to visit again soon.

The BOOK BOYFRIEND

Little voices and giggles filtered into the room and snapped her back to the present. "Miss Callie!" said Kendall, one of her students, running up to her. "My whole family came!"

Callie placed her hand on Kendall's shoulder. "That's wonderful. I can't wait to meet them."

Then families and other students started coming in. "Go get ready, and I'll be right there."

During their last couple of classes, they'd run through the steps of the recital… beyond the dancing. Each student picked their favorite ballet move that she had incorporated into one of her choreographies. They also knew to stay backstage, which in this case was marked off by a dark velveteen curtain hanging next to the makeshift stage.

Callie did her best not to keep looking at the door for Hudson, but she didn't even need to. As she had written in her book, she had felt him before she saw him. With her back to the door, she raised her gaze on the mirror in front of her. Their eyes locked in the reflection until he lowered his and sat down next to Isabelle.

God, she missed him. His hair looked a bit longer, his chest a bit broader, and his arms a bit stronger. That scruff she loved to feel against her skin was still perfectly trimmed. Her chest literally ached. Since the day he'd dropped her off, all she wanted to do was text him and say she was sorry for throwing his dream of architecture in his face. Especially after he told her why he hadn't pursued it. Still, she held herself back and kept silent.

Isabelle walked up to her with an excited Hailey by her side. "Hi, Callie."

"Hi," she said before looking at her student, who was ready to bounce out of her tutu. "Hailey, a few of the other girls are backstage. I'll be there in a minute. Jessica's mom is there helping everyone too." This morning one of the moms had offered her services, and Callie had gladly accepted.

"Okay, bye, Mommy. Don't forget to take pictures. Uncle Hudson said he wanted one for his desk." Emotion clogged Callie's throat, but she forced it down to give them both a smile.

"I will. Good luck, sweetie." Isabelle kissed Hailey, who scurried off to the back. She expected her to go and sit with her family, but she paused long enough for Callie to know something was coming... and it was. "Hudson told me before we got here that you two split up. I don't know what happened, but Hailey doesn't know. She'd be crushed, and she has been on cloud nine waiting for today."

Callie let out a breath. "I understand, and I wouldn't do anything to burst her bubble."

Isabelle nodded and headed back to her seat. Callie felt a sting behind her nose. Not looking at anyone else in the room, she adjusted one of the speakers and headed backstage to check on the girls, whose giggles could be heard from across the room.

She told them to line up and wait for Miss Jessica to send them out. Callie went to the center of the stage, and the chatter in the room silenced.

The BOOK BOYFRIEND

"Good morning, and thank you for coming to our recital. The girls have been working very hard and are so excited to show you what they've learned. At the end, each has selected their favorite move and will perform it before they take their bow." She had a longer speech planned, but when she addressed the group, it was difficult not to focus on Hudson. So she cut it short. "Without further ado, I present to you *Time to Sparkle*."

Applause and a couple of gasps rang out as the seven girls walked onto the stage in single file. Each wore a silver sparkle leotard with a bright-white tulle skirt trimmed in yellow ribbon that matched the one in their hair, white tights, and their pink ballet shoes.

Callie couldn't help but smile at her class. With her back to the audience, she looked at the girls and whispered, "You're all wonderful. Let's show them our dances." She winked and went over to where her phone was and started the music while Jessica adjusted the overhead lights that made their tops look like stars.

"Twinkle, Twinkle, Little Star" rang through the room as she watched the girls go through the steps. Even Callie couldn't help but smile when the two Haileys bumped into each other. It was typical and expected in a kids' recital. Neither were bothered by it. Both giggled and kept going. The song ended and applause rang out. Callie clapped her hands, gave her class a thumbs-up, and started the next song.

After the third and final routine, it was time to do their favorite ballet move before taking a bow. One by one they stepped out of line, performed, and curtsied. Families and friends clapped and whistled, and when it was Hailey's turn, her uncle was the loudest in the bunch. Callie couldn't help but turn her head to see him standing. "Bravo! Bravo!" he yelled.

Hailey blew him a kiss, eliciting laughter from the crowd, gave a wave, and ran offstage.

When the platform had cleared, Callie took her place center stage. "Thank you all for coming. There's coffee, juice, and breakfast pastries in the room next door. Please help yourselves."

Everyone clapped, and the parents thanked Callie before meeting their child and heading for the small reception. Dwight and Izzy were next. "Just wonderful, Callie. I can't believe how much better they got," Dwight said.

"Thank you." She looked beyond them, said hi to Mr. and Mrs. Newman right as Hailey showed up, and dragged them all away. All except for Hudson.

"Hi." She almost closed her eyes to absorb his deep voice and the scent of his cologne, which she had unknowingly missed.

"Hi, Hudson. How are you?"

"Good, thank you. You did a great job with the kids. Although you should have a boy in your class." He laughed.

"Yes, well, I did, but then it was this or flag football."

The BOOK BOYFRIEND

"Ahh, I see. One day he'll realize he could have had all these girls to himself."

She nodded and knew he was trying to make it easy on the both of them, but despite his best efforts, it wasn't working.

"I'm sorry for what I said. It was cruel, and after all you did for me that weekend, you didn't deserve that."

Hudson shook his head. "No, I did deserve it. I'm sorry too."

Awkward silence surrounded them. What else could she say? They were over. Still nothing had changed, not really. Yes, she missed him, but she knew giving him what he wanted… what he deserved… still was an impossibility.

"Well, I should let you go. I'm sure your niece is dying to see you."

"Aren't you going to the reception?"

"No, I'm going to clean up in here."

"It was good seeing you."

"You too."

Hudson pivoted and walked toward the door. He looked over his shoulder and gave her one more smile.

Monica waved to Callie as she walked through the front door of Birchwood Assisted Living. Callie didn't even need to ask Monica for her to say, "Priscilla had a nice breakfast, took a walk outside, and is in her room. So far it's been a good day. As always, I'm sure she'll be thrilled to see you. And I know how she loves her calla lilies."

"Thank you." Feeling a bit more relieved, Callie clipped on her visitor's badge and, with her bouquet in hand, went to visit her grandmother.

She knocked once before opening the door. The small room reminded her of her grandmother's bedroom when Callie was little. The same crocheted multicolor blanket covered the back of a chair, a dish full of butterscotch candies sat on the coffee table, and her nana's perfume in a green bottle that she loved so much lingered in the air.

"Hi, Nana." Callie took a few more steps into the room after closing the door behind her.

A pretty smile accented with well-deserved wrinkles spread across her face. "Callie, my beautiful girl." She stretched out her hand, and Callie couldn't take it fast enough.

She set the flowers down, then bent and kissed her grandmother. "How are you?"

"Good, good. Thank you for the flowers." Her head shifted back and forth, forcing Callie to turn around to see nothing. "Where's that handsome boyfriend of yours? What a dreamboat. And his name. You know they were two of my favorite movie stars. And he could give them a run for their money in the looks department. Well, almost." She laughed, and Callie did as well, even though her laughter was laced with sadness.

"Yes, he's a very good-looking man."

The BOOK BOYFRIEND

"Oh, dear. I may be old, but something tells me something is wrong."

"Hudson and I broke up. We just weren't good together."

Nana shook her head. "Not good together? The way that man looked at you, I'd say you were great together."

"The way he looked at me?"

"Callie, that boy loves you. And my sweet girl, I know I forget things, but I will never forget the way your grandfather looked at me. It was the same way."

Just hearing her talk about her grandfather brought forth all the reasons as to why Callie couldn't be with Hudson. "Don't you miss him?"

"Your grandfather?" Callie nodded. "Of course I do. When I can remember to." She winked, and despite her illness not being a laughing matter, it was better than the alternative. "That man loved me more than a ballerina loves to twirl. And I know you understand that."

"Yes. I do. What you and Grandpa had was special, I'm sure."

"Special. Yes." Her grandmother paused and stared at Callie. The fear that her internal switch would flip and their conversation would change terrified her. "You love that man, Callie. I see it all over your face. When your mother brought your father home to meet me, neither of them had that look in their eye. I don't mean to speak ill of them — they are your parents, after all — but they went through the motions of life. Maybe they loved each other in their own way, but after you and Tommy blessed my life, they... well, I don't know what they did. You aren't either of your parents, Callie. Is that what has you worried?"

Treading on a fine line, Callie tried to explain, praying all the while her nana would stay in the present. "No. I mean, I didn't need them. I had you. Something I wouldn't trade for anything. I never lost them. They lost me. It's different. Being with Hudson was different."

"Can I tell you something?" She laid her hands on Callie's. "My heart broke when your granddad passed away. I swear he took a part of it with him. Which he should have, because it belonged to him. But no matter how my soul ached without its partner, I wouldn't have traded one second of what we had. You can't not love something for fear that you will one day be without it." Callie gasped, hearing almost the same line that Hudson had said to her. "Love is such a special blessing. Do you know that some people search high and low looking for love and never find it? Imagine you telling one of them that you found it but didn't want it. Now"—she sat back in her chair—"I know I don't need to tell you all about what the birds and the bees do, but without your granddad, I wouldn't have the most wonderful granddaughter. We're meant to love, Callie. You have such a beautiful heart. Open it. Let love in, because loving someone isn't a burden—it's fun and unexpected. It's pure joy. You deserve love."

Tears flowed down Callie's cheeks as she listened to everything her wise grandmother said. "What about kids? Do you think I'd be a good mother?"

Nana's dentures were on full display when she said, "The best. And you'll have him. And me, sweet girl." She placed her hand over her cardigan-covered chest. "No matter what, you'll always have me. Is that what's bothering you? You are not your mother's daughter; you're your grandmother's." She patted Callie's hand. "Don't forget that."

"I won't." Then for whatever reason, or maybe trying to lighten the somber mood she'd created, Callie shared, "He'd never seen a Rock Hudson movie."

Nana's lips pursed, and Callie laughed through her tears. "I hope you sat him down and fixed that boy."

"Yes, of course I did."

"You've always loved Rock Hudson. That man would do anything for Doris in those movies."

"I wrote a romance novel and used the name Lily May," she blurted out. After the shock wore off, she told her grandmother about her pen name, which brought her to tears. And that the cover didn't have Fabio on it. "I'm not sure how it ends."

"I think you are." She took a deep breath. "Now I'm getting a bit tired. The next time you visit me, I want to hear more about that book. Actually, bring me a signed copy. Betty is always showing off her grandson. He's a football player or something." She rolled her eyes. "My girl wrote a book. Now go find your happily ever after. And if it comes with a cute butt, then that's even better."

"Nana!" Callie loved her grandmother's spirit. She had always been her cheerleader and still was.

"What? I'm old but not dead. Now scurry along. Alan will be home soon, and I need to make dinner."

Callie stood, leaned down, and kissed her goodbye. "I love you, Nana."

"I know, my precious girl. I love you too."

Feeling much better and having a bit more clarity, Callie headed home to finish her story with an open heart.

CHAPTER 33

It had been two months since Hailey's recital. Sixty-one days, to be exact, since he'd seen Callie. So often he'd wanted to call her to tell her that he'd quit his job and started his own architecture firm. Granted, Keira, whom he'd poached from Logan Enterprises, was his only employee, so "firm" was a bit of a stretch. But he'd risen to the challenge and done it.

He couldn't help wondering if she was seeing anyone, but in truth, he didn't want to know. Deep down, he didn't think she would be, but despite his curiosity, he didn't want to be the proverbial cat, so he left it alone. Well, sort of. After a couple of beers with Jack and hearing how he'd met someone and fallen head over heels for her, he lost his willpower and searched various social media platforms. First he searched her name, but the only public image on her page was a picture of her and Gina taken before she met Hudson. The date on it was a couple of years ago. Both women looked a bit younger, but all Hudson could focus on was the woman who owned his heart.

Wanting to know more, he reluctantly tapped in the hashtag #ReadyToFall, and a slew of posts populated. Some were about her character, some praising her, some asking when the sequel was coming out, and some were a bit miffed that the second book hadn't been released yet. He felt bad about that one. How could he not wonder if that book would be finished if things were different between them?

He landed on a reader group with Lily May's name on it, but he didn't dare join. For a split second, he thought about having Isabelle do it; then the term *stalker* flashed in his head, and that was that.

Putting away his phone, Hudson walked up to the worksite, loving the smell of freshly cut wood and hearing the buzzing of saws. Nail guns popped in the distance as he grabbed a hard hat and began to walk through the framed structure. Seeing his home develop wall by wall, beam by beam, brought him a great sense of accomplishment.

Of course he still craved order, but his priorities had shifted. Tony, his project manager, gave him a wave as Hudson stepped on the plywood-covered floor to shake his hand.

The BOOK BOYFRIEND

"Hudson, it's good to see you. It's going to be a beauty. I've worked on a lot of projects, but this home and its location are one of a kind."

"Thank you, Tony. You and your crew have been great. Any issues today?"

"No, surprisingly, we're right on schedule. I have most of my men here, so we'll be starting on the roof soon."

"Great, thank you. I'm just going to look around a bit before I head out."

Hudson started to walk each room, doing his best to visualize how the contemporary farmhouse would look. When he got to the double office, he experienced a vision of Callie sitting at her desk. How sexy she looked in her glasses was something he wasn't even sure that he had told her before.

"I'm almost done with the book," she said, standing up to move toward him.

"Oh yeah?" Hudson pulled her against him, her arms instinctively circling his neck. "How does it end?"

"Well, it's a romance, so... they're happy and in love."

"Like us," he offered with a kiss to the tip of her nose.
"Yes, exactly like us."

He blinked, only to find the room just as it was—empty, no walls, no floors or desks, and no Callie.

In each room that he went into, he wanted to see Callie. Having coffee with him in the kitchen, watching old movies in their family room while debating between sappy rom-coms and Westerns, knowing either would be fine because they'd be together. He carefully made his way down to the lower level, imagining her teaching their kids how to dance in her private studio. The home may be perfect in theory, but it missed the most important part—having Callie there to share it with him.

Hudson stepped outside, and a compilation of memories swarmed around him. He said goodbye to Tony and a few of his crew before he hopped in his truck. His phone rang, and Jack's name flashed across the screen. Ever since Hudson had left Logan Enterprises, Jack had been pulling double duty. It was the one part of leaving that Hudson hated the most.

"Hey, Jack. How's it going?"

"Good, hey, I have a favor to ask. Are you at the site?"

"Just getting ready to leave, why?"

"I want to talk to you about something. Can you meet me for lunch?"

Out of habit, Hudson glanced at his watch, knowing he had cleared his day to check on his house. "Sure, where and when?"

"Now, and Rocky's."

He should have gone home to change, but he hadn't seen or talked to Jack in a while, and Hudson started to feel like a horrible friend. "I'll be there. It'll take me a bit."

"That's fine. I'll be here."

Hudson wanted to ask if everything was okay, but he'd find out soon enough. Over the past several weeks, he hadn't been around. He and Jack would text occasionally, but Hudson had to cancel the last time they were supposed to get together, because a surveyor was coming to his property.

Jack, of course, understood. So at the very least, Hudson had no issues meeting his buddy for lunch despite not being dressed for it. Hudson brushed the sawdust off his jeans and was thankful that he kept a spare T-shirt in his truck. With a bit of nerves lacing his movements, he reached over his head and tugged. The almost-fall air kissed his skin before he slid the clean cotton over his head.

He slid in behind the wheel, started up the engine, and began his drive across town. Thanks to the upcoming shift in seasons, leaves had begun to change colors and flutter in the air, falling to the ground. That was one other thing he couldn't wait for... autumn at his home. Granted, his house wouldn't be done before the threat of snow, but even that would be serene.

Thirty-five minutes later, he parked in front of the restaurant, raked his hand through his hair, and stepped inside. Per usual around lunch hour, there were only a couple of vacant tables. The woman at the host station glanced up; then her eyes widened.

Hudson took a step forward. "Hi, I'm—"

"You're him," she said, placing her hand on her chest. "I can't believe it."

Hudson's first instinct was to cringe. Then he thought of Callie's success and nodded.

"Wow, you're just... wow."

He smiled. "I'm flattered, thank you. But it's really Lily May who deserves the credit."

She nodded. "Yes, totally. My favorite book."

"I'm glad to hear it..." He looked at the tag on her black vest: TAMI. She giggled, and he had a hard time suppressing a smile. "Can you tell me if you know where Mr. McAfee is sitting?"

"Yes, so sorry. Please follow me. I'll take you to them."

"Them?"

Tami ignored his question, but Hudson knew that Jack sometimes had lunch with his father, so maybe that was whom he was with. They wove their way by a few tables before he spotted Jack, who raised his hand.

"Thank you, Tami."

"You're welcome, Mr. Newman."

She walked away, and Jack chuckled before shaking his hand. "Still can't escape the 'book boyfriend' tag, can you?"

"Doesn't look that way." They sat down, and Hudson took note of the lipstick-marked glass, making it unlikely that Jack's father was the surprise guest.

A server came by, and Hudson decided to order an iced tea, not knowing what he had just walked into. Once it was just the two of them, Hudson pointed toward the object in question. "Who's here?"

"My girlfriend," Jack said as though it were obvious.

"Girlfriend? Who is she?"

"Well, I met her at Shadow Oaks." Hearing the

The BOOK BOYFRIEND

name of the country club where Callie worked made his heart pound. "You know her, actually."

Before he could continue his inquisition, Gina appeared. "Hello, Hudson."

Jack stood to pull out her chair while Hudson sat, stunned.

"Gina, it's good to see you. How are things?"

"Fine, fine. But enough of that." She leaned forward. "Let's cut to the chase."

Hudson's gaze flicked between Jack's and Gina's before staying on her.

"I am tired of you and Callie."

"There is no me and Callie," Hudson said, wishing he'd ordered a whiskey instead.

"Right, well, that needs to change. Are you in love with her?" Gina asked.

Hudson didn't feel right answering her before he said those words to Callie, which he most definitely wanted to. He just hoped he had the chance.

Gina waved her hand between them. "That was rhetorical. My one question is: What are you going to do about it?"

The server returned with his iced tea and asked if they knew what they wanted. Jack told him they'd need a few minutes, while Hudson looked at Gina, who cocked a brow.

Hudson didn't know how much Gina knew about their breakup. He assumed everything but didn't want to overstep. "I'm not sure how much she told you about our time away, but regardless, Callie wasn't very receptive to the idea of love."

"I know. I understand. But a lot has happened over the past few weeks—you know what, never mind. It's not my place to say."

Gina was right. Talking about Callie without her here wasn't what should happen. Hudson needed to talk to her, see her, hold her. He so desperately wanted to show her his house. He wasn't even sure that she knew he'd started his business.

"Sorry I can't stay." He stood. "I do want to hear more about you two, though."

"Go get your girl," Jack said assumingly.

Hudson nodded, and that was exactly what he was going to do. Right after he took care of a few details.

CHAPTER 34

Callie sat at her kitchen table, surrounded by hardback copies of *Ready to Fall* as she prepared for the launch of *Fallen for Her,* the rights to which she'd sold to a publishing house. Her hand started to cramp. She set down the silver signing pen that Gina had bought for her as a congratulatory gift. When really she should have been receiving them.

Since day one, she'd pushed Callie to first write the book, then publish it. Her life had changed overnight. Finishing the second book had been difficult, but after her visit with Nana, it had flowed a bit easier. Still, writing a romance about a character, the book's hero, no less, named Hudson Newman hadn't been easy. Then, after a while, it had become therapeutic.

Callie missed Hudson more than she ever

thought was possible. Especially since his friend was dating her best friend. The day they met in the parking lot of the country club after his round of golf, she knew by the shy, coy way Gina smiled that there would be something between them. At least it made her last day at the club interesting.

She smiled, thinking about the day she put in her resignation. Sadly, the first person she'd wanted to tell was Hudson, because before she walked out, she left a couple of copies of Lily May's book in the Founders' Lounge. The thought of women like Constance going ballistic made her laugh, and she knew that Hudson would have laughed too.

But she couldn't just call him and act like nothing had happened. Jack told her that he'd left Logan Enterprises and moved on. She honestly didn't think that meant another woman, but he didn't elaborate. Nor did she ask Jack or Gina. It wasn't her business. Yet every day she would look at their picture and wonder what would happen if she did call him, but she never did. She just hoped Hudson was happy.

Like the seasons, things changed — it was the way of life. One that Callie was starting to understand more and more lately. Since she was technically unemployed and living off her book royalties, she'd been spending a lot of time with her grandmother — who, of course, always asked about the boy with the cute butt.

Even the nurses knew about Hudson. How could they not? Nana made sure he was the topic of conversations more than once. It didn't matter that she went in and out of past and present; she made sure her granddaughter thought about the man whom Nana deemed the perfect Rock to her Doris.

Deciding she needed a break, she stretched before heading into her bathroom and ran a nice hot bath. It had been a while since she'd let herself indulge, but after being hunched over a table for the better part of the day, a soothing bath was just what the doctor ordered.

Callie pulled all her hair back into a ponytail, stripped out of her two-day-old sweats, smeared her favorite avocado mask on her face, immersed herself beneath the soothing water, and closed her eyes. She let out a sigh as her mind finally relaxed and drifted off. That was, until there was a knock on her door. Then another… and another.

On a groan, Callie got up, slid into her robe, and wrapped a towel around her head as a makeshift turban. She figured it was another delivery. The publisher wanted a ridiculous amount of books signed and was constantly sending her more and more.

Another knock.

"Coming!" *Why weren't they just leaving it in front of the door?* She yanked it open to find Hudson on the other side of it.

That devilish sexy smirk cracked his face. "Hi, Callie. Green looks good on you. Brings out your eyes."

Her pulse jumped, seeing and hearing the man she'd missed more than she ever knew she could.

Not even caring that she looked like a spa child, she tightened the belt on her robe. "Hi. I'm sorry, I wasn't expecting anyone."

"I'm not going to stay."

Her heart fell.

"I have a question for you."

She looked at him expectantly.

"Will you have dinner with me tonight?"

"You came all the way here to ask me that?"

"Yes, I did. So what do you say?"

"Yes, I'd like that."

She felt her knees give when he flashed her that gorgeous smile of his.

"Perfect. I'll wait."

"Wait?"

Hudson closed the gap between them in less than two strides. Not caring about the green mess on her face, he cupped her cheeks. Callie was certain she was about to combust. God, she missed him.

"I'll wait for you until time no longer exists."

She felt the slide of his thumb against her cheek.

"I should hold off saying this so you have a great memory of this moment," he continued, "but I suppose you'll have something to write about when you heard me say *I love you* for the first time."

Tears welled in her eyes. "You do?"

"Yes, even if you don't want me to, I do. I'm sorry I walked out. I'm sorry that I let my pride get in the way of me telling you everything that was in my heart. But, to be honest, I didn't understand it

The BOOK BOYFRIEND

myself. Until I didn't have you. Until I saw you at Hailey's recital, and all I wanted to do was pull you into my arms and kiss you. Until I realized I couldn't because I was dumb to let you go. Dumb for not telling you that I could never resent you for who you are. I'm here to tell you, green face and all, that I love you, Callie Richardson. It doesn't really matter if you love me back or if you say it's impossible. Nothing on my end changes."

She felt the same. Nana was right about him. He did look at her with love in his eyes. She'd seen it with Tommy and with Dwight. Callie realized it was more than missing him or needing to hear his voice. She was unequivocally in love with Hudson Newman.

"I do want you to love me. I love you, too, Hudson." Before she could recite eloquent lines that she had so desperately wanted to say to him, his mouth landed on hers.

When he pulled away, his scruff was tinted chartreuse. "You're a mess, and I need to rinse off."

"Want some help?"

"I thought you'd never ask."

Hudson helped her into his truck. "Are you going to tell me where we're headed?"

"No, I'd like to surprise you without needing to blindfold you again. I've missed your eyes way too much to cover them up."

"I've missed yours too."

"So Jack and Gina?"

Callie couldn't help but laugh. "Can you believe it? And they didn't tell me until last week. I knew they met, because I was there when they did. Then oddly, anytime I talked to Gina, it was about my books and nothing about her dates."

"How is your writing going? I couldn't help but see the stacks of books on your table."

"I finally finished the second book. I wanted so desperately to tell you." Not wanting to rehash anything negative, she added, "You'll be happy to know that Hudson got his girl."

"Maybe he is like me after all."

"Yeah, maybe. Hey, I never asked you… did you really have someone standing by to delist my book or did you make that up."

"Sorry, desperate times. Can't say that I wouldn't do it again. After all, I wouldn't have you, right?"

Callie felt as though she were floating. She couldn't take her eyes off him. He was always a good-looking man, but there was something about him that made him seem even more handsome. Hudson flicked his eyes in her direction and winked.

"You're staring."

She shook her head. "There's something different about you. I'd love to take the credit and say it's because we're back together, but something tells me it's more than that." Before he could reply, the truck turned and slowed to a stop, Callie took her eyes off him and looked out the window. Her brows pulled together. It looked so familiar, yet different. Then she gasped. "Hudson…"

"Come on." He hopped out of the truck and went to her side to help her out. Hand in hand they walked up to the framed structure.

She couldn't believe what she was seeing. Her heart soared with the realization that his dream had come to life. "You did it."

"Yes."

"It's amazing, Hudson."

Callie was in complete awe as Hudson gave her the grand tour. He introduced her to Tony and then brought her into the will-be office.

"For years I had a vision of how I wanted this house to look. Then I met you and things changed. So, on the original plan, this was a game room."

She scanned the room and could imagine a pool table, maybe a table to play cards. "What is it now?"

"An office… our office. One day when we're married, we'll live here. I'll draw house plans, and you'll write books. But we'll do it together. What do you think?"

She took a moment and looked around before turning toward him. "Married?"

He nodded and pulled her into him. "Yes, one day."

"And picnics with our kids?"

Hudson's eyes widened, and then a glorious smile blossomed across his face. With their bodies flush against one another, she looked up at him. "I would love nothing more than to have a family with you."

He cupped her face and kissed her.

"I love you, Callie."

"I love you too. This is incredible. I'm so proud of you."

"Thanks. I'm not sure I would have done it without you pushing me."

She smiled at him.

"Wait." Hudson tucked a few stray strands of hair behind her ear. "You never told me the title of the sequel."

"*Fallen for Her.*"

"Perfect."

Happiness flooded Callie's heart. Never did she expect to be able to open her heart and let someone love her and to love them back. Or contemplate marriage and a family, but Hudson changed all of that. He made her realize that love wasn't something to fear, but something to hold on to and grow with. And she couldn't wait to do that with him.

"Hey," he said, taking her hand and leading her outside. "In this new book, you didn't write about more red thongs, did you?"

Callie laughed, remembering all the gifts he'd received. "No."

He put his hand on his chest. "Thank God."

She sent him a sideways glance. "They're black."

Hudson sighed, and Callie laughed. "I'm just kidding. I didn't write anything like that this time."

"Why not?"

"Because you're mine."

"Forever."

Hudson speared her hair with his fingers and kissed her. Making her breathtakingly aware that she was finally ready to fall.

EPILOGUE

Nine months later

Steam rose from Hudson's mug as he stood on the back porch of his house, listening to the sounds of nature making their homes in the large leafy trees. Morning was Hudson's favorite part of the day, but as he looked out onto the dewy lawn that in a few hours would be filled with family and friends, he decided *this* morning was his favorite.

Getting down on one knee and proposing to Callie had been his most cherished moment, but there was zero doubt that the moment when she became his wife would surpass that. Everything had started to fall into place for both of them.

"I hope you're not having second thoughts."

The BOOK BOYFRIEND

Hudson turned and smiled. "Not a chance. Your sister is stuck with me."

Tommy sipped his coffee and stood next to Hudson. "I'm glad she has you. My sister is one of a kind. As is this property. It's incredible. No wonder Callie loves it here."

Hudson couldn't agree more. The property was perfect, and he knew it the first time he laid eyes on it. "I want you to know that Callie is my world. She will never want for anything, especially love. I've never been prouder of anyone in my life. That woman amazes me."

Since they'd been together, she'd published her second book, started a third, and helped him with every aspect of their house. That was why she deserved today.

Tommy nodded. "I was stunned to hear she became an author. Not to mention your involvement."

"Yes, my involvement." Now Hudson was the one laughing.

Hudson's phone rang, and a picture of Callie's pretty face lit up the screen. "It's your sister."

"I still can't believe you're surprising her with a wedding."

"We're engaged. It's not that much of a surprise."

Tommy almost spat out his coffee, and he shook his head. "Okay, if you say so." Tommy turned and walked away, giving Hudson some privacy.

Hudson pushed the green icon to connect the call. "Hey, sweetheart."

"Hi, I only have a minute because you know how Gina is with her spa days."

Hudson had never been so thankful for Gina's help. He needed someone to be his accomplice, and there had been no one better than Callie's best friend.

The idea of a surprise wedding hadn't come lightly, but the last time they'd visited Callie's grandmother, she seemed to have declined a bit. Wanting to make sure Callie had the most important person in her life there when they said *I do,* he'd talked to Tommy and Gina. Both of them thought it was a great idea.

"What are you and Tommy doing today?"

"Going over his house plans." That was the excuse for Tommy and Gretchen's visit. "Don't worry about us. Go have fun with the girls. We'll be here slaving over angles and rooflines."

"Okay, I won't. I need to go before Gina finds me on the phone. Love you and see you soon."

"Love you too."

For the next few hours, Hudson made sure everything was just how Callie had described the wedding of her dreams.

"Please, I just want to see you in it," Gretchen begged, looking at the gown in Callie's bedroom.

"Cal, just show her. Hudson is in the back having a beer with Tommy and Jack. He won't come in here.

Plus, you're all done up. It will be like a preview for your wedding day. What if you decided you want your hair up instead of down or vice versa. Better to find out now rather than later, right?"

"I agree," Gretchen said. "And I couldn't be here when you bought it."

Callie felt so badly about that. Her flight had been canceled due to bad weather.

After she and Hudson got back together, Hudson bought Callie tickets to Dallas for one of her Christmas gifts. She couldn't have been more shocked or delighted. While they were there, and Hudson got the "don't hurt my little sister" speech, Tommy and Hudson became fast friends. She found out later that Hudson had asked her brother and Nana for her hand in marriage. Something Callie found endearing. After all, they were her family.

"Okay, geez. You both are acting so weird about it."

"You should pee," Gina said out of the blue.

"What?" Gretchen and Callie both laughed. "I think I'm fine."

Gina shrugged. "Suit yourself, but once you're in that dress, you might wish you had. Don't forget all the water we drank at the spa. Hydration is important."

Callie had no idea what Gina was talking about, except that all her chatter had Callie walking toward her bathroom.

When she came out, Gina and Gretchen were wearing similar sky-blue dresses. Gina's was a strapless maxi dress that hit her midcalf and hugged her curves, and Gretchen's was the same length but had a halter top instead and was a bit more flowy. "We bought these and wanted to surprise you. Do you like them?" Gretchen asked.

She had asked the girls to stand up for her at her wedding and told them the color she liked, but they could pick what they wanted as long as they were comfortable.

"You guys look amazing!" A bit more excited to put her own on, she took it off the hanger, and within minutes she was ready. When she turned to show Gretchen, her sister-in-law's eyes filled with tears.

"It's stunning, Callie. Hudson is going to lose his mind."

Callie had decided to go with a romantic sleeveless A-line with embroidered tulle, a full skirt, semideep neckline, and a sheer back. "I hope so. Okay, let's change before they come looking for us."

Gina's phone chimed. "Oh no." Callie's head snapped toward her. "Something happened. We need to get out back."

"What? What happened?" Callie asked frantically.

Gina wrapped her hand around Callie's wrist. "Let's go."

"But I'm in my dress!"

Everyone ignored her and practically sprinted down the stairs. "Gina, slow down. I'm going to fall in these shoes!"

They flew through the house, Gina on one side,

The BOOK BOYFRIEND

Gretchen on the other. Callie's heart was beating a mile a minute. She had been so worried about what was going on and not falling down the stairs that she didn't notice anything else. Then they made their way outside, and Callie stopped dead in her tracks.

Tommy stood on the patio, wearing a tan suit, one that she knew he had bought for her wedding. His tie matched the color of Gretchen's dress.

"What's going on?"

A woman came out of nowhere and handed Gretchen and Gina small bouquets—and one made of calla lilies to her. That was when she spotted Hailey, who had a basket in her hands, and Izzy, wearing the same dress as Gretchen. Callie's eyes welled up. When she finally took a moment to breathe, she saw a few rows of white chairs filled with their friends. Her nana was in a wheelchair at the end, with Monica sitting beside her. At the center of it all was Hudson, wearing a black suit, white tie, and that killer smile of his.

"I think you might understand now," Tommy said. "Hudson did all of this. Now how about you go and marry that man before he bursts."

She looked at her bridesmaids, flower girl, and maid of honor standing in front of them.

"You got this, Callie," Gina said, giving her a wink.

The music started, and she looped her hand in the crook of Tommy's elbow.

"You ready?"

She nodded, and they began their stroll down the makeshift aisle, following the trail of flower petals tossed onto the ground by Hailey. Callie scanned the guests, happy to see Hudson's family. When they got to Nana, Tommy slowed down.

Callie bent over and kissed her on the cheek. "Thank you for being here, Nana."

"I wouldn't miss it, my calla lily."

When they were about two feet away from Hudson, he walked up to them and took Callie's hand. "You're beautiful."

"Thank you. So are you. I can't believe you did this," she whispered.

Tommy kissed her, shook Hudson's hand, and took his place next to Jack, who was Hudson's best man, and Dwight, who was a groomsman.

The minister welcomed everyone and prompted the couple to start their vows.

Callie realized she wasn't prepared for this part. Yes, she looked good because of the spa day, but that was trivial in comparison to this monumental moment.

Hudson must have sensed her nerves when he said, "I promise to love you forever, Callie. To always be by your side. To be the Rock to your Doris. I've never been prouder in my life than I am right now. You make me a better man, and I couldn't imagine my life without you."

Callie wiped a few tears that had trickled out of her eyes.

"That was beautiful. I should have something

eloquent to say, given my profession and all, but I usually don't like the first draft." Everyone laughed. "Hudson, you amaze me. From the first day you stepped into my office, you surprised me, and clearly you don't intend on stopping."

More laughs echoed in the air, and Hudson shook his head. "Never."

"I'm glad, because I need you in my life. Even when I didn't think so. I never considered falling in love before you, and my promise to you is that you have my heart forever. Thank you for never giving up on me. And for all of this. I can't wait for a lifetime of surprises with you. Thank you for being my rock."

Hudson nodded and brought her hands to his lips.

"I now pronounce you husband and wife. You may now—"

Before he declared them official, Hudson cupped her cheeks and kissed her. A kiss she'd never forget, and one for the books.

The End

Keep reading for a preview of
Once Upon a Kiss.

ONCE UPON A KISS

Every year Drew Mitchell looked forward to his holiday vacation. He loved the hustle and bustle of city life and his fast-paced job, but even he needed to unwind every now and again. That was why for the past several years Drew had traveled to the Spero Resort to relax.

It wasn't like when he was younger and his mission was to meet a beautiful woman... or on occasion, *women,* to enjoy himself. Now he used the time to appreciate the beauty of the water and the island—and to hang out with his friend Ethan, whose parents owned the property. Not that if someone caught his eye he wouldn't strike up a conversation or buy her a drink; it just wasn't his primary goal anymore. And his intentions never went beyond a drink.

The past year had been hectic, and his financial clients were demanding. He loved what he did, but he knew taking time for himself was just as important as making money.

As Drew stepped into Spero's lobby, Ethan's father, Jackson, greeted him with a firm handshake.

"It's good to see you, son."

Drew smiled at the older man. Jackson and his wife, Hanna, were like an extended family to him.

"Thank you, it's good to see you too. As always, the weather…" He lost his place in their conversation as a dark-haired woman, coming from the direction of the front desk, breezed past. His heart stuttered. Even Jackson glanced around, searching for what had made Drew's attention waver. She must have just checked in, because he definitely would have noticed her before.

"Enjoy yourself," Jackson said with a knowing grin as he patted Drew on the shoulder. All Drew could do was nod, suddenly speechless. Who was the last woman who had done that? Drew could have racked his brain for days trying to formulate an answer, but it would be… no one. No one had ever affected him so much.

As Drew watched her, his chest expanded with a breath that caught in his throat. He had never seen anyone so beautiful. Her bright smile further illuminated the already sunlit lobby, and her blue eyes reminded him of the sea, though with just one glance, he knew that, if given the choice, he'd take gazing at this woman over the gentle turquoise waves caressing the shore. Her floral-patterned dress floated around her long bare legs like the hibiscus blooms in the hotel's fountain.

Drew made his way toward the beauty, ready to introduce himself, but stopped when Fiona approached her with a tray of Spero's signature drinks. The mystery woman wrapped her perfect rose-colored lips around the straw, and every coherent thought flew from his mind.

Before he could acknowledge the tug he felt in his rib cage, like a tether pulling him toward her, she stepped into the elevator and disappeared behind the sliding brass doors. Knowing he would make a point of meeting her, he turned and walked out the back exit to the purity of the white sandy beach, her blue eyes still flashing through his mind.

Vacationers stretched out on lounge chairs, uninhibited by whatever stresses they had before their arrival, which was also Drew's ultimate goal—to leave the pressures of the city behind him.

When Ethan's family bought the once run-down resort and transformed it into a haven of tranquility and beauty, they put all their energy into creating a place where people could escape, where they could leave their troubles behind and get a new lease on life. It was wonderful to see them achieve their goal.

Drew took his time greeting the Caribbean water. There was nothing like the island's soft sugar-white sand. It was worlds better than the pavement his feet pounded back home in the city. He stood, staring at the waves, appreciating the wonder of it all and breathing in the warm salty air before heading back toward the resort to see his friend.

Ethan was behind the outdoor bar, working his mixing magic while joking with a few of the guests. Even though Drew missed seeing his friend back home, he knew this was where Ethan belonged. Part of Drew wondered if he should follow suit and give up the hustle of Chicago's financial district, but he knew he'd miss the excitement of city life too much. Luckily, Drew's salary gave him the means to spend most of his off time flying back and forth to the island.

Couples, singles, and locals surrounded the teak wood bar. A few of the twosomes appeared to be on their honeymoon and lost in each other. One pair barely came up for air to enjoy the fruity beverages in front of them.

Drew sat next to George, one of the locals who owned a condo less than a mile away. George had a deep-sea fishing charter that Spero contracted to take guests on excursions.

"Good afternoon, George. How were they biting this morning?"

Ethan smiled at Drew and set down a cold glass of lemonade in front of him while George tipped his captain's hat toward his friends. "Not too bad. It would have been better if one of the men didn't get queasy when the boat anchored." He let out a laugh. "You know the saying, the bigger they are, the harder they fall." After another hearty chuckle, he looked at Ethan's worried face and added, "Don't worry. The only thing the man injured was his ego."

The three of them shared an enthusiastic laugh. Drew looked up to ask Ethan how the day had been going, but his friend's attention was no longer on the pineapple he had been slicing. Following his line of sight, Drew found what had distracted his pal... stepping out of the resort was the same woman who had rendered him stupid only thirty minutes earlier.

Drew slipped on his aviator sunglasses before flipping his baseball hat around; he didn't want anything to impede his view. Ethan let out a whistle, and Drew was ready to call dibs right then and there as if they were still in college and vying for the same girl. But not wanting to tip his hand, he remained silent.

George finished his beer, glancing in the mystery woman's direction. "Well, gentlemen, duty calls. I'll leave you two to duke it out." After a hearty chuckle, a pat on Drew's back, and a handshake with Ethan, he was gone.

The woman walked to the beach stand, smiled at the young man who looked as though he'd swallowed his tongue after she thanked him, and grabbed two of the resort's fluffy white towels. Like fools, Ethan and Drew watched her head down the few stairs that led to chaise lounges.

"Wow." Ethan let out a breath as they watched her peel off her lavender cover-up, revealing a white-and-purple-striped string bikini. The triangular piece of fabric covering her backside had Drew shifting on his stool. "She looks thirsty," Ethan added.

Drew knew his buddy was prepared to woo her with his mixology genius. "Sorry, brother.

ONCE UPON A KISS

Remember your father's rule?" When Ethan graduated and moved to the island to run the resort with his parents, Jackson was adamant about Ethan not fraternizing with guests. *Be friendly, but not too friendly,* was his dad's mantra. Drew had never been happier to not be working at the resort.

Ethan glared at him. "Really?" When Drew's gaze floated back to the beauty, his friend grinned. "I have a feeling you'll be thanking your lucky stars you didn't join us in this business venture. It's been a while since I've seen you look like this."

"Like what?"

"Remember Debbie Kearney?"

Creases formed on Drew's forehead. "Debbie, the TA in our accounting class?"

Ethan smirked. "One and the same. Whenever she called on you, the A student, you couldn't even explain the difference between a credit and a debit."

Drew hadn't thought about Debbie in a very long time, but back in college, whenever she'd walked into the classroom, his baseball hat had gone right to his lap as if he was a hormonal teenager. "No one could. She looked like a centerfold." Drew shook his head. "Plus, if I'm not mistaken, *you* were the one who ended up getting an A in that class, and you hated accounting. It must have been all of that late-night tutoring."

Ethan smirked. "Sue me. My point is, you're looking at that chick the same way."

That was the last thing Drew needed to hear.

Drew was a confident man, but Ethan wasn't half-wrong about what he had been feeling. Something about her made Drew think he wouldn't be able to string together a coherent sentence when they were finally face-to-face. Forget the fact that Drew had a degree from Northwestern University; anything beyond introducing himself would tie his tongue into a sailor's knot. Then again, like a true sibling, Ethan loved getting under Drew's skin and over the years had made it an art form. Despite his pal's words, Drew knew he didn't have an issue with the ladies. If anything, he reminded himself, it was usually the opposite.

Ignoring his friend's comments, and without much hesitation, Drew rose off the stool. He brushed his shirt, smoothing it out, or maybe it was to wipe the beads of sweat that had formed in the life lines of his palms.

"Good luck," Ethan said with a tilt of his chin.

Drew's white deck shoes hit the sand; he was just taking his first step toward her when raucous laughter bellowed from one of the couples at the bar. The mystery woman raised her head, and when her eyes landed on the sound's source, they doubled in circumference right before they narrowed into slits. It was a strange reaction. Did she think they were too rowdy? Were they disturbing her? If so, he would tell Ethan to have them keep it to a dull roar. Hell, he'd pay for a charter on George's boat to guarantee her a peaceful day. At that moment, the same loud couple left their spot at the bar and walked hand in hand to one of the beach cabanas, kitty-corner to where the woman was relaxing.

In one graceful movement, she pushed herself off the chair and scanned the area until her eyes landed on Drew. His mirrored sunglasses prevented the woman from seeing that his focus was trained on her. Did she know how beautiful she was? How other men looked at her? How that bathing suit looked as though it was designed with her in mind? He watched, transfixed, as her hands clenched and unclenched, swinging at her sides.

What was going on with him? Never in his life had a woman made him *want* so much before—let alone a woman he didn't even know. But there was something in her eyes... her stance... that made Drew want to learn everything about her.

Leaving a trail of footprints behind her in the soft white sand, she strode in his direction, shocking him as she came to a halt, standing toe-to-toe with him. Drew's heart leaped in his rib cage, and he told his hands to stay put.

She tipped her head back. "Hi, I'm Lacey Winters. Are you single?"

Drew had met forward women before, but no one quite like this. Cute lines darted from the corners of her squinting eyes. The urgent tone of her voice and the softness of her face begged him to answer.

He raised his sunglasses, resting them on top of his cap. "I'm Drew Mitchell, and yes, I'm single."

Before he could reach out to shake her hand or ask if she wanted a drink, she let out a loud laugh, catching him off guard. That bizarre outburst should have sent him running in the opposite direction, but then she roped her arms around his neck and pressed her lips against his. If a bald eagle had swooped down and landed on his head, he wouldn't have been more surprised.

Lacey's lips were as soft as they looked. She tasted of sweet citrus, with a hint of salt, and all woman. Drew's body came to life at her touch; his heart restarted, he was able to breathe… and move. One of his hands rested on the thin knot tied at the center of her back, while the other cupped her head, drawing her closer to him.

Lacey was several inches shorter than Drew, but his firm hold on her raised her off the ground, allowing their hips to touch like a quiet whisper. If he didn't put a stop to this, Lacey would soon know how turned on he was.

Then she moaned into his mouth, and he was done for.

OTHER BOOKS *by* CARINA ROSE

Once Upon a Kiss
Once Upon a Dare
Once Upon a Duke

ABOUT THE AUTHOR

Carina loves everything about romance. To her, it's the little things that matter. She also believes in insta-love, since she knew her husband was *the one* the first day she met him. She loves writing about swoony heroes and strong heroines. She adores that moment when a couple comes together and the hurdles they jump to get there.

When it comes to books, Carina loves to read all types of romance, but she seems to lean toward dark romance. She sometimes equates it to chocolate—sometimes you need a little dark to balance out the sweet. Whether enjoying dark or sweet romance, she reads to escape reality (even if it's for a few hours) and get lost in a fictional world. It helps her relax, and she hopes her books do the same for her readers.

Carina looks forward to sharing more love stories in her future novels.

CONTACT

CARINA ROSE

I love hearing from my readers. You all truly keep me going.
Please stay in touch!
Instagram - www.instagram.com/author_carinarose
BookBub - www.bookbub.com/authors/carina-rose
TikTok! - www.tiktok.com/@carinarosebooks?
Facebook Group – Carina's Sweethearts - www.facebook.com/authorcarinarose

I also have a newsletter to help you stay up to date. I promise not to spam you. 😊
You can sign up here -
https://bit.ly/CarinasNewsletter
You can also reach me via my website www.carinarosebooks.com or email me carinarosebooks@gmail.com

A NOTE FROM THE AUTHOR...

Dear Reader,

Thank you so much for reading *The Book Boyfriend*. It means so much to me. I also love hearing from you. Please don't be strangers. Feel free to drop me a note to let me know what you thought of *The Book Boyfriend* or if you just want to hear about what I have going on. It's because of you that I get to do what I love.

Book reviews mean so much to writers, and I treasure each of them. If you have time, I'd love an honest review from you.

Once again, thank you for reading and for taking a chance on this book.

All my best,
Carina

ACKNOWLEDGMENTS

First, I'd like to thank my family for putting up with my long hours, my moodiness, and several nights of getting takeout for dinner. I truly could not do this without your support. I love you all with everything that I am.

To my critique partner, Ann Marie Madden, thank you so much for being my sounding board and my shoulder to lean on! Thank you for putting up with my many changes and for talking me off a ledge a time or two. I am so appreciative of our friendship. I love you and am very grateful to have you in my life. You're more than a friend — you're family.

To James Gallagher at Castle Walls Editing, thank you doesn't even cut it. Once again, your flexibility, knowledge, attention to detail, and putting up with my many changes are invaluable to me. I feel extremely fortunate to work with you. You're the best even beyond the pages.

To MJ, thank you for beta reading for me again! Thank you for your honesty, comments, and suggestions. I'm so happy we met through books and have become friends. I adore you.

Tami at Integrity Formatting, thank you for making this book pretty! I truly appreciate you. You're the best!

Sommer Stein at Perfect Pear Creative, I have zero words for this cover. No, I take that back. I have a few words… you're incredible. You always surpass my imagination. I couldn't love this cover more.

Thank you to Danielle Sanchez at Wildfire Marketing for your help in promoting *The Book Boyfriend,* and for everything you do for me. I truly appreciate you.

To all the bloggers, thank you for the time you spend supporting authors and reading our stories. You take time out of your personal lives, and I am very thankful.

To the ladies in my reader group, Carina's Sweethearts, you are all wonderful. Thank you for joining me on this journey.

To Rock Hudson, Doris Day, and Paul Newman, whose films bring back wonderful memories. You may be gone, but you'll never be forgotten.

Most important, I'd like to thank the readers. We all love to read and talk about the books and characters we love, and I am so thankful for all of you. If you have time and would leave a review, I'd be very appreciative. Thank you! Xoxo

In this book, I touch a bit on Alzheimer's disease. It was one of those moments when I let the harshness of the real world into my book. Like my character, Callie, so many of us either have known, know, or will know someone with Alzheimer's. If you'd like to learn more about it or what you can do to help fight the disease, please go to the website for the Alzheimer's Association www.alz.org

Printed in Great Britain
by Amazon